SECRET
ALPHA

ISBNs as follows:
Paperback — 9781923173705
ebook — 9781923172746

A catalogue record for this
work is available from the
National Library of Australia

*We acknowledge the traditional owners of the land
and pay respects to the Elders, past, present and future.*

KATHRYN ROYSE

SECRET ALPHA

To my wonderful son Samuel and daughter, Katie, their awesome partners, Tracey and Zac, my gorgeous new grandson, Zander, my amazing friends, most notably Jean, Wendy, Adam, Donna and Alison, and, my best friend, cheer squad, and partner, Michael who left this world too soon, thank you for always believing in me.

Thank you to everyone who has supported and encouraged me through my years of dreaming about writing, the times when I was discouraged, then finally putting pen to paper and creating the stories. A big thank you to Terry Spear for all the advice and online writing lessons, I couldn't have realised my dream without you all.

CHAPTER 1

Panic shone in the black wolf cub's eyes as the ominous shadow loomed closer. Fearing not for himself but for his playmate, Reine, Tere refused to cower, lifting his chin defiantly when a large, roughened hand shot down, grabbing him by the scruff. Trying to free himself from the vice-like grip, he wriggled, his eyes dropping to the smaller, silver male cub, his friend, Reine who he'd been playfully stalking only moments ago.

Reine twisted attempting to halt the trajectory of his playful attack on Tere. Realising too late whose long legs blocked his path, he landed in a tangle at the scowling alpha's feet. Reine's gaze tracked fearfully up the muscular legs clad in black leather to the face so like Tere's, but so very angry, snarling down at him. Scrambling away, his tail between his legs, Reine paused a moment to cast a worried look back at Tere before he scurried to safety, avoiding the wrath of the pack alpha. Tere cringed, whining a small apology to his friend as he watched Reine hurry away

Lacas spat at Reine's disappearing form and scowled as he roughly lifted Tere to eye level, growling.

'Tere, I've told you, *do not* associate with the betas!'

Holding him at arms-length, as though Tere were something

1

disgusting, Lacas stomped inside and savagely tossed the cub at his mother's feet, snarling.

'Keep him away from the subordinates, or I'll teach him a lesson he won't soon forget.' Lacas stalked into the bedroom, slamming the door.

Tere's eyes narrowed as he watched his father leave the room. Anger simmered within his small body. His heart clenched at the thought of never spending time with Reine again. Tere swore to himself that when he was the pack alpha, everyone would be shown respect, no matter their status.

Despite feeling like a young alpha moments before, Tere scrambled into his mother's loving embrace, soaking up her offered affection. Touch and the bonds of the pack are as necessary as breathing to a wolf changeling. Tere craved both with an almost unbearable intensity. Burrowing into her lap, he nuzzled into her.

'Tere, you must listen to your father.' Alika released her son with a deep sigh. 'Now shift, little one, and climb into the bath.'

Tere's body transformed into a small boy, a shower of silver and gold sparks surrounding him, evidence of his royal breeding, of both a mother and father of alpha lineage. Eyes flying to the bedroom door, he darted behind the metal tub, fearful his father would see the colours of the lingering sparks. Tere wasn't sure why, but deep down, he knew it wasn't a good idea to let his father know he was already displaying strong alpha tendencies.

Climbing into the metal tub near the open fire, he met his mother's sad, brown eyes.

'Sorry, Mama. Reine and I were just playing. He's my best friend, my *only* friend. He doesn't run away like everyone else.'

The water was warm, yet Tere shivered, momentarily missing

his fur and the increased body heat of his wolf form. Dipping his body beneath the soapy surface, Tere quickly became distracted by the bubbles around him, the soft pops spreading their tickly, foamy splatters over his body.

Dragging his attention back to his mother, he watched her gaze flick nervously to the bedroom door. A deep sadness filled Tere. The unfairness of them both living in constant fear washed over him like a wave threatening to drown him in its inky depths.

In a tone that left no doubt of his resentment, he asked, 'Mama, who else should I play with?'

His ice-blue eyes lifted, meeting his mother's sad and worried gaze. 'Shhh, Tere.'

Alika's gaze darted around.

'You need to play with the cubs of the pack leaders. You are the son of an alpha. You know your father hates it when you go anywhere near the betas.'

Tere scowled, momentarily distracted from his exasperation as his mother scrubbed him clean. Motioning for him to climb out of the bath, she wrapped his tiny body in a large, soft towel, rubbing his black, unruly hair vigorously.

'Mama,' he whispered, 'the cubs of the pack leaders ... They're mean and always cross. Why don't they like me?'

Alika sighed deeply, dressing him in his soft night pants and answered in a low voice, 'Tere, just try for me. Please?'

Tere's head drooped. 'Yes, Mama.'

Tucking Tere into his bed, she kissed him goodnight and ruffled his hair his eyes quickly drifting closed.

* * *

Alika's gaze wandered around their small but functional cottage. It had one main bedroom and a separate sleeping area for Tere, closed off with curtains and the kitchen was along a corridor, separating it from the lounge area. It had been her family home and Lacas hated it because he maintained that the pack alpha should have a grand home, commensurate with his status in the pack. Lacas was a powerful alpha with a temper to match who always seemed to want more than he currently had. She worried about Tere's future with Lacas's expectations and almost constant anger.

Tere displayed an intelligence beyond his years, a legacy of the times he'd cared for her after one of Lacas' alcohol-fuelled rages. Her heart ached for her young son, for the joy and freedom he should be experiencing as a cub yet forbidden by the cruel and controlling alpha that was his sire.

Alika's thoughts briefly drifted to happier days, and she allowed herself a rare, small smile remembering her father. He had been a loving father and an adored, respected leader of the prosperous Inare wolf pack, who had forged mutually beneficial alliances with the fae and elven folk. She pictured herself playing as a cub with many other younglings, but her eyes suddenly widened with realisation. How many cubs had been born during Canis' leadership? The streets had been filled with them romping, tussling, their parents chatting, laughing. After Canis' untimely death, Lacas had immediately assumed control of the pack. She hadn't thought about it before, but a new alpha taking over leadership without being challenged was unusual. There was always more than one wolf who wished to fight for leadership, especially in a prosperous pack with lots of cubs.

Alika had been too distraught over the loss of her father to question why Lacas had simply stepped into the role of alpha. Alone and miserable, she'd initially welcomed Lacas' advances. He was incredibly handsome with a hard, muscled body, piercing ice-blue eyes and a magnetism that drew women to him. Proud and strong, he held himself like a leader. She'd counted herself lucky that he'd chosen her ... until she'd glimpsed his true nature.

While Alika reflected, Lacas strode out of the bedroom and through the front door, slamming it as he left. She watched him swagger down the dusty road. Through the window, she noticed the betas shrinking back into the shadows as he passed by, fear shining in their eyes. And where were the pups? Inhaling sharply, Alika realised there were no more than eight pups in the entire pack and no newborns. Crushing dread inched its way down her spine. Lacas had broken all the alliances nurtured by her father. Trading with the elves and fae had ceased and the only non-wolf she'd seen recently was the Sorcerer that Lacas and the pack leaders kept company with. She'd only met him, Rantec, once and he'd made her skin crawl. She had no idea what business he and Lacas conducted together but she was certain it wasn't good. She was certain that if Lacas remained as their alpha, the pack would not survive.

As Alika busied herself tidying up after Tere, Lacas returned. Cringing when she scented his arousal, her wolf struggled for its freedom. Alika tamped down her wolf's fury, knowing she wasn't strong enough to defeat Lacas' beast. Straightening, she turned to him, schooling her features into a practiced smile, slipping off her shirt in preparation to fulfil his needs. Waiting to be told to undress would only earn her a beating.

Her eyes flicked to Lacas' face. She no longer saw his features as handsome, recognising only the cruelty and anger reflected there. An icy shudder passed through her like a spectre of evil sucking any remaining joy from her life. Lacas roughly grabbed her arm and hauled her to his bed. Her jaw set, she fisted the sheets to hold back the tears. Forcing herself to move beneath him, Alika whimpered and moaned, knowing that feigning pleasure as Lacas relentlessly pounded into her without foreplay was the only way to avoid his wrath.

When he fell asleep, temporarily sated, Alika slipped out of bed and into the sleeping area beside Tere. Warming some water, she washed herself thoroughly, unable to bear Lacas' scent on her. Feeling more comfortable, she settled down into the soft bed she'd made when she'd birthed Tere, keeping it set up in the lounge area next to the window where the warmth of the sun filtered through on the pretence of using it for a nap during the day.

Sometime during the night, Tere woke and padded over, slipping into bed with her and snuggling into his mother's loving arms. When she woke just before dawn, she smiled at Tere's little body tucked into hers. She had not long drifted off to sleep again when Lacas sought her out.

Alika sighed inwardly. Lacas' lust was never sated for long. With no regard for Tere's presence, he flipped her onto her belly and yanked her up onto her knees, taking her from behind. Alika bit her lip hard, desperately trying not to cry out with the pain of Lacas' violent invasion of her body. With her free hand, she gently tucked the blankets over Tere's head, praying he wouldn't be disturbed. However, Lacas' loud grunts and the thumping of the bed against the wall woke Tere. He whimpered, eyes wide.

Terrified, Alika's heart thumped wildly, fear slicing through her as she tried to quiet her cub. The moment Lacas finished with her, he grabbed Tere by the scruff, slapped him and flung him cruelly to the rough wooden floor. Tere howled, his eyes flashing with hatred, snarling at his father as Lacas raised his hand for a second strike.

Alika stepped forward, blocking Lacas' access to Tere, her love for her son breaching her fear as she attempted to intervene.

'He's young. He doesn't understand. Please, Lacas.'

Lacas lashed out. His fist connected with her jaw, sending her sprawling across the floor. Grabbing Tere, he opened the door and tossed him out into the cold. The door slammed so hard the walls of the cottage rattled. Lacas stalked back towards her, fury contorting his features.

Closing her eyes, Alika readied herself for the beating she knew would follow. Shaking uncontrollably, she opened her eyes to face Lacas, forcing herself not to cringe as his claws sliced out from his fingertips. She prayed that she'd live through this to watch Tere grow, knowing this time would be worse than the others. Trying unsuccessfully to stifle a scream as Lacas' claws bit into her side, the metallic scent of blood filled the air. Her blood. Viciously, he slammed her into the wall. Alika slid to the floor and lay on her side, winded, sucking in air to fill her lungs. Tears poured down her cheeks. Burning pain seared through her body.

Lacas snatched up his leather belt and stalked towards her, his lips curled in disgust. Her wolf snarled demanding release, but Alika knew Lacas could easily best her. The scent of leather and old blood, as well as Lacas' fury, reached her nose. He was out of control. Her wolf understood that this beating would be far worse than the rest, silently howling its fear for their life.

Before Alika could regain her breath enough to scramble away, Lacas flicked back the stiff brown leather and slashed it across her exposed back. The buckle ripped through her skin. Her scream echoed off the walls of the small wooden cottage. White-hot pain ripped through her. Teetering on the edge of consciousness, a tear escaped as Lacas raised the belt for a second blow. With the blinding pain of the next lash, she heard a distant scream laced with pure agony. She realised the scream was hers a moment before blackness clouded her vision, plunging her into the depths of oblivion.

* * *

Outside, Tere shook uncontrollably, his mother's screams curdling his blood. Bile rose in his throat. Unable to stand it any longer, he tore off his clothes and shifted, then ran as fast and as hard as he could. To where, he wasn't sure. His wolf ran farther than he had ever dared venture before finally halting, exhausted, under the stars in a sheltered copse of young trees. Terror and helplessness warred within his small body as he shook, unable to stop his mother's screams from replaying over and over in his head. Too distressed to be afraid of being alone, Tere finally fell asleep, exhaustion claiming his tiny body.

Waking in the early hours, the crisp coldness of the approaching winter chilled his naked, human form. Still too young to hold his wolf form while he slept, his tiny body quaked uncontrollably, his skin a pale shade of blue from the bitter cold. He looked around, briefly wondering where he was. Remembering, desolation threatened to overwhelm him, but he steadfastly refused to cry anymore. He must return home.

Tere called the change, feeling his bones shift as they elongated and popped easily into place. As young as he was, the change came easily. He knew others found it much more difficult, some even experienced pain.

Afraid of what he might find, his heart pounded against his ribs as he raced home. He'd never seen his father so angry. Stopping at the front steps of the cottage, he listened. Quiet. Dressing quickly in the cold, slightly damp clothes he'd tossed on the ground the night before, Tere huddled on the front steps, shivering, not daring to enter until he was granted permission.

He jumped when the door was yanked open. Lacas walked out, grunting as he noticed his son, and left on what Tere assumed was pack business. He watched his father stride down the wide, dusty street, all those in his way, lowering their eyes and scattering. Tere hurried inside as soon as Lacas was out of sight. His mother was so badly hurt, she was unable to stand for long. Tere helped her as best he could to the bed near his. Sitting quietly on the floor, he held her hand and gritted his teeth against the tears that threatened until finally she told him to go outside and play. Rummaging around in the cupboards that he could reach, Tere managed to make himself a simple breakfast of bread and some soft, juicy berries that he found in a bowl on the kitchen bench.

Carrying his meal outside, Tere sat on the step. Eating, he watched the small, green-eyed girl, Ileia, who lived in the cabin across the wide, dusty street, wrestling with her brothers. He looked away, kicking the dirt at his feet, angry at Lacas for hurting his mother. He was alone and miserable. Hearing a scuffle and a shout, Tere lifted his gaze. Despite his mood, he couldn't hold back a smile as Ileia bested her much bigger brother, then let out a victory whoop. How he wished he could play with them, but he didn't dare. Angrily he dashed away the lone tear trickling down his cheek. If his father saw him crying, he'd probably be rewarded with a beating, too.

It was several days before Alika was able to walk or even stand for any length of time. Tere ate what he could reach, drinking water from the well outside. He'd found his mother some bread and cold, salted meat to nibble on, which she'd gratefully accepted. As Tere watched her chew carefully with her split lip and swollen jaw, his anger and hatred of his father grew. Lacas had not yet returned ... thankfully. Tere wondered where he went during these long absences. It was rumoured that his sire consorted with a Sorcerer at an encampment some distance away, for what purpose Tere had no idea, but he was grateful for the reprieve his absence provided no matter the reason.

Soon, Alika was well enough to shift, to hasten her healing. While cooking Tere his favourite meal of roast lamb, she talked quietly to him as she moved around the kitchen.

'Tere, you must understand that adults, especially males, have physical needs. You must never get in the way of that. If your father comes to me again, leave the room and try to go back to sleep or, if it happens during the day, stay outside.'

'Mama...' – he eyed the bruises on her arms – 'why does Papa hurt us?'

Tears welled in Alika's eyes. She paused, as if attempting to phrase her answer carefully. Tere was just a cub, but he'd seen and experienced more pain and anguish than anyone his age should ever have to. Alika held back the sob that constricted her throat.

'Some males become cross when things aren't as they expect, especially alpha males.' She paused again. 'Leading a pack can be difficult. So, you must be especially good, so everything is always as your papa expects.'

Tere nodded and gazed into the distance, obviously pondering her words.

'Now, go and play.' When he started to walk away, she added. 'And please stay away from Reine.'

'Yes, Mama.'

Tere slowly padded outside, barefoot. Dejectedly, he scanned the street, unable to find anyone he really wanted to be with at that moment. Sitting on the rough wooden steps of their front porch, he quietly watched the activities of the village.

The red female, Ileia, romped happily in her front garden with her older brother, both in their wolf forms. She tumbled over as her brother headbutted her flank. When she rose, her eyes settled on Tere. She yipped at him and Tere ventured a small smile. Her emerald, green eyes held his for a moment, then she chased after her brother, disappearing through the door of their home. He pondered that word for a moment. Home. His eyes misted, desiring something he'd never have.

Swallowing hard when he noticed his father striding towards him, Tere stood and lowered his eyes, though he had to fight hard against his alpha nature to do so. He was determined to be good and make things as his Papa expected so Mama wouldn't get hurt anymore.

'Good afternoon, Papa.'

Lacas stopped, eyeing him suspiciously as he walked past and into the house. Tere's mother gasped in fright as Lacas slammed the door, then he heard a few cries and groans. Knowing his father was doing what adults did to each other, he stayed outside just like his mama had told him, until Lacas opened the door and allowed him in for dinner.

Life improved a little while Tere attempted to avoid doing anything that irritated his father. Though that was difficult, Tere worked hard at it. Lacas could rarely find cause to be angry or beat Tere or his mother.

* * *

As Tere grew, so did his anger and resentment toward his father. It festered inside him like an open wound, but he still steadfastly refused to give Lacas any reason to hurt his mother.

One sunny afternoon, Tere returned home from a session of hard training. As soon as he'd reached his teens, he'd started training, quickly building strength, agility and determination far beyond his years. Today, he felt tired, satisfied … and ravenous. Lifting one foot to begin climbing the steps to the front door, he overheard Lacas speaking to his mother.

'Damn woman! It must be your defective lineage that has made Tere into a subservient beta. What a disappointment you both are! All I asked of you was to produce an alpha heir. One who could follow in my footsteps and lead this pack as it should be lead. He should have been killed at birth.'

Stomping up the front steps, Tere's mood sank. Then he heard the unmistakable sound of Lacas beating his mother. He wanted to burst through the door and help her. However, he knew from experience that if he tried to intervene, it would be worse for her so he shifted and ran until he was so exhausted he could hardly move. Guilt warred with the need to wait to take his revenge on Lacas. His body shook. His muscles burned. His tongue lolled out the side of his mouth as he panted, catching his breath.

When he could run no further, he found a shaded area and lay on the cool grass just beyond a stand of young elm trees, his head resting on his paws, flanks heaving, his energy spent from his emotion-fuelled run. When a twig snapped behind him, he lifted his weary head, sniffing suspiciously. Dragging himself up onto his haunches, his keen wolf eyes scanned for danger. The scent he caught was familiar, yet foreign. Snapping his head around, he tracked a red female wolf padding slowly between the trees. He waited, alert. His ears twitched as he listened. Her emerald, green eyes caught his attention, held his gaze as she approached. Her movements were smooth and unhurried, her bearing almost regal.

Ileia?

She whined, stopping a short distance away.

Why is she here?

Memories of watching her wrestle with her brothers as pups flooded his thoughts. He'd been afraid to join in because he hadn't wanted to bring them to Lacas' attention, but he'd ached for the happiness they shared. She hadn't given him any indication that she'd really noticed him since, or had she? He'd certainly noticed her. Her rich, red coat and vibrant green eyes were incredibly beautiful. Her movements were filled with an assurance and grace that mesmerised him. At the sight of her, his heart thumped a staccato beat. He desperately wished they could at least be friends. What he truly wanted was much more with her but that could not be because if Lacas knew that Tere cared for her...

Pushing those thoughts aside he allowed himself a wolfish smile as he recalled his first real erection when he'd seen her change from her gorgeous wolf form into her naked human form after running with her friends. He'd stopped breathing for a moment. Both of her forms were stunning, but her luscious human body – creamy white skin, firm breasts, long, lithe legs and softly curled, waist-length, deep auburn hair – had his heart thundering against his ribs and his body hard, aching with need. She'd laughed with her friends as she'd dressed, and he'd been forced to swim in the icy river.

Pulling his focus back to the present, he growled low. A warning. He didn't want her to see him like this. She stopped a short distance away, her gaze assessing him before she dropped onto the cool grass. Her head resting on her paws, her eyes held warmth, compassion and something else that Tere could not identify. The sighed and turned away laying on the edge of the outcrop overlooking the vibrant green valley below, not seeing its beauty. Anger, sadness and fear spiralled through him, but something unexpected coiled low in his belly. Desire.

He didn't protest when she moved up beside him. Surprise filled him at her gesture of support. He'd learned not to expect anything like that from the pack. Her presence was an unexpected but welcome comfort.

When he finally rose, ready to return home, Ileia stepped close, nuzzling him. Startled, he sprinted away. Pausing as he entered the forest, he looked back over his shoulder, then loped away. Ileia watched him, he felt it and heard her wolfish sigh as the red wolf trotted home behind Tere's midnight black wolf.

* * *

That night, Tere crept inside to tend to his mother after Lacas left. Breaking down in her son's arms, unrestrained sobs racked Alika's body. After a few minutes, she raised her face from his shoulder. Tere cursed at the sight of her blackened, swollen eye and the dried blood down her neck.

'Tere, you must leave soon, or your father will find an excuse to kill you. He'll find out that you are really an alpha and—'

Tere smoothed her hair, whispering, 'No, Mother. I will kill him and take my place as pack alpha.'

Alika's eyes widened. 'No, Tere. You are too young. You must not challenge him. Please, I couldn't bear to lose you. Please, promise me you won't.'

Tere sighed. 'All right, Mother. I promise ... for now.'

Tere knew he was a strong alpha, but he must hide it from Lacas until he was ready. He grew bigger and stronger every day and would soon challenge Lacas, freeing them from the tyrant who ruled their lives and was slowly destroying the pack.

The months passed quickly and Tere increasingly struggled to hide his alpha tendencies. Every day, he held back the wolf straining to exert its dominance. It snapped and snarled within. More and more often he was forced to shift and run until exhaustion overtook them both just to maintain control.

Today, Lacas had taunted him, accusing him of being homosexual like a few of the other male wolves in the pack Tere had seen engaging in intimate acts with each other when they thought they were out of sight of the pack. Tere did not judge them but knew Lacas' words were spoken solely to provoke him. He had come so close to shifting and fighting Lacas, he'd run farther than ever before to burn off the anger and frustration.

Not yet, he told his wolf, *but soon. Very soon.*

Strolling back past the river, the soft gurgling sounds of the water flowing between the smooth rocks calmed him. Deep in thought, he startled a little when he heard splashing. He parted the tall, brown rushes separating the well-worn path from the river and froze at the magnificent sight before him.

Ileia

Tere found himself unable to drag his eyes from the delicious sight of Ileia bathing. Her creamy skin glistened with jewel like droplets of water. Tiny rivulets sparkling in the sunlight slid enticingly between her firm, round breasts. His throat suddenly dry, Tere swallowed. His heart pounded as he watched her dip below the water to rinse the soapy bubbles from her sleek, red locks.

She stood, the water lapping around her upper thighs and the thatch of curly, red hair between her legs, working a glistening, damp trail through it. A soft moan slipped unbidden from Tere's lips. Ileia gasped, dropping beneath the water's surface. Her arms crossing over her breasts, her eyes frantically searched the area for the source of the sound.

Feeling guilty, Tere stepped from the cover of the bushes, averting his eyes. 'Forgive me. I was passing and heard splashing. I didn't mean to—'

'Tere.' Her voice sounded both relieved and annoyed. 'Were you watching me? You scared the hell out of me. How dare you. You—' The utter desolation Tere felt at upsetting her must have shown on his face because she abruptly halted her rant. 'Tere?'

'I'm truly sorry. I didn't mean to startle you. I heard a sound. I didn't intend to watch, but...'

Her voice gentled. 'But what, Tere?'

His eyes met hers, holding them for several minutes. 'I just wanted to thank you for sitting with me the other day.'

Ileia smiled. 'You looked so sad. I wanted to comfort you. But ... you seemed angry that I was there.'

'Not angry. Surprised. Nobody has ever tried before.'

She nodded. 'Not because they don't care, Tere. Because of Lacas.'

Tere sighed, not wanting to discuss Lacas in front of this very beautiful, very naked woman.

She regarded him, clearly assessing his mood. 'You didn't finish what you were saying earlier.'

His eyes drifted over her nakedness, barely hidden by the water. Ileia shivered and Tere wanted to howl as desire coiled through him. Her nipples hardened and her neck and cheeks were flushed despite the cool river swirling around her.

Tere took a step closer, his resolve growing. Dragging in a deep breath, he decided to let her know what was in his heart. 'I was going to say that you are so beautiful, I couldn't drag my eyes away once I saw that it was you. I've wanted to speak with you, join in your games with your brothers ever since we were cubs but was afraid for you in case Lacas noticed,' he paused, 'that we were, well... friends.'

Ileia paused as though making up her mind then slowly rose out of the water. Tere's heart thumped as she held her hands out to him in invitation, her gaze capturing his. She spoke, her words like a salve to his battered heart.

'I have wanted to be your friend too but had witnessed and heard the result of Lacas' anger and was afraid to. I no longer wish to be afraid. Will you join me, Tere?'

His body ached for her touch as it had since he'd first noticed her so long ago. *How long had it been?* Then he'd wanted the touch of friendship, now he wanted much more. For a moment he did not move as he wrestled with the fear of what Lacas would do if he discovered them together. His eyes held hers as she waited for him to make his decision.

Moving towards her, hesitated briefly, then ripped his shirt over his head, tossing it onto the grassy bank. Ileia's eyes watching his every move made his member twitch and harden. Her eyes, now large and darkened with arousal, tracked his every movement as he tore off his trousers and released his throbbing member. Her lips parted on a gasp. Tere groaned softly. He couldn't wait to taste the soft sweetness of them. He knew he was big, but it didn't matter. They weren't permitted to have full intercourse, or they'd be mated, but they could do everything else. His heart hammered against his ribs. Changelings were used to seeing each other naked as they shifted, but this was different. Desire assaulted him, battering hard at his prided self-control.

He prowled toward her, walking into the water and his heart leapt when Ileia lunged forward, into his arms. Groaning at the feel of her wet body pressed against his, he slid his hands down her back to cup her firm bottom, holding her close. Tere slanted his mouth over hers, tasting honey and cinnamon. The curves of her slim body fitted perfectly against his and she was unbelievably warm, despite the cool water sluicing around them. When her lips parted, allowing his tongue entry, Ileia moaned. Smiling against her lips, Tere's heart thumped, and his hands shook as they slid over her soft skin.

Moving deeper into the water, Tere lifted her. He didn't think it possible, but his body hardened more as she wrapped her legs around his waist, rubbing against his rock-hard erection. He kissed her deeply, one hand sliding between them to cup her breast, gently rolling the nipple between his fingers. Ileia threw her head back, softly crying out as Tere bent his head to lave each tight bud with his tongue. She moaned softly as he suckled, bucking against him, the movement almost bringing Tere undone.

Tentatively sliding his hand down her soft, flat belly, his fingers found her sensitive nub. Supporting her with one hand under her luscious bottom, he began a circular motion that soon had her writhing. He shifted her slightly, to gain access to her feminine folds, thrusting two fingers inside, groaning at the slick tightness. He couldn't stop the rhythmic thrust of his hips in time with his pumping fingers, his swollen member sliding between her thighs. How he wished he could just fill her with his throbbing manhood. Ileia moaned and wriggled against him, telling Tere that she was close. Within moments she bucked hard and cried out, arching against his hand as her climax washed over her, her muscles clamping around his fingers. She clung to him as the ripples subsided, their lips locked in a long, wet, passionate kiss.

Releasing her ankles from behind his back, she paused, looking into his eyes before she slithered down his body, then urged him to the riverbank. Encouraging him to sit on the soft grass, she dropped down between his knees, wrapping her hand around his erection. He moaned, closing his eyes, and leaned back on his elbows allowing the sensation of her hand sliding over his aching member to wash over him. His heart pounding, the spiralling heat of his climax built quickly.

He couldn't stop himself from thrusting into her hand as she worked her magic on him. The exquisite sensations rolled through him, turning his blood to lava, stealing his breath. His climax about to erupt, he tried to pull away. Ileia lifted her eyes to his and continued sliding her hand along his length, squeezing gently. Certain that his heart would burst, his head lolled back. His eyes drifted closed as he savoured this long-awaited moment with the woman he had desired from a distance as long as he could remember. Both intense pleasure and a sense of long sought after peace combined, curling through him like the heat rising from a fire. Fisting the grass around him he exploded in an intense, mind-blowing climax, biting his lip to stop himself from crying out, but unable to silence the groans.

Once the waves of his release subsided, Tere pulled her up to cradle her against his chest. Ileia's sigh of contentment filled him with a sense of happiness that he had never experienced before. Gently cupping her chin, he lifted her chin to look into her expressive eyes, not bothering to wipe away the moisture gathered at the corners of his own. Tenderly, he captured her lips for a searing kiss.

Lifting his head, a hoarse, emotional whisper slipped from his lips before he buried his face in her damp hair.

'Thank you.'

Ileia's eyes filled with tears, and she hugged him tightly. Pulling back, she looked into his eyes.

'I will always be here for you, Tere and I will never again let fear come between us.

She ran one hand down his washboard abdomen, causing a sharp intake of breath as his body sprang to life again. Urging him to stand, she drew him back into the water. When they were chest deep, she slid her arms around his neck and kissed him with a heat that stoked a renewed fire within them both.

CHAPTER 2

The Coming-of-Age celebration was one of the biggest events of the year. When the young wolves of the pack turned eighteen, they were considered adults and able to participate in pack rituals, including fighting and mating activities. The ceremony consisted of each wolf being paired with a partner of their parents' choosing. The festivities would begin once each couple returned, having lost their virginity. A feast for the entire pack followed. This was the only time in a wolf changeling's long life that full intercourse didn't indicate a permanent mating. Rather, it was a rite of passage.

The initiates gathered, nervously anticipating the impending pleasures of the evening. All were excited, some were anxious, others fearful at the fact they'd not had any input into who their partner would be. A few were fortunate that their parents had worked hard to pair them with someone they liked. Others were paired with those who would increase their parents' standing in the pack. Tere's chosen partner, Anya, was a beautiful chocolate brown wolf, the daughter of Lupus, one of the high-ranking pack council members; however, Tere desperately wished Ileia had been chosen for him.

Tere worried for Ileia, suspecting her partner, Rand, would not be gentle. Rand had an evil reputation not unlike Lacas where females

21

were concerned. Holding back a possessive growl Tere shook himself, his black fur glistening in the last rays of the day's sunlight. Frustration welled within him, but he clamped down on it. He hated that he couldn't help Ileia, but he vowed he would find her as soon as the initiation was over.

Cocking his head, Tere listened as the ancient ceremonial words were spoken. Despite his frustration, he was looking forward to his first full sexual encounter. Even though he had enjoyed several intimate trysts with Ileia they had never dared complete the act in case she became pregnant, and it was forbidden before the ceremony that he anticipated now.

The Coming-of-Age was a critical ceremony for young wolves. Tere didn't want to be the last to shift back to his human form when the time came, mostly because he didn't want Lacas to see the gold and silver that was indicative of his alpha status, and because being last would provide his sire with a reason to humiliate him. He was determined to not provide his father with any reason to spoil his pleasure this evening. As the last words of the blessing were spoken, Tere initiated the shift back. Wishing he could hide the silver and gold sparks that betrayed his heritage, his body stretched and reshaped itself as the change took hold. Fearful Lacas would realise that he was pure alpha, Tere slipped cautiously behind Anya, his partner for tonight, completing the change. The cool breeze fluttered across his naked body, carrying a myriad of odours to his heightened senses. Annoyance flared within him as he immediately scented the interest of some of the females, Anya included. There was only one whose attention he truly desired.

Later, he told himself, focusing on the pleasures to come.

Anya sidled up to him, desire gleaming in her eyes as she slipped her arms around his neck. Pressing her soft, sexy nakedness against him, her wavy brown hair whispering over his chest, his body stirred to life. Tere stole a glance over her head at the gorgeous redhead with green eyes and sun-kissed skin.

Ileia was trying to smile as Rand, a sleazy silver wolf, ran his hands over her body. Her green eyes were wide, her panic evident. Tere could smell her fear as her gaze lifted to meet his. He tensed, fighting the urge to pull her away, to be the one to make love to her for the first time. His frustration at having to hide his alpha wolf soared. He would never allow this to happen if he were pack leader. *When* he was pack leader! One day, he would destroy Lacas for every hurt he'd caused his mother and the pack.

Tere's hands fisted at his side and he forced himself to suck in a deep breath to calm himself. For a moment, he held Ileia's gaze, allowing himself the luxury of watching her. His beautiful Ileia, the only one he'd been intimate with, until today. They had explored each other many times, the last time, only a few days ago when they had managed to slip away together unnoticed. She would be his mate one day, he had no doubt. He already knew how her long, slender legs felt wrapped around him, her luscious, kissable mouth on his. His body hardened in response. He sent her a tiny reassuring smile, and quickly glancing around to ensure no-one was watching mouthed his love for her.

Oblivious to Tere's distraction, Anya pulled his attention back, running her fingers through his spiky black hair, unaware that the emotion she witnessed in his eyes, his reactions weren't directed at her. She was obviously not displeased at her father's choice for the ceremony and her position in the pack would improve after tonight.

Tere's excitement bubbled up at the prospect of finally losing his virginity, even though it wasn't with his beloved Ileia. He slipped his hand into Anya's, leading her toward the privacy of the forest, casting one more glance back at Ileia before she disappeared with Rand. The howls and moans of the other pairs already mating stirred his loins into action. Anya was not unattractive and seemed nice enough. She certainly had a sexy body, and he could smell her arousal. Once he thought they were far enough, Tere stopped, his desire spiking. His staff hardened, jutting out from his naked loins and his heart began thumping erratically. Anya eyed his length, gasped and backed away, covering her mouth, a look of fear replacing desire.

'Don't be afraid, Anya. I promise I'll be gentle.'

Tere prowled slowly towards her. Motionless, save for her shaking, she watched him. His muscles flexed as he moved like the predator he truly was. Stopping mere inches from her, Tere inhaled her sweet scent. Her anxiety was obvious, he could smell it, but he also smelled the sweet scent of fresh flowers. Tere's wolf strained for release, desperate now to take her. Knowing that he needed to be gentle, he struggled to contain the rising desire coiling through him like a snake ready to strike. It was his first time, too although he had some experience having already shared great pleasure and intimacy with without taking her virginity. When he heard a pain-filled scream, he growled. *Ileia?* God, he prayed she was all right. With a great effort, he yanked his focus back to Anya. Her eyes were wide, her naked breasts rising and falling with each breath, obviously frightened by the scream, fearful of its cause.

Even though his fingers twitched, desperate to reach out and caress her, Tere waited. For a moment, he was certain Anya was going to run as her breathing quickened further. He slowly reached out resting his hands on her arms to calm her, but also to grab her if she attempted to run. She would be shamed by the pack if she ran, and quite simply, he wanted her. Her body was rigid, her hands clenched at her side. After a few moments she realised that he wasn't going to force her. Dragging in a deep breath she unclenched her fists and tentatively slid her arms around his neck, eventually relaxing her shapely body against him.

The intimate contact elicited a rumble deep within Tere's chest. He slowly lowered his lips to hers. His body hummed with the heat of her response. Lowering his hands to her backside, he eased her body closer and kissed her deeply, his tongue sliding between her soft, moist lips. When she rubbed her slender body against his throbbing arousal, his control threatened to slip.

'Lie down on the grass, Anya. Please.' His voice was husky with his escalating desire.

Anya glanced down, leaning over to brush aside the dried, fallen leaves from the small fern-like bushes surrounding them. The grass beneath was soft and damp with the early evening dew, the air cool and crisp. Dropping to her knees, a shiver rippled through her body. Whether it was desire or the chill of the ground, Tere wasn't certain.

Anya's long brown hair contrasted starkly with her pale skin as she lay on the grass in front of him, her legs spread in invitation. Her chocolate brown eyes were huge and round in her pretty, elfin face. Tere smiled reassuringly as he lowered himself over her, resting his weight on his elbows. Kissing her lips, his tongue sought entry. Anya opened for him, and their tongues duelled in an age-old mating dance.

Emboldened again, Anya slipped her hands around him and down his back, exploring his sculpted body. Tere sucked in a sharp breath, fighting for control as her hands traced the lines of his buttocks then trailed between their bodies. Shifting his weight to one elbow, he halted her progress pulling her hands up to his chest as his arousal nudged at the entrance to her womanhood. Pleased at the dampness that greeted him, his body hummed, his rock-hard member twitching in anticipation. Anya was warm, willing and ready for him, although her body stiffened as he circled his hips, rubbing against her slick core.

'Try to relax. I'll be as gentle as I can. I'm told there'll be a little pain as I breach your virginity but that will quickly pass.'

Anya nodded as he trailed his lips down the sensitive area on her neck. Leaning on one elbow to give him access his other hand took a slow, teasing journey down her flat stomach to the damp thatch of hair between her legs. Anya wriggled, moaning. Tere responded to her unspoken request, slipping two fingers into her slick heat. His body clenched with need, but he gritted his teeth and held onto his self-control, pleasuring her with his fingers, his thumb working her sensitive nub as he suckled first one, then the other taut nipple.

When Tere scented that Anya's climax was imminent, he lifted his body over hers, replacing his fingers with the tip of his now aching member. Anya let her hand drift down between them, almost bringing him undone as she grasped his throbbing erection guiding him into her body. Moving slowly, inch by inch he slid into her tight sheath. Her tightness was exquisite torture and he struggled to hold back the urge to surge forward.

Slowly Tere pushed deeper until he met the barrier of her virginity. His lips captured hers before he jerked his hips, pushing through it. Anya gasped and with great effort Tere stilled, lifting his head to watch her. Tears squeezed from the corners of her eyes. Tenderly, he wiped them away with his thumb, kissed her, then began moving slowly and gently until she became used to the feeling of him inside her. Emotion welled up, urging him to slant his mouth tenderly over her soft lips. Sweeping her arms around his neck, her tongue tangled with his as her hips began rocking against him.

Tere's muscles shook with the effort of holding back. Setting a tortuously slow rhythm, her little whimpers urged him on. He'd waited so long for this, and although he wasn't with Ileia, Anya was sweet, sexy and stirred his desire. The spiralling tingle of his climax began deep in his loins and although he'd experienced climaxes when he and Ileia had been intimate, he was unprepared for the intensity of the powerful heat and pleasure building so quickly that it threatened to overwhelm his control. Pushing aside thoughts of Ileia he focused on the sensations, the rhythm and Anya. Gritting his teeth, Tere tenuously held on, determined to ensure Anya's pleasure first. It wasn't long before she thrashed and moaned, desperate for release. Her hands moved frantically over his body, her nails leaving tiny, bloody scratches down his back. Increasing the tempo, he was barely able to control the thrust of his hips. At the same moment that his control finally splintered, Anya screamed, shuddering and bucking as her climax washed over her. Her muscles clenching around his throbbing length catapulted him into a powerful climax that rolled over him like a tidal wave. His howl of satisfaction pierced the night. Answering calls echoed around him, shattering the silence of the forest.

Tere's breath came in quick gasps, his pulse hammering as he moved to lay beside Anya on the cool grass. She snuggled into him, draping one leg over his, her fingers tracing circles on the smattering of black hair on his chest.

'Thank you for being so gentle and considerate, Tere. It was wonderful.'

He grinned. 'Thank you, Anya. I loved that you were so ready for me...'

Rolling over, he slid one leg between hers and planted a long kiss on her lips. His body sprang to life again as he tasted her. His desire-fogged brain registered something different. She tasted of sweet apples. Even as he lowered his head to kiss her neck, he remembered what was different. Ileia tasted of honey and cinnamon. He forced that thought away so he could focus on Anya as she deserved. She arched into him, and a satisfied smile curved his mouth as he nibbled his way back up to Anya's lips for a searing kiss before they made their way back to join the others for the feast marking the completion of the ceremony.

There were cheers as each couple returned. Tere grinned as his long-time and only real friend other than Ileia, Reine stepped forward and gave him a congratulatory slap on the back, then slipped back into the throng and away from Lacas' view. Hand in hand, Tere and Anya skirted the gathered crowd to retrieve their clothes. Noting Lacas' appreciative expression as Anya wafted past him Tere gripped her fingers a little tighter, not yet willing to let go of their newly forged emotional connection.

Annoyance spiked through him, and he frowned as Anya slid Lacas a seductive glance while she dressed. An involuntary growl rumbled from deep within Tere's chest and he caught himself moving forward to challenge Lacas. Despite being in his human form, the hair on the back of his neck stood up and his spine became ramrod straight. His posturing clearly displayed his alpha status for the briefest of moments. Forcing himself to relax, he sucked in a deep, calming breath. He would not allow Lacas to spoil this evening. Dressing quickly, Tere excused himself and went in search of Ileia.

At the edge of the forest, he found her. Naked. Washing herself. The metallic scent of blood reached his nostrils, as he approached.

Despite the waning light, his wolf's vision located its source. Blood trickled between her legs. He noted her damp eyes, a look of shame on her face. *Why?* His fury spiked. His hands fisted. He spotted Rand in the distance, laughing with a group of his mates, their eyes flicking in Ileia's direction as they made lewd gestures. A low, warning growl rumbled deep in Tere's chest. Why hadn't he pushed back against Lacas' choice for him? As the son of the pack alpha, he should have been given a choice of partner for the ceremony. If he had, Ileia would be uninjured. Guilt over having enjoyed his experience with Anya, and a deeper hatred of Lacas assailed him. He lowered his gaze.

'I'm sorry.'

'Tere.' Ileia rested her hand on his arm, pulling his attention back. 'This is not your fault. Don't, please.' Her tone pleaded with him to not beat Rand senseless for what he'd done to her. Dragging in a calming breath he moved closer. Gently taking the sponge she had been washing herself with, he rinsed it out in the warm water. Handing it back he sat on a nearby fallen log, turning to allow her privacy while she finished washing even though he'd seen her naked many times.

'Are you ... all right, Ileia?'

'Yes.'

Tere grunted in frustration. He knew she wasn't.

Quickly dressing, Ileia sat beside him, leaning into him a little. 'Thank you.'

His head snapped up, his eyes flashing. 'I didn't do anything. I should have, but I didn't.'

She rested her hand on the tanned skin of his arm, quelling his anger. 'You care. That's something.' Pausing, she turned to meet his eyes. 'I wish it had been you.'

No accusation. Just a statement.

The silence stretched between them until Tere slipped his arm around Ileia's waist and whispered, 'Me, too.'

'Tere?'

His gaze shifted to her face, then her lips. She looked away for a moment, then looked back, avoiding his gaze. Opening her mouth to speak she closed it again. Tere placed his finger under her chin and gently raised her head so that she met his gaze.

'What is it, Ileia?'

She didn't speak for a moment then looked meaningfully into his eyes before her words tumbled out.

'Would you make love to me?'

Tere's heart leapt with joy before he remembered her injuries.

'Nothing would make me happier, but you are injured. I would never forgive myself if I hurt you more.'

Ileia did not respond she just leaned into him and kissed him before pulling back.

'Tere, being with you will take away all the hurt and replace that memory with love and pleasure.'

Without hesitation he pulled her onto his lap, capturing her mouth in a passionate kiss that unleashed the depth of his feelings for her. He rose, swept her up into his arms and carried her into a thicket far into the forest. She weighed almost nothing, but her sweet curves against him awakened his body, sending desire and fierce protectiveness surging through him. Carefully lowering her to the soft, mossy forest floor, he covered her body with his. With tenderness that he hadn't thought himself capable of, he gently made love to Ileia, unofficially claiming her as his own.

Pleasuring her felt right, like pieces of a puzzle sliding together.

What wasn't right was the terror that consumed Tere when he thought about what Lacas would do to Ileia if he discovered their tryst.

* * *

The next morning, Tere was a little sore. Remembering his evening with Anya, then Ileia, he smiled as he pulled on some loose trousers and padded barefoot out of his room. Despite the crisp chill of the morning, a contentment he hadn't expected warmed him. He entered the worn, yet spotless kitchen to find his mother and Lacas seated at the table, silently eating bacon and eggs.

Immediately, Lacas eyed him. 'So, you managed to get it up.' He laughed and continued eating his breakfast.

Annoyance slid through Tere, but he tamped down his reaction preferring to hold onto the beauty and ardour of the previous day's events. 'Several times, actually.' He refrained from mentioning that the several times was with Ileia. *Mine.*

Turning away, he grinned as he grabbed some bacon and dropped it into the pan, then cracked an egg into it and watched it sizzle. He registered that, for once, Lacas had not felt the need to respond to his comment. He should have been suspicious of that.

Hearing a grunt, Tere turned, placing his plate on the table. His mood plummeted. Lacas had Alika's dress up and was taking her from behind as he leaned over, fondling her exposed breasts. She shook her head at Tere, warning him, tears rolling down her face.

Tere knew Lacas was baiting him. Bile rose in his throat. His body stiffened. He didn't think he was strong enough to kill Lacas yet. Oh, how he wanted to, to stop the abuse. Pulling in a sharp breath and averting his gaze, Tere yanked the pan off the stove. As it clattered noisily to the floor, he stomped out of the house, banging the door shut behind him. Tere stripped, taking the front steps two at a time as Lacas' cruel laughter and his mother's screams rang in his ears.

He shifted, running until he could run no farther, exhaustion halting his flight. Shifting back to his human form, he perched on the same outcrop where Ileia had comforted him once. Oblivious to the cold and rough stone cutting into his naked backside, he stared over the vast plain that led to the Kingdom of Therin, not seeing the beauty below. All he could see were visions of the cruelty both he and his mother had endured at the hands of Lacas. His anger exploded.

He clenched his fists around the sharp stones surrounding him, growling at the feeling of the blood oozing through his fingers as they cut into his palms. The guilt he harboured at not being able to help his mother lanced through him. He embraced the physical pain.

Alone. Desperate. Empty.

Throwing back his head, Tere howled until he was hoarse. His face was wet with the tears of years of abuse. Finally, he dropped his forehead onto his knees, exhausted from the outpouring of grief and anger, and slept. He did not move again until well after dark. Eventually, he shifted back and reluctantly padded home, wishing he had somewhere else to go but unwilling to leave his mother alone with Lacas for too long.

When he finally returned to the dark house, he assumed his mother and Lacas were in bed. He checked his mother's bed. Empty. Then he heard a whimper and a groan and realised Lacas had her in his bed again. Tere did not know how much more of this he could take. Stripping out of his clothes, he slid into his own bed and yanked the pillow over his head to block out the sound. Even muffled, the sounds ripped at his heart.

When it was finally quiet, Tere lay on his back, staring up at the ceiling. He hadn't eaten all day and considered getting up to make himself something, but his emotional and physical exhaustion was so complete, he didn't want to move. Unable to sleep, despite the almost overwhelming tiredness ravaging his body, Tere planned his revenge.

A few days later, Tere's mother told him she was pregnant again. He knew he must act soon or live each day wondering when Lacas would try to kill him so that the new alpha son Lacas hoped for would be his only offspring and inherit leadership of the pack. Lacas would then finally have what he would deem as a valid reason to dispose of his inferior offspring and remove the embarrassment of siring what he believed was a beta wolf.

It seemed Alika's belly swelled daily, bringing an unexpected blessing. Lacas returned home less often, preferring to lay with the young, slim females of the pack. This gave Alika and Tere time to relax. Tere seized the opportunity to spend time with Ileia, exploring the forest and each other. She made him happy. He was different around her. Ileia was a calming influence, and her sexy body and loving ways fulfilled him in a way he was unable to explain. He so dearly wanted to claim his gorgeous she-wolf officially but dared not for fear of drawing Lacas' attention to her.

* * *

One peaceful afternoon, Tere and Ileia lay on the large, soft sofa in the centre of his lounge room, their bodies entwined, enjoying a Lacas-free day where they could all relax. Sunshine streamed in through the almost sheer, crisp white curtains adorning the window warming Tere's exposed back. He knew his mother had slipped away for a nap. She slept heavily these days and would not hear them, but they still made sure they were quiet. Lacas was thankfully away on business for a few days. Time enough while his mother slept, he hoped, to satisfy his and Ileia's escalating desire for each other. Gazing at Ileia's incredibly beautiful face and into her soft green eyes, he felt an all-consuming contentment he'd never known before he met her.

Damn, I love her.

His body hardened with desire as their lips locked in a long kiss, her tongue wrestling with his. Ileia wriggled against him, teasing, rubbing herself against his already rigid erection. A groan rumbled up through Tere's chest as he hardened to an almost painful degree. He moved a little, allowing them both better access to each other. Focusing on the carnal assault from Ileia's kisses and her hand between them, stroking him through his trousers, the tension of an exquisite climax slowly curled through him. One of his hands lazily circled and tweaked Ileia's dusky pink nipples through her sheer, pale green blouse

Groaning as Ileia shoved his trousers down a little for better access and wrapped her fingers around his rigid member, Tere flexed his hips into Ileia's soft and talented hand. Pleasure spiked through him, his climax close. He couldn't resist lowering his head to suckle one tightly beaded nipple, making Ileia gasp and moan as he drew it into his eager mouth.

Somewhere through the fog of his desire, Tere heard a cry and the clatter of something falling in the kitchen. His heart jumping, he reluctantly slipped free of Ileia's warm, welcoming body, shaking his head to clear his thoughts. Ileia frowned, her gaze lifting to his before she stood, straightening her clothes.

Yanking his trousers up, he called out. 'Mama, are you all right?'

No answer. His heart clenched as he sprinted to the kitchen. His heavily pregnant mother lay on the floor, doubled over in pain. A pool of blood spread between her legs. Heart pounding, Tere swore, quickly kneeling beside her. He sensed Ileia pad up quietly behind him and heard her soft intake of breath.

'Mama, what's wrong?'

Tere's gaze flicked over his mother, checking for injuries as cold fear slid up his spine.

Alika's face contorted in pain as she clutched at her stomach. Gasping, terror filled her expression. 'The baby … Oh god, Tere. Get Merico. Quickly.'

Tere scrambled to his feet.

'Ileia, can you stay here with Mama, please? I'll be as quick as I can.'

She nodded, kneeling beside his mother and taking her hand. Tere wrenched the back door open, letting it slam shut behind him. Leaping down the six steps he raced down the dusty, unpaved street towards the healer's house. The houses, trees and people blurred as he streaked past them. He heard someone call out to him, recognising Reine's voice.

'Tere, what's wrong? Is everything all right?'

Grateful, yet not able to spare much breath to respond, he shook his head. 'It's the baby. Something's wrong. Let Lacas know. Please.'

Reine took off at a run as Tere sped towards the healer's cottage, his pulse racing, his chest tight with fear. He'd kill Lacas for this. He'd heard of women who had died in childbirth. He couldn't… wouldn't let that happen to his mother. He barrelled past the fifty or so cottages, the five minutes it took to get there seemed like much longer.

He banged furiously on the large, blue, wooden door. When

Merico opened it, it took no more than one look at Tere's expression before she grabbed her medical bag and hurried back with him. A few people had gathered in the street to see what was going on, watching as Merico and Tere raced past. He hated that none of them would offer to help for fear of upsetting Lacas. He heard snippets of their conversation as he tore past them, and the scent of their concern reached his nostrils. All he cared about right now was his mother. All this—his mother, the baby, the fear in the pack—was Lacas' fault.

Bursting through the door of the cabin, they found Alika writhing in agony on the floor. Ileia had placed a pillow under her head and covered her with a blanket, holding Alika's hand to comfort her. Ileia looked up, tears streaking her face. Tere squatted beside her, gently pulling Ileia against him. His eyes fixed on his mother, he felt simultaneously helpless and furious at Lacas.

Merico took in the situation. 'Get some old cloth or towels and place them on the bed, then help me lift her onto it.'

Ileia ran for the cloth. Tere bent, silently cursing Lacas as he easily lifted his mother, carrying her to the bed. Merico then shooed them outside, her face grim. He and Ileia waited, cuddled together on the dusty wooden front steps of the cabin.

Tere gripped Ileia tighter each time he heard his mother cry out. Head hanging, he struggled to fight the overwhelming sadness for his mother's suffering.

Damn Lacas.

Tere's free hand fisted around the edge of the rough, wooden step as white-hot fury took over, settling deep within his soul. His wolf snarled and lunged, seeking freedom to take revenge on Lacas. Tere barely managed to hold the beast back, gritting his teeth, his hand flexing rapidly, his feet digging into the dirt. Finally gaining some semblance of control, he realised that Ileia had pulled away from him. Glancing at her, her eyes wide, he realised she'd witnessed his struggle.

No! He prayed she wasn't frightened by what she'd seen because without her love, her calming influence, Tere was lost. He'd give in to the anger and be just like his father.

Ileia frowned, then rubbed her thumb back and forth across his now dusty fingers. He turned his hand over and his fingers reflexively clenched around hers. Leaning into him, she rested her head on his shoulder, her closeness comforting him. Tere struggled to hold back his alpha wolf daily, though he knew she didn't truly understand how difficult it was for him. Eventually, his shoulders relaxed and his vice-like grip on her hand loosened. Ileia relaxed into the heat of his body, staying like that for what seemed like an eternity, waiting.

When Merico emerged, wiping her hands on an old cloth, they both stood quickly, eyeing her expectantly. She shook her head.

'Your mother has lost the baby, Tere. She's going to need your help over the next few weeks until her body fully recovers.'

Tere nodded sadly, and Ileia leaned into him, offering silent comfort. Wrapping his arms around Ileia, he kissed the top of her head.

While Tere was sad for his mother, he couldn't help being relieved for both her and the unborn child. He wouldn't want another child going through what he had with Lacas. He refused to think of him as his father any longer. Lacas had not even bothered to see if his mate was all right, despite being told there was a problem. Lacas was probably disgusted with her for losing the baby. Tere almost snorted in derision.

He and Ileia headed inside. Would losing the baby be another excuse for Lacas to assault his mother? Gritting his teeth, he swore and vowed that he would never again allow Lacas to touch her.

CHAPTER 3

By the time Tere turned twenty, he was more muscled than most males his age. He was lean, yet at least as powerful as his father in both human and wolf form. To hide his alpha tendencies, he spent much of his spare time in the forest, usually with Ileia. He continued to keep their relationship discreet to protect her from Lacas.

Tere's lack of obvious female companionship caused rumours to circulate through Lacas' followers, doubting his sexuality. He ignored them without bothering to comment because he really didn't care anymore. He only waited for the day he would challenge and kill Lacas.

Returning home one Saturday night after spending time swimming at the lake with Ileia, he found his mother alone by the fire, sewing. Kissing her cheek, he noted several bruises on her legs and arms. Tere gritted his teeth, forcing himself to refrain from commenting.

'I'm going to bed, Mother.' He turned towards his room.

'Wait a moment please, Tere.' Turning back, he perched on the arm of the chair, his long legs hanging casually to the floor, his hands resting on his knees. Alika ran her gaze over him.

'Tere, why aren't you out with the other young ones? I know you have some in the pack willing to be your friends despite Lacas. I want you to enjoy yourself while you are young, before you have responsibilities.'

'Mother, you know that if Lacas has his way, I'll never be the leader of this pack, and I've been in the forest with Ile—'

The back door banged open, interrupting their conversation. Lacas weaved in, drunk, his clothing dishevelled, as if he'd dressed without caring what anyone thought after being with one of his many casual sexual partners.

'I brought the pup someone, so he can have some fun.'

Alika jumped from her chair, bravely protesting as five huge males pounced on Tere. He fought furiously, but Lacas' thugs managed to subdue him, drag him to his bed and secure him to the bedposts, spread-eagled, the man he once called his father helping them. This was a new low for Lacas. Tere briefly wondered how far he'd go with his cruelty. He didn't have to contemplate long.

Lacas used his claws to rip Tere's clothes off, cutting his skin deeply in the process. Blood trickled down Tere's sides and onto the crisp, white sheets. Tere roared, struggling furiously as four of the men pulled on the roughly hewn rope securing his limbs even tighter to prevent his escape. Alika screamed, begging Lacas to stop, but he backhanded her, then punched her, sending her sprawling to the floor, unconscious.

Cold fury coursed through Tere. Had he not been tied so tightly; he would have unleashed his wolf. Uncaring of his own predicament at that moment, he cried out, fear for his mother foremost in his thoughts.

'Mother!'

While Lacas' henchmen struggled to hold him down, Tere memorised each of their faces for the day he would take his revenge.

Fury and betrayal initiated a power within him that he couldn't identify, but it too was leashed by his bonds. Tere recognised that whatever was growing in his soul fought against those bonds, something elusive, a strength just out of his grasp. It seemed to be stretching his skin, trying to burst free. Could it be magic? Straining to hear the whisper floating across his thoughts, a voice, so like that of his paternal grandfather's, the one he'd often heard in his dreams, momentarily broke through the barrier. Tere twisted violently. It wasn't enough.

Fear and hatred coiled through Tere as Lacas roughly shoved a small, red-haired male into the room. This was the wolf they called Manny. Bile rose in Tere's throat. His heart thudded furiously. Tere knew that Manny had been reviled by the pack since he'd been caught rutting with human males. Tere had tried not to judge him. He knew what it was like to be misjudged.

Manny approached the bed, licking his lips nervously. His eyes darted around the room. Tere shook his head at him, but Manny's fear of Lacas drove him down onto the bed. Manny avoided looking at Tere except for the briefest of moments when his eyes lifted, and a look conveying an apology flicked across his expression so quickly that Tere doubted he'd seen it.

Gods, no. Surely even Lacas couldn't be that twisted.

Lacas stood back, a sick grin curling his lips, arms folded across his chest, body swaying slightly from the alcohol he'd consumed. Even from here, Tere could smell the whiskey on Lacas' foul breath. He knew now that there were no bounds to his evil and that he must be stopped. He vowed to himself at that moment that Lacas' life was forfeit.

Lacas roughly grabbed Manny, shoving him down on top of Tere.

Tere grunted and writhed, attempting to dislodge Manny, but his movements only seemed to incite the pale, anxious looking male.

Manny slid down, kneeling between Tere's legs, running his hands along his bare inner thighs and up to his groin. His eyes flicked nervously to Lacas, then back to Tere. Tere bucked hard, attempting to dislodge Manny's hands, which began rhythmically sliding up and down Tere's flaccid member. The friction forced an involuntary erection, sending Lacas' thugs into uproarious laughter. Tere swallowed against the bile rising in his throat.

Unable to watch, Tere closed his eyes, all the while fighting the visceral response of his traitorous body. A wisp of magic wrapped around him, sending shivers of unwelcome arousal spiralling through Tere. His eyes flicked open, focusing on Lacas. Tere couldn't hold back a vicious growl when he realised Lacas was using his magic to make it appear as though Tere was enjoying Manny's attention. Tere's eyes bored into Lacas, conveying his hatred.

Tere shuddered and swallowed hard against the nausea, praying it would be over soon. Slamming his eyes shut once more, he felt Manny's flesh rubbing against his. Only one thought slipped across his consciousness during this ordeal.

Revenge.

Moments later, Tere heard a grunt as Manny climaxed, his hot seed spilling onto Tere's groin. Tere turned his head, retching violently. Manny's weight lifted, and he sent Tere another brief look of apology before leaving, the back door banging shut after him. Tere's eyes blazed, focusing on the laughing men walking away, leaving him tied to the bed, defiled.

Gritting his teeth, he yanked furiously at his bonds. His wrists and ankles bleeding, his anger burning like wildfire. He wanted to howl in frustration but would not give Lacas the satisfaction. His wolf clawed from within, demanding its freedom, wanting revenge. Oh, how Tere wanted to set his wolf free, to rip apart those responsible for this, but the bonds prevented him from shifting, which probably saved his life.

After what seemed like hours, Alika crept into the bedroom slicing his bonds away with a razor-sharp knife. Tere couldn't hold back the anger and frustration, wondering why she hadn't used it on Lacas. He instantly regretted his ire when he noticed her split lip and a gash over one eye. She moved tentatively, hunched over, protecting bruised or possibly broken ribs, sobbing uncontrollably.

'Tere, I'm so sorry. I'm so sorry.'

Tere's hatred for Lacas burned so fiercely, he couldn't bring himself to speak. Rising awkwardly, he headed to the kitchen to heat some water until it was so hot it almost burned his skin as he tried to scrub away the smell and residual feel of Manny. While he bathed the deep cuts Lacas had ripped down his thighs, Tere's stomach revolted. Rushing outside, he dropped to his knees behind the closest bush and vomited until his belly ached and there was nothing left in it.

Eventually, he walked back inside and towelled himself dry. The smell of the sheets on his bed produced another bout of retching. Ripping them off the bed, he tossed them onto the floor and crawled onto the bare mattress. Sleep refused to come, disgust, fury and shame warring instead for his attention.

* * *

The next morning, Tere was exhausted, yet determined that things would change. He couldn't let the evil creature that was his father destroy his or his mother's life any longer. When he walked into the kitchen, he stopped short, witnessing Lacas taking his mother on the table.

Tere's temper exploded, twenty years of hurt and anger erupting. Launching himself at his sire, he grasped his hair and yanked Lacas' head back, his fists flying with the ire of a lifetime of cruelty. The force sent Lacas flying across the room. Alika screamed for Tere to stop, but now that he'd started, there was no way he could. The control that he'd so carefully built and prided himself on shattered like glass in a storm.

Lacas snarled viciously. Jumping to his feet, he pounced, knocking Tere to the floor, but Tere had grown strong without Lacas realising it. He was more than a match for his father. Snarling and snapping, they rolled on the floor, clawing, biting. Tere was very close to overpowering him when Lacas launched himself backward to where Alika cowered in the corner. Pulling a wicked looking knife from his boot, Lacas grabbed Alika by the hair and held the blade to her throat. Her eyes bulged with terror; mouth opened on a silent scream.

'One step closer and your mother dies.'

Tere froze, unwilling to risk injury to his mother, yet not daring to show the fear he felt for her. Panic threatened to overwhelm him as his heart pounded and his fisted palms grew damp with the sweat rolling down his body.

Tere held Lacas' glare as his eyes narrowed in challenge. Lacas' expression betrayed surprise at his unspoken defiance. An instant too late, Tere registered an almost imperceptible nod from Lacas. The same wolves who had held him down last night stood behind him. His fury had obviously clouded his senses because he should have smelled their presence sooner, should have known that Lacas never fought alone. Whirling around, Tere took one burly male down with a kick between the legs, sending him to the floor howling, clutching his genitals. Adrenaline pulsed through Tere as Lacas dropped the knife, launching toward him.

'Mother, *run!*'

Before she could, Lacas' henchmen surrounded her, dragging her away screaming and struggling to no avail.

Tere bellowed. It took four wolves to contain him however, he wasn't the only one battered and bloody. Hauling him to the village square, they viciously tied his hands above his head and attached the rope to a wooden frame. Yanking it up, they pulled until his feet were off the ground. His arm muscles straining and burning, he hung there, unable to move as they dragged his mother out by the hair. Badly beaten, Alika was hardly moving or making a sound. Her chest barely rose and fell with her laboured breaths.

Lacas' eyes never left Tere's face as Tere twisted violently, struggling to free himself. Without warning, Lacas drew his knife and drove it into Alika's belly. She screamed in agony. He leaned down, saying something that only she could hear. She shook her head violently, mouthing, *No,* as he slit her throat without pause, a sick grin on his face.

Tere could not pull his eyes from his mother as he watched her die, her lifeblood draining onto the ground. Her eyes, wide with pain and terror, lifted to Tere's one last time before fluttering closed.

His heart shattered. Realising the screaming he heard was his own, he drew a deep breath, tipped his head back and howled, a long, mournful sound filled with a lifetime of pain and suffering.

Through hot tears of fury, he saw Lacas wielding a vicious whip and stilled, readying himself for the pain to follow. Lacas laughed maniacally. Raising the lash repeatedly, he didn't stop until the blood ran down Tere's back, the skin shredded. The pain was excruciating, but Tere refused to utter a sound. His last thoughts were of bitter revenge before the blackness of oblivion consumed him.

* * *

When Tere woke, it was to the inky darkness of an almost moonless night. His shifter vision allowed him to see that his mother's body was gone, leaving only the stain of her blood on the ground. Spatters of his own surrounded him and the pain in his back was agonising. Closing his eyes, Tere attempted to regain control of his spiralling emotions so he could focus on healing. His efforts faltered as a deep, rolling swell of something resembling the heat of an open fire filled him. His body tingled, just as it did around wolf healing magic, but there was a subtle difference this time. Probing it carefully, it brought Tere a welcome distraction from the searing pain ... did he feel just the tiniest bit stronger?

Unable to get any real rest with his full weight hanging on his arms, stretching and straining his muscles, his raw and bleeding back sent shards of agony screaming through him. The tight, unforgiving knots of the ropes bit into his already raw wrists. He didn't care. He only cared that his bonds stopped him from shifting. If he could shift into his wolf form, he could heal himself. Only then could he find Lacas and take his revenge.

Sometime during the night, exhaustion claimed him, and he slept, fitfully dreaming of his grandfather. He had never met Canis, but his mother had told him stories of her father's leadership. The pack had been a good place to be then, prosperous and happy, blessed with many cubs and everyone looked out for each other. That was what being part of a pack should mean.

While the true meaning of pack filled his dreams, his grandfather appeared before him.

Tere, you have become a fine, powerful young wolf. Do not destroy yourself or those who love and would follow you with thoughts of revenge. Your mother is safe with me now. Embrace your destiny. You are an alpha. Draw the other wolves to you. Show them your strength and valour and they will follow you. Only then can you truly fulfil your purpose. Bide your time, Tere. Your opportunity will come. Do not let your anger drive your actions ...

Tere startled awake, his grandfather's voice fading. He peered into the darkness, trying to determine if the voice he'd heard was real or an hallucination. Despite his injuries, he felt an odd calm settle over him as a surge of strength rippled into his battered body.

A twig snapped to his left.

Pain shot through him as he swivelled his head around and tensed, ready to lash out with a kick. He winced as the muscles in his arms and neck protested the tiny movement, the ropes biting deeper into his already bloodied wrists. To his surprise, Ileia crept towards him, a sponge, a water bottle and a small jar of salve in her hands. His heart leapt at the sight of her.

Reaching up to caress his face, her hand trembled as she sobbed quietly. 'Oh, Tere. What has he done to you?'

Ileia offered Tere some water, tipping the waterskin up for him to drink, then gently washed the wounds on his back, applying a little salve to ward off infection.

Tere did not speak or cry out in pain, gritting his teeth instead. Tears pricked the back of his eyes, grateful as she so carefully did what she could to help. When she stood on her tiptoes, softly kissing his parched lips, his body trembled with the myriad of intense emotions flowing through him. Tears filled her eyes again, streaking down her cheeks. He wished he could kiss them away.

He swallowed hard, his throat dry and whispered, 'Thank you, my love, but you must go. Ileia, if they catch you here...'

His words trailed off. Pain stabbed his heart at the thought of what Lacas would do if he caught her. Nodding, she offered him some more water, then took a few steps away. She paused to look back over her shoulder, sadness in her expression, then disappeared into the shadows.

Even though she couldn't hear him, he whispered, 'I love you.'

Closing his eyes, he remembered Ileia's kiss, wondering if it would be his last.

*   *   *

The cold light of morning pierced the chilly dawn, and the thud of booted feet stirred Tere from his pain-infused sleep. Several of Lacas' armed soldiers surrounded him. Steeling himself for a killing blow, he was surprised when they cut him down and threw him into a cage, keeping his hands tied so he could not shift to heal himself. They locked the door before he scrambled to his feet. Tere growled, hurling himself at the bars of his prison. His captors laughed as they walked away. Lowering himself to the dry, dusty ground, the pain making him dizzy and nauseous, he couldn't help wondering why Lacas had not ordered him killed.

Attempting to gauge the extent of his wounds, Tere twisted, wincing as pain lanced through him. He tentatively poked at a large, blackening bruise on his abdomen. Broken ribs. Those would heal eventually, quicker if he could shift. Damn Lacas. His plan must be to keep him in a weakened state, so he was no threat. The hell he wasn't. A long, low growl rumbled from deep in Tere's chest. Lacas had underestimated him. That would be his downfall.

Chewing and pulling at the bindings around his wrists, Tere smiled when he finally worked them free. Then his alpha wolf took control, unleashing twenty years of pain and fury. Its strength surged through him. A wave of pure power swelled and burst over Tere, bathing him in white light, filling him with its gift of familial magic. Tere stripped quickly. Long denied its freedom, his wolf howled, stretching within. His bones popped and cracked, and a satisfied wolfish smile stretched his lips. The alpha power immediately began healing and strengthening him, but he dared not stay in his wolf form too long.

Restless beyond measure, Tere shifted back, dressing rapidly. Pacing around the perimeter of the cage, he assessed its strength. An iron mesh floor buried beneath the dirt prevented escape by digging, and the criss-crossed iron bars were too thick to bend or dislodge. This was a prison designed to ensure that even the strongest and most resourceful captive remain interred.

Determination lanced through him. His wolf snarled, finally free to give voice to its frustration. Placating his wolf, even as his own vehemence protested his inaction, he forced himself to sit and take a deep breath. He glanced around, noting the only shelter from the elements was a rough wooden structure, a hole dug in its centre. Given the unpleasant odour, he could guess what it was used for. Tere wrinkled his nose in disgust.

With his back resting against the bars, he mulled over his grandfather's words. He would honour his grandsire's words, embrace his destiny and bide his time while he grew strong enough to prove himself worthy of becoming the future pack leader. Lying face down on the dirt floor of his prison, the muscles in his arms tensed as he began a punishing regimen of exercise.

The days passed. His jailers came by once daily to bring dirty water and mouldy bread for him. Despite this and aided by the food and clean water his beautiful, brave Ileia brought every night, Tere's wounds healed, his strength gradually returning.

Each evening after dark, Ileia brought as much food as she could and warmed water to wash him. Calling to him quietly, she would lean in close to the bars. Sharing kisses through the cold iron, they spoke in soft whispers. Ileia spoke to Tere about the activities around the village. Of Lacas and his growing army. Of her suspicion that a Sorcerer and other foul creatures had rallied to them, although she had no inkling of their purpose.

One night Ileia came but did not move up to the bars of Tere's prison as usual. Instead, she slipped quietly to the door of the cage and began working at the lock. Tere hurried to the cage door.

'Ileia, no. What are you doing?' he whispered.

'Hush, my love. I have the key.'

'How did you—'

His words were cut off when Ileia wrenched open his prison door and swept into his arms. His heart thudded loudly with both fear and the joy of holding her close. Wrapping his arms around her, he buried his face in her hair, inhaling her sweet scent. Gently lifting her chin with his roughened hand, he placed a tender kiss on her honeyed lips. His pulse quickened as his body responded to her warm, soft curves pressed against him. Savouring the taste and feel of her, he momentarily allowed himself to believe they could be together.

Gods, she tastes so good.

Despite the joy of holding her, he forced himself to pull back, brows furrowed. 'This is too dangerous, Ileia. You must leave before someone catches you.'

Her laughter tinkled quietly through the cool night air.

'I paid a witch for a sleeping potion, my love. The guards will sleep until morning.'

He blinked. 'You what?' At her smile, he pulled her close, kissing her lips hard, excitement pounding through his veins. 'You are incredible, Ileia. You must come with me. If Lacas realises that it was you...'

He couldn't finish that sentence. Cold dread filled him at the thought of what Lacas would do to her. Ileia grabbed Tere's hand, turning towards the open cage door. Icy fingers prickled up Tere's spine moments before someone in the shadows applauded slowly, deliberately.

CHAPTER 4

'Well, well, well. It was you all along, lovely Ileia. I was convinced it was that sexy vixen, Anya.'

Lacas' voice was calm. However, Tere knew it belied a viciousness that was about to reveal itself in the worst possible way. Tere shoved Ileia behind him.

'Ah, so it appears you *can* get it up, or does she just pity you?' Lacas laughed cruelly.

Fury surged through Tere. His entire body shook with it. He readied to attack his sire, lunging forward before his grandfather's words penetrated his thoughts.

Do not let anger drive your actions...

With a great effort, Tere halted his forward motion, cocking his head at his father. 'Why don't you fight me, *Lacas*? Are you afraid that I'll beat you?' He spat out his father's name as if it were distasteful.

Lacas snarled. 'Why you little...'

Standing his ground, Tere smirked, achieving his purpose to enrage Lacas even further. Lacas lunged, but Tere was ready for him. Easily stepping aside, he pushed Ileia out of the cage.

'Run! I'll meet you ... You know where.'

He desperately hoped that she did. Not daring to voice that he'd meet her at the cave under the waterfall where they'd spent time enjoying getting to know each other both emotionally and physically. He feared if Lacas knew their meeting point, she'd be tracked. Turning his attention back to his father, Tere fought a grin of triumph.

Time for you to know fear, Father.

Tere's lips pulled back into a snarl, his teeth elongating, sharpening. Holding his shift back with the practice of twenty years, Tere's wolf strained for release, salivating for revenge.

Soon, dear friend. Soon.

Charging at Lacas, Tere tucked his head in, his muscled shoulder slamming into Lacas' abdomen causing Lacas to fall, sprawling backwards along the dirty cage floor. Palpable fury rolled off Lacas in waves as he scrambled back to his feet and launched himself at Tere. Lacas was driven by rage, rage that would be his downfall.

Tere's anger remained controlled and focused. Avoiding Lacas' furious punches, he landed a few powerful blows of his own to Lacas' jaw. A cracking sound echoed. After several more blows to his stomach, Lacas doubled over, struggling for breath. Tere brought his knee up under his sire's chin, sending him flying backward, splintering the wooden structure that surrounded the cess pit and knocking him unconscious. Yanking a long, thick, sharp splinter from the shattered timber, Tere lifted his arm to plunge the makeshift weapon into Lacas' heart. Hearing booted feet clumping hurriedly towards him, Tere hesitated.

Cursing under his breath, he stabbed the wooden dagger through Lacas' upper thigh, pinning him to the ground. Lacas' limp body jerked. Tere leaned down, inches from Lacas' still form.

'When I kill you, you will be looking into my eyes so I'm the last thing you see before you die.'

Snarling, Tere landed one last savage kick to Lacas' ribs, the sickening crack pulling a cry from Lacas. Tere felt no remorse as he sprinted from the cage and shifted, his dirty clothes ripping off his body as he transformed and sped to meet Ileia.

Finally reaching the cave at the side of the waterfall, Tere's heart pounded with fear. Had Ileia arrived safely? His skin and clothes were damp from the droplets that the immense waterfall sprayed far and wide as it roared down the craggy cliff face. The rough, rocky path that led to the cave and ran beside the edge of the precipice overlooked the roaring river far below. Foam created by the water as it pummelled the worn rocks accumulated along the water's edge. The grass and foliage surrounding it was vibrant green, long, and slick from the mist the waterfall sent through the air.

Tere looked back to ensure he hadn't been followed and spied the small stream off to the side, between the trees and undergrowth that he and Ileia had enjoyed this past summer. He briefly wondered if they'd ever spend such happy times there again.

Peering cautiously through the cave entrance that was partially concealed by huge fern fronds and long tendrils of ivy, he saw her standing just inside the cave, panting hard. Quickly moving into the cool, dank of the cavern he scooped her into his arms. She gasped as he hugged her tightly. He held her for some time, not speaking, just needing to feel her soft warmth against him as reassurance she was safe. Finally, having caught their breath, Tere tipped Ileia's chin up, kissing her gently. His love for her swelled, heating his blood. His brave Ileia.

'How can I ever thank you, Ileia? You put yourself in great danger to help me. I love you more than words can explain.'

Ileia's green eyes sparkled with a love so powerful, warmth washed over Tere like the healing rays of the sun. 'I love you, Tere...'

It seemed that she wanted to say more. Instead, her words trailed off, her eyes filling with tears.

'Ileia?'

Tere groaned when she pressed closer, moulding her body to his. Lowering his head, he captured her sweet mouth in a long, passionate kiss. She eagerly opened for him, their tongues tangling. Sliding his hands down her back, he urged her legs around his waist, settling her over his burgeoning erection. Ileia wiggled against him, evoking a deep, possessive growl that rumbled through him like thunder in a storm. His heart thumped so hard; he was certain she could feel it.

Running her tongue over his lips, Ileia teased and kissed the corners of his mouth. Tere's desire escalated, and his thoughts turned to mating with his sexy, red wolf. Reason won out, the danger too great right now.

Reluctantly, he lifted his head from her swollen, damp lips. Her molten, darkened eyes held his, dragging a groan from him as he pulled back.

'I need to check that we weren't followed. Stay here while I look around,' he said before kissing her again and cocking his head in a very wolf-like gesture. 'Do you have any food in that pack? I'm starving.'

Ileia's laughter tinkled through the cave, echoing softly into its unknown, inky depths. 'Of course. I knew you would be. I'll have something ready for you when you return.'

Stealing another kiss, Tere grinned as he moved cautiously out of the narrow entrance, the bracken scratching at his skin as it rustled into place behind him, shielding the entrance. He slid between the dense stand of trees near the pond, shifting, using his wolf senses to search for any sign that they were followed. Scenting the damp leaf litter beneath his paws, the clean moisture of the fine spray covering everything within several hundred feet of the waterfall, landed gently on his fur. The thundering of the water as it pounded onto the rocks far below reached his ears, a staccato beat rumbling through him.

Sniffing the zephyr that lightly ruffled his long, black fur, he could not detect any sign of pursuit. Tere extended his search, skirting the lush, green plain that undulated gently down to the edge of the precipice. The long grass cushioned his huge paws as he carefully scanned his surroundings. Satisfied that nobody was around, for now, he turned back. His pulse quickened as he finally allowed his thoughts to return to Ileia waiting for him.

When an unsuspecting rabbit exiting its hole caught his attention, he shifted into stealth mode. *Our next meal.*

Nuzzling his way into the cave, several freshly killed rabbits in his mouth, Tere's heart stuttered when he couldn't immediately locate Ileia. He caught a whiff of her sweet scent to his left, seeing her holding up a knife, ready to stab whoever entered the cave. Releasing the rabbits, he gave a little yip.

Ileia let the knife fall from her fingers, a cry slipping from her lips. Running to his side, she dropped to her knees, flinging her arms around the thick fur of his neck in a fierce hug. Whining quietly, he licked her face, making her giggle and release him. Shifting in a shimmer of gold and silver, relief washed over him at no longer having to hide his alpha status. Tere stalked towards her without thought of his nakedness, gathering her to him for a searing kiss.

When they broke apart, Tere grabbed clean breeches from the pack Ileia had brought, quickly dragging them on to cover his arousal.

He wanted more. Wanted to mate with Ileia. How much longer could he hold back?

Ileia smiled, watching his hard muscles flex as he dressed. 'You didn't have to dress for me.'

Raising his eyebrows, Tere turned and grabbed the rabbits. His control was tenuous right now, so he focused on cleaning the rabbits. When he turned to her and saw the tears in her eyes, he felt guilty for hurting her. He hadn't made love to her or asked her to formally mate with him because it wasn't safe right now. He opened his mouth to explain but she grabbed the rabbits from him, not making eye contact and began cleaning them. Once finished she wrapped them in a piece of linen and stuffed them in a crevice in the cave wall.

'I'll cook them for tomorrow,' she said in a clipped voice.

Tere gathered some wood to light a fire near the back of the cave, so the smoke was drawn backward instead of out the entrance. Silently, they nibbled the food Ileia had brought, then settled in beside the fire to warm themselves and relax. After their meal Tere laid down and pulled her close hoping that the animosity between them earlier was forgotten. He smiled as she curled into him, and they slipped back into their usual relaxed way. They chatted easily, discussing their next move.

'We can stay here for a while, but Lacas will eventually come looking for us.' Tere said as his hand moved up and down one of her arms.

Ileia rolled away and onto her stomach, her gaze sliding over him. 'So, we go where they won't expect. Why don't we head for Therin? I've heard it's safe there?'

Tere had always wondered what Therin was like. He'd heard many stories about the castle, its' knights, its' people, and the surrounding villages and was keen to see it all. He wasn't certain if they'd be accepted as wolves because he'd also heard that the previous king of Therin had not tolerated magic. Nonetheless, the reports indicated it was largely a peaceful place now with potential opportunities for them.

'Hmmm, yes. I would like to see Therin. I've also heard there's a fae kingdom to the east of Therin. I've never met one of the fae. I wonder if they'd be accepting of us. I haven't heard much about them except that Lacas caused some trouble with them. It's quite a lot further than Therin so perhaps that could be our second choice? There are elven kingdoms too according to Reine's father, so we have several options.'

'Well, let's start with Therin and see what it holds for us,' she replied.

Her long, red hair curled softly over her shoulders, and her emerald, green eyes watched him, love shining brightly in their depths. A smile curved the corners of his mouth.

'You are so courageous. I love you, Ileia.'

Leaning in to kiss her, he hauled her onto his body. His heart thumping as Ileia stretched out on top of him. Wrapping herself around him, their lips and tongue tangled until they were both breathless. With great effort, he pulled away, rolling Ileia off him.

'You should sleep now. I'll keep watch.'

Tere could see the frustration in Ileia's expression, feel it in the way her actions toward him changed. He felt it too. He loved her, so why wouldn't he mate with her? They'd explored and enjoyed each other many times before, but ever since the Coming-of-Age ceremony two years ago, Tere hadn't let it go any further. He ached for her, surely she knew that. He knew there was something that she wanted to say but also that she held it back. He wasn't sure why or what it was.

'Wake me when it's my turn,' she snapped at him.

Tere started to protest, but Ileia pinned him with a determined stare. He sighed. The conversation about mating would have to wait, their lives depended on it.

'We will survive only if we work as a team. Wake me when it's my turn,' she ground out.

Ileia rolled over and closed her eyes. Tere watched her for a moment, a smile twitching at his lips, wondering at her strength and valour, then he took position at the cave entrance.

In the early hours of the morning, when he couldn't keep his eyes open any longer, Tere reluctantly woke Ileia to take her turn at the watch. Rubbing her eyes, she kissed him lightly, hopefully indicating she'd forgiven him, at least for now, then moved to the cave entrance. Tere stoked the fire, then lay down, quickly falling into a deep sleep.

After several hours sleep, he woke to the delicious aroma of rabbits cooking over the fire. Ileia smiled at him, making his pulse jump. Tere rose, prowling towards her.

Ileia stood and wrapped her arms around his neck. Leaning her warm body against him, she nibbled at his lips, telling him silently that she wanted him. Growling, Tere captured her mouth, holding her close for a long moment. When his stomach rumbled loudly, breaking the moment, they both laughed. Ileia pulled away and filled a dish with some of the stew, which Tere ate heartily, making little appreciative noises. Giggling, she lowered herself gracefully to the ground beside him.

* * *

They lived in the cave for several days before deciding the safest thing to do was to start for Therin. They had heard that the new king, Aidan, was a fair, compassionate and reasonable man. A man in touch with his people. They'd also heard that significant numbers of Elves and Fae had started making their way to Therin. On the fourth day since their escape, they packed up their meagre possessions in preparation to leave for a new life in Therin.

Tere moved up behind Ileia as she worked, sliding his arms around her. Leaning back into him, she sighed when he kissed her neck, lifting her hair to drop tiny kisses around her neckline. She shivered, turning in his arms. Looking down into her beautiful green eyes Tere lowered his head, injecting all the passion he possessed into the kiss. When he lifted his lips from hers, his breathing was ragged, his blood raging through his body, and without a second thought he opened the last piece of himself to her.

'Did I tell you today how much I love you? When we find somewhere safe, I'm going to spend all day making love to you to show you just how much.'

Ileia gasped then smiled with such joy Tere's heart leapt. She leaned into him and whispered against his ear. 'I can't wait, my love, it is what I've wanted since the Coming-of-Age ceremony.

Swallowing hard, Tere forced himself to move away from her because they needed to leave. He dropped a quick kiss on her lips and grabbed their water skins. Before they exited the cave, he stowed a spare set of clothes in a small crevice in wall in the hope that they'd be able to return to the pack one day. Tere left Ileia to finish packing her belongings and made his way to the nearby stream to fill their containers before they set out. Squatting on the bank, he dipped the leather water skins beneath the surface of the cool, clear water, smiling to himself at the prospect of their new life together. But his pleasant thoughts were interrupted by a blood-curdling scream that pierced the silence of the forest. Tere dropped the containers, leapt to his feet and raced back to the cave, fear slicing through him.

As he neared the cave entrance, his heart stopped. Lacas and six men from the village were hauling a struggling Ileia along the path from the cave and towards the precipice. He leapt forward hurling himself at Lacas, driving his sire to the ground. The others stood back, holding Ileia as Tere and Lacas fought a vicious battle. Finally managing to pin Lacas under him, Tere was pounding his bloodied face with his fist when the largest of Lacas' followers, a huge, silver-haired wolf, one of Lacas' most loyal followers named Baras, wrenched Ileia's arm so hard, she cried out.

Tere, momentarily distracted by her cry, paused his assault long enough for Lacas to shove him off and draw a knife from one of his long, leather boots. Lacas slashed wildly, but Tere moved quickly, rolling and twisting to avoid the blade. At that moment several things happened, Baras forced Ileia's face into the dirt, twisting her arm behind her back to stop her struggling, the other five men circled behind Tere, capturing his arms. Despite Tere's violent struggle, they eventually subdued him.

Lacas lashed out with a vicious kick to Tere's stomach, winding him. Tere struggled to breath as Lacas spat out, 'That's partial payment for what you did to my leg.' Lacas' men dragged Tere and Ileia further down the winding path beside the waterfall. When they reached the precipice, Tere stilled. His heart pounding his gaze locked with Ileia's.

Bravely, she raised her chin, mouthing, *I love you.*

Lacas nodded at his henchmen. Baras dragged Ileia closer to the edge and, without pause, hurled her over the bluff. Tere's eyes flew wide open. Despair, terror and white-hot fury enveloped him. Biting back a cry, Tere pinned Lacas with a deadly stare, instinctively drawing strength from the force of Mother Nature. Time seemed to slow as his body filled with the power he had been trying to grasp since he'd dreamed of his grandfather. He closed his eyes and swept a wave of familial magic down the almost vertical cliff face, attempting to stop Ileia plummeting to her death. After moments that seemed like an eternity, he sensed her trajectory slow, then finally halt. Seeking her essence, Tere sensed her, injured but alive, on a narrow, jagged ledge. Ileia was safe for now.

He turned his fury towards Lacas.

Releasing a blast of power fuelled by pent-up rage, he threw the five men off him sending them sprawling backwards. The force stole the breath from their lungs, smashing their bodies against the rock-hard ground, rendering them unconscious. Turning to see Lacas' eyes wide with shock and Baras fearlessly stalking towards him, Tere pushed his palms out, chanting in an ancient tongue that spilled from a place deep within his soul. A swirling vortex of power whipped around him, and Lacas and Baras froze, unable to move. For the first time, true fear shone in their eyes as understanding of Tere's strength penetrated their awareness.

Closing his fist as though gripping the throats of his adversaries Tere propelled them towards the edge of the cliff with his new-found magic.

Experiencing neither remorse nor compassion, Tere lifted Baras over the edge, holding him in midair momentarily, then released his magical grip, sending Lacas' henchman to his death. He stilled, listening to the screams as Baras plummeted to the jagged rocks below.

Turning his deadly gaze on Lacas, Tere partially released the magical bonds holding his sire. The terror in Lacas' eyes was somewhat gratifying. He whined and pleaded, revealing the coward Tere always knew him to be.

'Tere, you are my son. Surely you cannot do this to me. I have raised you as best I could and given you a home. Come, Tere. Let us sit together and talk as men.'

Tere's fury was palpable and barely contained. 'You bastard. You beat Mama and me. You killed her in front of me. You had them hold me and watched while Manny violated me. You flogged me almost to death, imprisoned me, and have all but destroyed the pack. I refute your paternity. Why would I wish to hear anything you have to say?'

Lacas, realising Tere was beyond listening to his words, responded by attempting to use his glamour. Tere shut him down viciously, driving him to his knees with the power of his magic. Lacas eyes rolled with terror as the realisation of how powerful his son was penetrated his narcissistic view of life. A joyless smile touched Tere's lips.

'You should know, Lacas, that I am alpha. I possess the magic handed down to me by my maternal grandfather. I will be the pack leader and will restore peace and happiness to the pack you almost destroyed. We will rejoice in your death, and my mother can finally rest peacefully.'

Gathering his magic, Tere briefly marvelled at the strength he wielded. Silently thanking his grandfather, he shoved Lacas over the edge of the cliff, listening until his screams could no longer be heard. Turning his attention back to Ileia, he searched for her life force, finally locating it. It was weak, but there. He projected his thoughts to her.

Ileia, don't move. I'm coming to get you.

Locating a nearby tree stump, Tere looped the rope from the pack Ileia had brought for him around it so he could lower himself down to the ledge where Ileia lay injured. Tere prayed the rope would be long enough. Slowly lowering himself over the edge of the precipice, desperately wanting to go much faster, he finally saw her crumpled and bleeding form lying deathly still on a narrow shelf.

Reaching the ledge, he carefully braced his long legs on either side of her, testing the stability of the rocky surface. He leaned down, using his magic to probe for injuries. Her leg was broken, probably her ribs too, and he detected multiple deep cuts and bruises. Her head wound, which bled profusely, worried him more than the other injuries.

Realising he needed to heal her ribs before he could move her, he removed his shirt, tying her legs together to support the broken one. Despite being unconscious, Ileia's face contorted in pain as Tere tightened the knot on the makeshift splint. He wanted to cry for the pain he knew racked her petite body. Whispering reassuring words, even though he wasn't certain she could hear him, Tere placed his hands over her ribs, allowing a gentle stream of healing magic to flow into his beloved she-wolf. A tiny sliver of relief worked its way through him when her laboured breathing eased a little.

Edging around to place his back against the wet cliff wall, Tere untied the rope around his waist. Securing it around Ileia, he grabbed the end, looping it around his waist again. He lifted her as gently as he could and tightened the rope so she was secured against him and began the slow, agonising journey up the slippery, black rock. Sparing a glance down the almost sheer cliff, he hoped to see Lacas' body in the maelstrom of white water of the river below. His eyes quickly scanned the slick, moss covered rocks, unable to dismiss the doubt that plagued him. Surely nobody could survive a fall like that.

Forcing his attention back to the climb, his feet flat against the cliff wall, his legs either side of Ileia, he inched his way upwards. His muscles strained, shaking with the effort of hauling their combined weight up the almost sheer cliff face. Finally, after what seemed like hours, the edge of the cliff came into view.

Tere's fear for Ileia grew. She had not moved or made a sound since he started his ascent. Despite her tiny frame, the strain of pulling them both up the sheer side of the cliff had taken its toll on his arms. He paused, his breathing laboured and arms shaking. Sweat dripped into his eyes blurring his vision. Dragging in a deep breath, he gathered the last remnants of his strength and hauled them the last few feet up the slick rock face, straining until they were both safely over the edge.

He untied the ropes securing Ileia to him and laid her down gently, then flopped on the grass a few feet away to catch his breath. For a scant few moments he lay panting on the damp grass, every muscle in his body screaming in protest. When Ileia groaned, Tere crawled to her, ignoring his own aches and pains. Carefully untying her legs, he bent over, chanting a healing spell over the broken one. Until a few days ago he hadn't known that he possessed such strong healing magic, the words of the incantation still foreign to him. Focusing on the power now coursing through his beloved Ileia, healing her, he allowed a finger of his scent to wrap around her, to calm and reassure her.

After a while Ileia sighed as the pain obviously eased under his ministrations, and Tere felt a little of the tension lift from his shoulders.

You're safe now, Ileia. I love you. We're going to leave for Therin and our new life together as soon as you're well enough. I'm going to carry you to the cave now so that you can rest.

Despite his protesting muscles, Tere lifted her into his arms, carrying her back to the cave. He placed her gently on some tufts of dried grass they'd brought in during their stay to protect them from the sharp rocks on the cave floor, lay out her bedroll, then carefully lifted her onto the too thin bedding. Reluctantly leaving her for a moment to build a fire at the back of the cavern, he covered the cave entrance with bracken before he settled down beside her, exhausted, tenderly curling himself around her body to keep her warm.

In the middle of the night, terrified screams woke him. Holding her tightly, he whispered words of reassurance, then gently turned her to face him. The fire was low but provided enough light so she could see his face. Calming immediately, she burrowed herself against his chest and cried, releasing the terror of her ordeal. Tere held her close until her sobs subsided, his own eyes moist with the realisation of how close he'd come to losing her, his heart aching for what his precious Ileia had endured for him. Finally, the she-wolf changeling, who he loved more than life itself, fell into an exhausted slumber.

Holding Ileia in his arms, he tenderly stroked her hair as she slept. He gazed down at her, an ache spread across his chest, his breath catching at her beauty and the incredible strength of spirit she possessed. Silently, he thanked his grandfather for the powerful ancient magic gifted to him that had allowed him to save her.

After dozing fitfully, Tere, woke a few hours later to barely glowing embers. Untangling himself from Ileia, he added more wood to the fire and retrieved another blanket from her pack. Dropping to his haunches to drape the blanket around her, the memory of her haunting screams as she was shoved over the cliff's edge replayed over and over in his head. He squeezed his eyes shut, attempting to block out the image of the panic shining in her green eyes moments before she disappeared over the crag. His heart had stopped, horror gripping him and rendering him unable to think or act for what had seemed like long minutes but had in reality only been seconds before he'd instinctively flung out his power to save her.

His thoughts turned to the moment he'd shoved Lacas over the cliff, using nothing but his magic. The dread and intense fear reflected in Lacas' eyes as he'd realised what was happening had not provided the satisfaction Tere had expected. And he couldn't shake a nagging suspicion that, despite seeing Lacas disappear over the edge of the precipice and hearing his screams, it wasn't the last he'd see of the cruel wolf who'd sired him.

CHAPTER 5

The current slowed, the rocks that had been worn smooth from the constant motion of the water rushing downstream from the waterfall cradled his battered, bleeding body. The gentle wash of the water around him a welcome relief from the violence of the icy waterfall and jagged rocks ripping at him as he'd hurtled down jagged cliff and then the unrelenting rapids. Teetering on the edge of consciousness images of his terrifying plummet over the cliff played disjointedly through his thoughts.

Separating dream from reality was difficult, until a sudden rush of cool water brought some clarity and rolled him onto his back. His eyes fluttered open. Quickly squeezing them shut against the bright, fiery, rays of the sun, he groaned, pain lancing through his skull. What the hell happened?

He slowly turned, wincing as he struggled to his hands and knees, his body protesting every move, the sharp stones on the riverbed biting into his knees as he pushed himself up. Coughing violently, he doubled over emptying his lungs of water, white-hot pain slicing through him as he struggled onto the damp, grassy bank. Clarity induced by the sharp agony stabbing in his chest presented Lacas' brain with the memory of Tere shoving him over the edge of the precipice using his new-found power, courtesy of his maternal grandfather.

Lacas swore, spitting and growling in response to the image, then immediately wished he hadn't as he sucked in a pain-filled breath. Who knew the pup was an alpha possessed with such powerful magic? He would have never let him grow into adulthood, had he known. He briefly wondered how Tere had managed to hide his alpha status, then vehemently cursed Alika for helping him.

The painful throbbing in his leg returned his attention to his injuries. The metallic odour of blood permeated the air. Moving slightly, testing his body, he gritted his teeth against the pain in his side. Broken ribs. Hauling himself into a sitting position against a large rock, his eyes followed the trail of bright red blood to the deep gash on his thigh. His breath came in little gasps as he slipped back into the abyss of unconsciousness swearing revenge against Tere as blackness engulfed him once more.

Lacas woke again as the sun hung low in the sky like a giant, perfectly round, red and gold apple. Panting hard, he pulled himself into a sitting position. Groaning, he began assessing his injuries. The open wound on his head caused a wave of dizziness and he fell onto his elbows, vomiting what he hoped was the last of the contents from his stomach. Crawling a little way up the bank and under the protection of a small outcropping of rocks, Lacas winced and grunted at the pain in his chest as he ripped his shirt to bandage his bleeding leg.

Several of his ribs were broken, his head throbbed. He was battered and bruised, but surprisingly, that was all he could identify. Leaning back onto the rocks heated by the setting sun, he closed his eyes and his world spun. Swearing out loud, his bloodshot eyes flicked open until the spinning settled, then he closed them again and quickly dropped into a deep, exhausted slumber.

* * *

Waking at first light, Tere was surprised he had dozed off again. He guessed that use of such powerful magic must take a toll on his body. Turning his attention to Ileia he was pleased to see that she was breathing more easily. He let his hands skim the length of her body, assessing how well she was healing. Tamping down his physical reaction to her, he inspected her limbs carefully to be sure that he hadn't missed any injuries. Satisfied with her progress, he moved away to rummage through their packs for something for breakfast. Finding some oatmeal, he grinned as his stomach rumbled, thankful, not for the first time, that Ileia had packed exactly what they needed for their journey under extremely difficult circumstances. He placed the oats in one of the small pots, along with some water and a little honey he'd found in a container, then set it over the fire. He stoked the fire again for warmth, then gently woke her.

Ileia opened her eyes slowly, her lips curving in a smile as she woke to him hovering over her. He helped her sit up, urging her to shift to hasten her healing. She shifted then stretched as the last of her external wounds healed, the skin closing, the pain ebbing away. A wolfish smile curved her lips as she paced around inside the cave testing her ability to move, her strength. When she shifted back, Tere's eyes flicked away, his attention fixed on the oatmeal warming over the open flame.

Perplexed by his lack of interest, Ileia sidled up to him, leaving the lacy cream-coloured shirt she'd slipped on, unfastened, her breasts exposed. After everything they had been through, now was not the time for subtlety. Moving around to face him, she squatted so that he had no choice but to meet her gaze.

'Why won't you look at me, Tere?'

The confusion in her eyes almost undid him completely. He felt compelled to return her honesty, his voice husky with desire.

'If I'd looked at you while you were naked, I might have lost control completely. I couldn't bear it if I hurt you.' He dropped his eyes, ashamed, fearful of being like his father.

'You would never hurt anyone, Tere. Look at me ... please.'

Slowly, he lifted his eyes to see her blouse open, exposing her soft, heaving breasts. His breath caught. Raising his hand, he gently touched her cheek.

'I want you so much, but you were so badly hurt, I ...' He trailed off, unable to finish.

Moving closer, Ileia took his hand and placed it between her breasts. He groaned, gently pushing her to the ground, kissing her with such passion that they both gasped at the intensity. Unable to get enough of her, Tere quickly but carefully had her naked beneath him still afraid he may hurt her. Moaning and squirming as his mouth followed his hands down her body, Ileia climaxed twice under his attention before he finally yanked off his trousers, releasing his rock-hard erection. He hesitated, swallowing.

'Ileia...'

'Tere, we were meant to be together. Please, take me as your mate. I love you.'

Tere growled, her declaration shattering the last filaments of his control. He settled himself between her legs, his erection nudging the damp entrance to her body. He lowered his head to suckle each dusky pink, beaded nipple as he moved his hips against her. The little mewling sounds she made when he rubbed against her most sensitive spot drove him wild. When she lifted her knees and angled her hips, he slid into her. Breathing heavily, her hands kneaded his buttocks, her ankles locked around him urging him closer, deeper. He couldn't hold back any longer. Slipping deep into her heat, he gasped as her tight sheath massaged his length.

Tere set a slow rhythm, drawing out their pleasure, never wanting this exquisite feeling to end. Ileia writhed and panted beneath him, her hair deliciously tousled, her lips swollen from his kisses. His heart soared. Quickening the pace, he sensed her approaching climax. When she slid her locked ankles higher around his waist, she opened further, and he slid deeper, lost to everything except the two of them and this moment. Ileia moaned his name as his hips surged forward. When her muscles clamped around him, a powerful climax swept through Tere stealing all rational thought. Eventually, he lifted his head from where it had been nestled into her neck as he caught his breath.

'I love you so much, Ileia. I thought I'd lost you.'

His eyes momentarily filled with tears, his voice a hoarse whisper. Taking his weight on his elbows, he kissed her again before. himself off her, smiling at her happy sigh. Rising, he retrieved some warm water from another pot he'd put over the fire to boil some time ago. He'd remembered to lift it off before they'd made love, so it had already started to cool. Grabbing a clean rag he gently washed her, paying extra attention to her most feminine parts. Her eyes shone with tears, and he leaned forward to wipe them away with his thumb before placing a tender kiss on her damp lips. When he had finished, she sat up reaching for him and captured his face between her hands, kissing him passionately. They spent some time kissing and cuddling, then dressed, ate the oatmeal he'd prepared then just leaned into each other's warmth for a little longer, both yet unwilling to surrender the intimacy of physical contact.

Finally placing the empty bowl down Tere stood, 'I'd like to leave here as soon as we can. The pack will soon come looking for us and Lacas.'

Ileia nodded, watching him with a smile. Tere held her gaze. His love for her swelled and leaning down, he circled his hands around her tiny waist drawing her to her feet. The warmth of her skin and her soft curves caused a renewed surge of desire but he tamped it down. Their safety was the priority.

Ileia gazed into his eyes. 'Let's leave now. This cave unsettles me like it never has before. It feels as though something bad is going to happen and I can't explain why.'

Nodding his agreement, he asked, 'Are you certain you're strong enough?'

'Yes.'

Pulling her close he held her tightly, focusing on their newly forged bond shining brightly between them and growled possessively. *Mine.* He knew he should formally ask her to be his mate to make the bond unbreakable ... except by death. But that would require him biting her to draw a small amount of blood as they made love, and he wasn't convinced that she was strong enough to lose more blood yet. He swore to himself that he'd perform the final ritual to seal their bond as soon as they were safe. They were technically mated now because they'd had full intercourse anyway. He smiled. Ileia was his at last.

Collecting their meagre belongings, they cautiously headed down the side of the mountain, leaving the cave and the evil memories of Lacas and his followers behind. One day they'd return to their home so Tere could claim his rightful place as pack alpha.

* * *

Lacas awoke and tried to stand, but his legs refused to support him. Too weak to shift, he lay there, his back against a rock, battered and sore from both the beating Tere had given him and his fall over the precipice. Landing miraculously in a section of water clear of rocks had saved his life. He cursed vehemently. Tere had surprised him with his strength and power.

That damn woman had produced an alpha male and hidden it from him so well, he'd had no idea. Lacas knew he had to kill his son or Tere would challenge him for leadership, most likely defeating him.

Who'd have guessed the pup actually had balls?

Lacas sneered at the thought. Dragging himself to the water to drink, he slaked his thirst then crawled back to the rock to rest and heal. The pain eased a little, allowing him to drift off to sleep. It wasn't long before he woke in a cold sweat, his breathing erratic following a vivid nightmare of his terrifying plunge down the side of the cliff. The pain and fear had been real as he'd dreamed of the water pulling him deeper and deeper until he was certain he would drown. Lacas closed his eyes, attempting to gain control of his breathing. With every inhale, a knife-like stabbing pain screamed through his chest.

The damn pup would pay for his suffering.

Heaving himself to his knees, Lacas' head spun, and his stomach roiled threatening to expel what little water was in it. He gritted his teeth and slowly, determinedly hauled himself into a standing position, supporting himself against a nearby tree. His vision blurred, but he remained on his feet despite swaying a little. After a few moments, he sat again and slowly stripped out of his torn clothes so he could shift. Running his hands over his naked body to feel for other injuries, he lingered a little too long over his semi flaccid manhood. Shifting in a shower of silver, a wolfish grin played across his face, despite the pain the shift caused. He sat on his haunches, panting, allowing his body to heal.

When the pain subsided and he could breathe more easily, he slowly loped back towards the village and his pack. His first thought was to fulfil his rising lust, then he would gather his pack leaders, find the pup and destroy him.

It took much longer than Lacas anticipated to travel the distance to the village due to his injuries. After several hours, he heard the familiar sounds of the pack. Several of his leaders rushed towards him as he limped along the main road. Growling, he shook off their sycophantic attention and shifted into his human form hobbling battered and naked, towards his cabin. The much larger cabin he'd ordered built for himself because he deserved something commensurate to his rank, after Alika's death He'd always despised the tiny cabin where he'd lived with her.

A lecherous grin stretched his lips as he spied the nubile and delicious Anya sitting on the porch of her home. The daughter of one of his most loyal leaders, Lupus, and young enough to bear him healthy pups, she would make a perfect new mate and her family would be happy for her to mate with the pack alpha. He'd noticed her at the Coming-of-Age ceremony and had wanted to show her what an experienced lover could do, even then. He doubted that his offspring had shown her the joy of true lust and grinned as his thoughts turned to exactly what he would do to show her. Trudging over, Lacas stopped within inches of her luscious young body. She gasped as he grabbed her, claiming her mouth in a punishing kiss.

Pulling back, he spoke close to her ear, 'You can be my playmate from now on. I will show you what real coupling is. You're young and tight and can bear me some strong alpha pups.'

His hand brutally grabbed her belly, then slid lower, as though testing her ability to bear him pups. Yelping, Anya's eyes widened with fear. A scream tore from her lips as Lacas roughly shoved her head to the side. First kissing her neck then allowing his wolf teeth to extend as he drew in her scent, he sank his teeth into the sensitive area beneath her ear. Drawing blood he claimed her as his mate. Her father, Lupus, rushed out of the cabin to see why Anya had screamed and looked on, hands fisted, knuckles white, fury and fear written across his features as he watched Lacas mate-claim his only daughter.

The taste of her blood fuelled Lacas' lust. His body was rigid, and he barely restrained himself from taking her right there. He growled, holding eye contact with Lupus, daring him to challenge his claim. When Lupus lowered his gaze and his stance drooped Lacas grinned before he spoke close to Anya's ear.

'Clean yourself up and be at my cabin before sunset.'

Invigorated by the desire pulsing through him he turned away, striding home with renewed zeal to bathe, dress and plan his son's death. Pack members averted their gaze from his body. Not from embarrassment, but from fear. Mothers hurried their daughters inside before they drew Lacas' attention. In his aroused and angered state, he may choose to sate his lust with one of them. Age did not matter to him.

Several hours later, a terrified Anya and her anxious father stood at Lacas' door. Lupus attempted to negotiate some terms to ensure his daughter's safety, but Lacas grabbed Anya and shoved Lupus out the door. Lupus grasped the handrail to stop himself from falling down the steps and stood on the other side of the door, listening to Anya whimpering. He wanted to rush in and rescue his daughter, but fear and misguided loyalty warred against his paternal instinct.

Turning slowly, his fists opening and closing reflexively, Lupus forced himself to walk away, vowing revenge. His wolf fought for release in response to Anya's screams echoing down the dusty street.

* * *

Anya was barely through the door when Lacas started stripping her, ripping her clothes off with his exposed claws. He panted, his lust out of control. Anya attempted to kiss him to slow things down, though it was difficult with the panic slicing through her, making her heart pound furiously. Even through the fear, she wanted him, wanted the status that came with being the alpha's mate, but she was well aware of what had happened to Alika.

Lacas' eyes were glazed. Knowing she couldn't break through the haze of violent lust, she steeled herself, her heart thumping with terror. She swore she'd show him that she wanted him, too. Lacas slipped a razor-sharp claw along the front of her dress and ripped it off, her breasts now exposed to his teeth. Lifting her, he dropped his trousers and entered her with such force she was sure he'd torn something inside her. A scream ripped through her bleeding lips. Pain knifed through her lower body. Panting to stay focused, she clung to his broad, powerful shoulders, locking her ankles around him as he pounded into her.

It only took a moment for Lacas to finish. He stomped away,

grabbed his trousers and yanked them up his muscled legs. Despite the pain Anya couldn't help admiring his firm backside as he walked away and dropped into an armchair. She searched the kitchen cupboards to locate a pot, warmed some water and using a soft cloth she found in the bathing area, washed away the blood between her legs. Despite the fear still radiating through her after the agony of their first coupling, she carried some warm water to Lacas, offering to wash him. He leaned back in the huge, dark green armchair and eyed her suspiciously, then nodded his approval.

Coaxing him to lift his hips so she could slide down his trousers, Anya moved between his legs washing him carefully, laving him with long, slow strokes of the warmed cloth. Holding his darkening gaze, she lowered her head to take his already burgeoning erection into her mouth. Lacas' eyes widened with surprise as he drew in a sharp breath. Throwing his head back, he allowed her to pleasure him, his body pulsing under her ministrations. She took him to the pinnacle of pleasure, then boldly reached up and kissed him.

Lacas smiled almost appearing surprised that he had, shook his head a little and moved his hands to her tiny waist, pulling her naked body closer.

'Hmm ... I smell both your fear and your arousal. Because you are so brave, I will let you rest. But later, I want to hear you scream with pleasure instead of fear.'

Anya stood, sashaying away. She looked over her shoulder. 'Oh, you can be guaranteed of that. I'll do my best to make you shout my name in ecstasy, too.' She grinned, wiggled her backside at him and moved into the kitchen to warm some more water to finish washing herself with. Before she looked away Anya noted his surprised expression followed by something that almost resembled tenderness, then he laughed suddenly, the first true laugh she thought she'd ever heard from him.

'I knew I made the right decision when I claimed you. Continue as you have tonight and we will give each other great pleasure,' he called out to her.

Anya had just finished washing when he grabbed her arm and hauled her to his bed. Strangely, he didn't seem to want her again. He just wanted her near. She smiled, knowing she'd already made progress in taming the sexy alpha. She vowed to show everyone that there was more to Lacas than the vicious wolf they knew.

*   *   *

Waking in the early hours of the morning, her body stiff and sore, Anya smiled at Lacas' sleeping form, his leg draped across her. When she tried to get up to go relieve herself, he grabbed her, a deep growl rumbling through him.

'I need to relieve myself.' She shoved at his arm's, vice-like grip across her belly.

'Come back when you're done,' he growled, releasing his hold.

She grumbled, 'Where else did you think I'd be going?'

Lacas' head snapped up at her tone, but she ignored him, heading out into the cold to the toilet area behind the house.

The area between her legs burned as she squatted over the hole. She could see by the moonlight that she was extremely red down there. Certain Lacas would take her again as soon as she climbed back into his bed, she realised that she wanted him too. Grinning, she shifted into her wolf for a few minutes to heal, then changed back and washed before sliding back into bed.

Anya's willingness and pleasure in their frequent coupling seemed to please Lacas. He was more relaxed and pleased her in return. They had just coupled again when Anya noticed Lacas looking at how red and sore she was despite having shifted to heal. His eyes met hers briefly revealing something that appeared to be remorse.

'I'll lay with some of the other bitches today so you can heal.'

Anya was surprised by the pang of jealousy that ran through her. 'No, I'll be fine. I'll shift and heal so I'm ready for you.'

Lacas frowned at her tone. 'Others have suffered after speaking to me thus, however, your jealousy pleases me. I will not lay with others unless you cannot satisfy me. Does that please you, little one?'

Anya nodded and sashayed up to him, desire curling through her again, surprising her with its intensity. Wrapping her lithe, naked body around him, she planted a long, seductive kiss on his lips. Lacas growled, running his hands up and down her body, pausing to squeeze her firm buttocks.

'Be ready for me later.'

Fisting her hair, Lacas kissed her brutally, then dressed and left to organise the search for Tere, leaving Anya to plan her next move to win over her alpha.

CHAPTER 6

In preparation for Lacas' return, Anya shifted into her wolf form, allowing herself to heal for several hours. When he walked through the door of the cabin, she was waiting for him in a sexy pose on the sofa, naked, her legs wide and inviting. Lacas' eyes widened. He pounced with a deep growl, pausing only to yank down his trousers and expose his straining member. He took her hard and fast and they howled their climax together. Anya knew, despite her initial fear, and inexperience, Lacas was her true mate and she his.

They lay together, their limbs entwined. Plucking up her courage, Anya dragged in a deep breath and ran a fingernail down the black hair on his chest. 'Lacas?'

'Yes, little one?'

Lacas' languid response encouraged her. He pulled her close and grazed her neck with his teeth, his kisses travelling towards her swollen breasts, making her gasp and almost lose focus on what she wanted to ask. She forced her attention back.

'Lacas, will you honour me and take my wolf as yours, too?'

Abandoning his lazy trail of kisses, Lacas scrambled to his knees, disbelief etched across his face. Taking her wolf meant that if one of them died, the other would likely die, as well. Few had survived the death of their mate, but those who had were never the same again.

Anya watched as Lacas made his decision. His body pulsed to life again, his phallus harder than she'd ever seen him before. He scraped his hand through his hair, a gesture she'd seen Tere emulate many times. But this was not Tere, this was Lacas. Her Lacas. A piece of her heart hardened against Tere as she watched Lacas stand. His voice husky, but surprisingly gentle he asked.

'Shift for me, my little one.'

Surprise briefly registered at his possessive endearment. Anya willingly did as Lacas asked and they howled loudly for all the pack to hear as they sealed their fate as bonded mates.

Finally moving apart, they shifted back to their human form and collapsed in a tangle of limbs. Lacas turned Anya's face towards him kissing her tenderly and with such passion, it brought tears to her eyes. Before he drifted off to sleep, Lacas spoke quietly.

'You, my Anya, are my true mate, my one true love. It seems I have been waiting for you all my miserable life.' Closing his eyes, his limbs wrapped possessively around her.

Anya slipped out from beneath him as he slept, relieving herself and washing before she returned, snuggling into his heat, clean and ready for him when he woke.

* * *

Lacas lay awake, the pale rays of the early morning sunshine streaming through the window. He listened to Anya's soft, rhythmic breathing. For the first time in his life, here was someone whose passion matched his own. He revelled in the knowledge that someone cared, actually desired him. Not out of fear, but out of ... Dare he believe that he was finally truly loved? Maybe Anya would be the one to erase the terrible memories of his sire's cruelty. When her eyes fluttered open and she smiled at him, he whispered.

'You can come with me when I meet with the pack leaders today if you wish, little one.'

Lacas wasn't sure why, but he wanted Anya beside him. The thought shocked him, a deep growl rumbling in his chest. Hauling her to him for a bruising kiss, his inexplicable anger settled when she responded willingly, biting the corner of his mouth. A chuckle slipped past his lips. *When was the last time he had chuckled with real pleasure?* A sliver of true happiness thawed a tiny corner of his damaged heart.

Anya beamed at him jumping out of bed and quickly dressing. Lacas felt her eyes on him as he slid his leather pants up his legs and over his backside and grinned as he turned to see her ogling him.

Grabbing her hand, he laced their fingers together as they walked down the street, drawing many disbelieving stares. Anya strutted beside him, displaying her pride at being the alpha's mate, especially when some of the females dropped their eyes in deference. Anya sent Lacas a seductive smile. His lips curved in an appreciative grin as he yanked her closer, anchoring her to his side.

When Anya's father, Lupus approached, Lacas couldn't help himself, he pulled her hard against him for a long, wet kiss. Anya slid her arms around his neck, rubbing herself against him and kissing him back, deeply, her tongue exploring his mouth. Lacas' body sprung to life and a low, possessive growl rumbled through him. One hand freed a breast from the confines of her dress, his fingers rolling its turgid nipple. He was rewarded with a moan, then a sigh as he tucked her firm breast back into her dress and slapped her backside playfully. He laughed, speaking loudly enough for her father to hear as Lupus averted his eyes from the scene and emitted a strangled growl.

'Now, we have pack business, but later, we'll run together and pleasure each other again as wolves.'

Anya stretched up, claiming another kiss and whispered against his lips. 'Hurry your business, my Lacas.'

Another low growl rumbled through him, and he grabbed Anya, kissing her with such force that her lips turned bright red. Grinning at her father's stunned expression she walked by Lacas' side to the meeting hall laughing openly at the open-mouthed pack members.

The pack leaders had no choice but to acknowledge her as the new mate of their alpha. Anya sat close to Lacas, her hand draped over his thigh, shamelessly drawing tiny circles with her finger in full view of the council of pack leaders, moving ever closer to his, once again, burgeoning arousal while Tere's capture and subsequent death were planned. Most averted their gazes, but her father stared, disbelief etched across his face, one eye ticking slightly betraying his growing anger.

Scenting her growing desire, Lacas leaned back and placed his hand possessively over her belly. Ending the meeting, he pulled her into his lap, his fingers trailing up the inside of her leg, grazing the place where he knew she most craved his touch. She moaned softly and cast a glance over his shoulder, before turning her head and kissing him passionately. Lacas heard a deep growl from Anya's father as the room cleared and felt her mischievous grin against his lips.

As promised, Lacas lead her to the forest's edge and stripped off her clothes. Dropping his own in a pile at the base of an old elm tree, they ran together as wolves, mating in the woods several times.

Unbeknown to them, they were not alone. A lone wolf watched from downwind, unable to believe what he was seeing. Running through the trees, Lacas and Anya playfully nipped at each other, then lay in the cool leaf litter to rest and nuzzle. When Lacas mounted her again, the watcher had seen enough.

Within a few months Anya's belly began to swell with his offspring. Lacas was filled with pride, and when she begged him to promise not to lay with any other bitch, he honoured her wish. It pleased him so much that she wanted him even more during the pregnancy that he did not feel the need to be cruel or vindictive towards the pack members and found himself being gentler with her. That was when he realised, he truly loved her.

CHAPTER 7

Tere and Ileia made their way down the steep, grassy path, staying alert for signs of pursuit. Briefly stopping to allow Ileia to catch her breath, they finally reached the flat, dry plain beneath the jagged outcrop. Despite how quickly she'd healed, her injuries had taken their toll on her stamina. Ileia flopped down in the shade of a large, leafy elm tree. Tere sat beside her, stretching his legs out in front of him. To his surprise, she scooted onto his lap, his arms automatically snaking around her.

'Is something wrong, Ileia?' He brushed her hair from her face and dropped a kiss on her cool cheek.

'I just needed to be close to you, to feel your heat.'

Her honesty never ceased to surprise him. That, combined with her soft curves on his lap, caused a spike of yearning in his heart and his loins. Wrapping his arms tightly around Ileia's tiny waist, he pulled her hard against him, crushing her breasts against his chest and claiming her lips with a long, wet kiss. Reluctantly, Tere broke the kiss and rose, helping Ileia to her feet so they could be on their way to Therin.

Travelling through the thickest part of the forest offered the safest path, but the spiky brambles, uneven ground and many animal holes made it slow going. They were both scratched, bleeding and exhausted when they finally reached the edge of the plains of Therin. Camping in a small copse at the edge of the forest seemed the best option for now as they were reluctant to move out into the open while the last remnants of the day's light remained for fear of being seen.

Tere eyed the path they must take across the vast expanse of vibrant, green grass damp with the settling dew of the early evening.

'We'll camp here for a few hours, then cross the plain under cover of darkness.'

Looking up at the clear, indigo sky, Tere scanned for clouds, hoping that some would appear and hide the luminescence of the almost full moon. His wolf was restless. It wanted to run so badly, Tere's skin felt stretched with the effort of holding back the shift. He gazed at Ileia. She seemed edgy, too. He wondered if they should spare the time for a short run as wolves. When Ileia let loose a small cry, her hands fisted at her side, he made his decision.

'I think we'd both be less on edge if we shifted and ran as wolves for a while.'

Ileia nodded, her eyes already glowing bright green as her wolf clawed to the surface. She stripped quickly, her teeth elongating, and body thickening and lengthening into her beautiful red wolf. Tere smiled, running his hand through the thick, soft fur of her neck. Shrugging out of his clothes, he closed his eyes, setting his wolf free. Immediately, the tension coiling along his muscles eased. Shaking his thick, black fur, he paused, then turned and sprinted around Ileia further into the forest. She yipped softly and followed, a wolfish smile curving her lips.

Chasing each other playfully, they frolicked in the twilight among the fallen red and gold leaves of early autumn. Tere ached to howl but didn't want to alert any wolves within hearing distance of their presence. Finally returning to camp, panting and more relaxed than they'd been for days, they shifted and collapsed onto their bedrolls.

Tere's gaze drifted over Ileia's creamy skin, which contrasted with the long curls of her dark red hair, then lower to the short curls at the apex of her thighs. His heart raced, his body pulsing with a fierce yearning, an all-consuming need. Scooting closer, he captured her lips in a searing kiss. Ileia returned the kiss with a fiery passion of her own, rolling on top of Tere. His heart almost burst from his chest when she wriggled, rubbing herself against his hard length.

Flipping her beneath him, he settled his hips between her legs, positioning his body over hers. Sighing, he slid into her, his body humming as their bodies moved in unison. Before long the heat of his impending climax spiralled through him. When Ileia's body pulsed around him, her gasps filling the air Tere wasn't ready for the moment to end, he slowly circled his hips and leaned closer, capturing her lips in a long, simmering kiss. There was nothing at that moment but the two of them.

When a distant howl pierced the silence, Tere stilled, his desire-fogged brain processing the danger too slowly. His eyes narrowed, scanning the tree line as he protectively caged Ileia with his body. Scrambling up, he grabbed his clothes and yanked his trousers on, then pulled Ileia to her feet. He simultaneously tossed her clothes to where she stood, fear freezing her momentarily in place, and snatched up the rest of their belongings.

'Run!'

She threw him a frightened glance as they slung their packs over their shoulders and burst out of the trees at a dead run.

Tere's wolf snarled for release, but he dared not stop to shift. Slowing a little, he dropped behind Ileia to protect her, sparing a glance over his shoulder. His heart leapt into his throat when he spotted five wolves hurtling towards them. Making a snap decision, he stopped, turned, and planted his feet wide, preparing for the fight of his life. He would not – could not – let them take Ileia.

'Ileia, run as quickly and as far as you can. Don't stop until you reach Therin. I'll follow you as soon as I can. I love you. Never forget that.'

She skidded to a stop. Sobbing as she looked back, she screamed, 'Tere, no! Come with me. Please.'

Tere looked over his shoulder. 'No. Do this for me. Please. *Run*!'

His eyes pleaded with her as he gathered his magic.

He knew the moment she made her decision to do as he asked. She drew in a deep breath and tears glistened on her cheeks. Turning. she called out to him as she sped away. '

I'll be waiting, my love.'

He nodded, wheeling back around to face the wolves, his magic swirling around his powerful body like the vortex of a tornado.

*   *   *

Not daring to look back, Ileia turned and ran until her sides ached, legs burned, and lungs threatened to burst, then ran some more. The snarls and howls behind her faded into the distance. Twilight darkened the sky before she dared stop to rest. Dropping to the cool grass in the centre of a thick growth of silvery leafed bushes, she struggled to catch her breath, her chest heaving. Digging her water skin out of her pack, she drank deeply.

Her wolf senses scanned for danger while she focused on Tere, attempting to sense his presence. She could barely feel him and hoped it was just because he was too far away. A tear slid down her cheek. *Please be safe, Tere.* No matter how far away, the mating bond should allow her to communicate with him via their thoughts. At least it still connected them, which meant he was alive. She shivered. Ileia wasn't normally afraid to be alone in the woods, but she was afraid for Tere, terrified Lacas' henchman would capture and torture her, as well.

Settling onto her bedroll in a thicket of small trees, her head resting on her pack, she pulled the blanket up around her chin and closed her eyes. Sleep eluded her. Her wolf was agitated. She jumped at every unfamiliar sound. Rising, she relieved herself, then returned to the warmth of her blanket. The night was clear and crisp, the stars blazing in the blackness of the cloudless night sky. Her thoughts wandered to Tere and the nights they'd spent together, gazing up at the stars. A tiny smile pulled at her lips.

A sound close by dragged her from her reverie sending shivers up her spine. Holding her breath she silently rolled onto all fours, ready to shift and fight. Her body quaked with fear, though she'd made up her mind that she wouldn't let them take her. Her wolf snarled, ready to break free. Heart pounding, she moved to gain a better view between the bushes catching sight of leather clad legs creeping past her hideout. Barely managing to stifle a gasp she lifted her head, silently inhaling. Her nostrils flared hoping to identify the intruder, though she wasn't sure how that would help the situation. *Damn, he was down wind!*

Sniffing sounds reached her ears. *Wolf!* Suppressing a growl she initiated the shift, her wolf launching at the intruder, aiming for his throat. At the last moment, the intruder twisted wrapping his arms around her before he dropped to the ground, pinning her wolf beneath his hard, powerful body. Her teeth snapped at his neck. Her claws scraped against his leg. Panic filled her. She would not let him capture her.

'Ileia, it's me.'

She struggled for a moment longer before Tere's words and scent penetrated her terror. The moment she stopped fighting Tere released her and she shifted back into her human form, flinging her arms around him.

'Tere ... Oh, Tere.'

As she clung to him, uncontrollable sobs racked her body. Tere moved into a sitting position and scooped her into his arms, capturing her mouth in a gentle kiss. Finally lifting his head, he gazed into her watery eyes.

'My brave, Ileia. I'm so very proud of you. I love you so much.'

Driven by the intense emotion still swirling through her, Ileia shoved him backwards, pinning him beneath her and dropping her lips to his in a kiss that momentarily stole both their rational thought. Finally, Tere gently pushed her away and drew in a long, deep breath.

'Ileia, we need to leave here. I've delayed them, nothing more.'

She pulled back, her body still thrumming. Tere's gaze drifted over her and she knew that he struggled with the same longing that she harboured. Forcing herself to sit up she moved away. They stood and his arms slid around her hauling her close. He brushed his lips over hers again.

'I wish we could make love right now, but it isn't safe. Get dressed, my love. Please.'

Before grabbing fresh clothes from her pack, Ileia pressed herself against him once more. Hands snaking around her, Tere captured her in a hug, his hands sliding down, to cup her bottom as he pulled her hard against him, leaving no doubt of his desire.

Turning away to dress, she glanced over her shoulder as she shimmied into her undergarments. She watched as he gulped and closed his eyes, obviously fighting for control. She knew that powerful feelings of protectiveness warred within him against the almost overwhelming desire to satisfy their mutual need. When she had finished dressing, she turned to him but this time he held himself away, his teeth clenched. She understood. The same longing burned within her but was frustrated by their situation. *When they reached Therin...* she promised herself.

Shouldering their packs, they broke into a run and left the cover of the trees, bursting out onto the open plain. They would have preferred to run as wolves so they could cover more ground, but they had no easy way to carry their gear that way. Pausing briefly, they scanned the shadows of the forest, both raising their heads, sniffing the breeze but did not detect any scents nor hint of pursuit so they pushed on.

Only steps away from the forest's edge at the far side of the Plains of Therin, a chilling chorus of distant howls pierced the silence. Ileia barely stifled a scream. Lacas' wolves were only hours behind them. Panic gripped her. She knew she couldn't run much farther. Tere motioned for her to stop in a heavily wooded area. They hoped the trees would afford them some measure of cover for the moment. Stopping, chests heaving, Tere grabbed his water skin and offered her a drink of the now warm liquid.

Swallowing a few gulps, Ileia handed the container back to Tere, who took a swig and resealed it. Her sides burned as she struggled to catch her breath. Leaning against a tree to support herself, her body ached and her legs shook from the exertion.

'Deep breaths, sweetheart. Suck in the air, slow and deep; otherwise, you'll become dizzy.' Tere squatted in front of her, concern wrinkling his forehead. Working hard at doing what he asked, she managed a tiny smile.

'We can't outrun them, can we?' she asked. The expression on Tere's face said everything. A tear escaped as she bit back a sob. 'What are we going to do? They'll kill us ... or worse.'

Pulling her into the warmth and reassurance of his hard body, he rubbed her back. She buried her head into his shoulder soaking up the much-needed comfort. After a few moments, he pulled back and lifted her chin with his roughened fingers so that she looked up into his eyes.

'I'll do everything I can to keep you safe, Ileia. I love you. You're right that we can't outrun them, but perhaps we can outsmart them.'

Tere slowly bent his head touching his lips to hers. It started as a gentle, melding of mouths, but turned into a searing kiss of desperation, as though it may be their last. Ileia clung to him, neither of them willing to move from the comfort of their embrace, but knowing they had to. Maybe if they wished hard enough, their flight would all turn out to be just a very bad dream.

* * *

Tere desperately wished that Ileia hadn't become involved in any of this. He would do everything in his power to ensure her safety, even sacrificing himself if it came to that. Closing his eyes, he remembered the first time she had smiled at him. He'd known he needed to keep his distance from her to ensure Lacas didn't notice her. If he'd thought Tere was interested in her, Lacas would have targeted her with his cruelty, perhaps even raped her. Tere's anger boiled just beneath the surface.

A snarl curled his lips. Tere opened his eyes to see Ileia gazing at him, her brow furrowed with concern. Her hands shifted to his forearms. 'Tere?'

Dragging in a calming breath, he forced the fury of his wolf down, clenching his fists at his side as he battled the anger threatening to steal his finely honed control.

'I'm fine,' he ground out between clenched teeth. Ileia's hands moved slowly up and down his bare arms, her gaze holding his. Her touch both soothed and aroused him. His wolf settled, a modicum of peace descending over him. Breathing evenly, his hands slid to her waist. 'I don't know what I'd do without you, Ileia. We need to keep moving, but I want to set some traps for Lacas' henchmen first.'

Ileia nodded. Gripping her arms tightly, he stared into her eyes. 'I need you to run and keep running while I set the traps. I won't put you in any more danger than you are already. I'll catch up with you as soon as I am able.'

Tere watched as Ileia struggled not to argue. She closed her eyes briefly, then opened them to focus on him, her gaze stormy and troubled. Ileia didn't speak as she began gathering her meagre belongings but before she left, she cupped his face in her hands and kissed Tere so tenderly, he had to fight back tears. Dragging in a ragged breath, she turned, sprinting away without looking back.

Watching her leave ripped Tere's heart in two, but he needed to ensure that she was as far away as possible, just in case Lacas' thugs caught up with him. A howl, much closer than before, sounded, spurring Tere into action. Pulling out the six blades he'd managed to steal during his last encounter with the pack masters, he set them up several feet apart from each other on a flexible, low-hanging tree branch. He then anchored it to the ground with a few strands of the rope he'd brought with him. Stringing a similarly fine braid of strands a few inches high across the path and into the thick underbrush, he connected it with those that he'd anchored to the ground so, when broken, it would pull and release the branch. This would fling the knives at whomever broke the rope. Tere prayed it was Lacas' and his accomplices.

Uttering a few words of magic to disguise his scent, Tere sprinted away to set his next trap. He'd have to be especially clever because after encountering the first one, they'd definitely be more cautious. He knew he needed to hurry. They weren't far behind him now but Tere had magic on his side, and that brought a small grin to his lips.

Thank you, Grandfather!

Halting about half a mile down the well-worn track, Tere closed his eyes, calling the magic his maternal grandfather had awakened within him. He felt it swirl around him before unleashing it at the path in front of him. Silently he blasted a long, narrow trench that spanned the track and extended either side of it for several feet. Next, he drove sharpened stakes into the bottom of the deep trough, the vicious spikes reaching upward to impale anything that was unfortunate enough to fall in. Finally, Tere dragged out a long piece of cloth that he'd used as bedding, cut it into two pieces long enough to cover the trench and stiffened it with magic so he could lay it over the hole in the well-worn path then covered it all with a thin layer of loose dirt.

Pleased with his diversion, Tere spoke a few words to erase his scent from the scene, then exploded into a run. He was determined to catch up to Ileia before dark. Pushing himself until his heart threatened to burst, it wasn't long before he spotted Ileia's lithe form up ahead, setting a good pace.

Stopping, she turned when she sensed his approach. She sprinted towards him, launching herself into his arms, her momentum knocking them both to the ground. Tere landed on his back with a thud. Laughing, his arms clamped around her, pulling her against him. Barely aware of the sticks and pebbles digging into his back, he kissed her hard. A kiss born of fear, relief and passion rolled into one heart-stopping melding of mouths.

Sighing he rolled her to the side and jumped deftly to his feet. As he pulled her to her feet he threaded his fingers through hers, unwilling to completely break the physical contact.

'We need to keep moving. Can you run some more?'

He eyed her for signs of fatigue. She was strong, but they had run a long way and her injuries had not yet fully healed.

Ileia nodded. 'I'm all right. I'm tired, but I can run for a while. Did you set the traps?'

'Yes, but I can't guarantee they will delay them for long, so we need to reach Therin as soon as we can and seek refuge there.'

Lifting his pack over his shoulder, Tere pulled Ileia close stealing one more kiss before they began their race towards Therin. After running for almost an hour, they stopped briefly for a drink. Just as they were about to set off again, a chill ran up Tere's back howl pierced the air sounding much closer than he'd anticipated.

'*Run!*'

Tere glanced at Ileia. Her shoulders hunched, her breaths short, sharp gasps, he knew she was close to her limit. He wasn't sure how much further she could run without a rest. Urging her along, he stayed close, determined to not let Lacas and his men capture her.

They'd run almost a mile when Tere smelled them. He couldn't believe it. Predators like wolves never ran downwind of their prey. They were obviously so sure of catching them, they didn't even attempt to conceal their approach. Swearing under his breath he whispered a few words of magic to mask his and Ileia's scent. It wouldn't stop them, but it might confuse them long enough for Ileia at least to reach the safety of Therin. He would forfeit his life to block their pursuers' path to ensure she reached Therin, but only if there was no other choice.

Cresting the hill, the plains of Therin came into view. Tere dared to hope they'd make it. They burst into the open just as Lacas and his men erupted from the forest on either side of them. Tere briefly registered surprise at seeing Lacas alive but he'd harboured a niggling suspicion that it would take more than shoving him off a cliff to kill his sire.

'Run, Ileia. Run as though your life depends on it.' And it did.

Tere counted. Only five men, including Lacas. Perhaps his traps had worked after all. Tere's legs pumped hard as he gathered what was left of his strength and reached for his magic, sucking it into his body like water given to a man dying of thirst. Before he could hurl it at Lacas and his followers, an enormous pulse of magic enveloped Tere, crushing the breath from his lungs and the magic from his grasp.

The last thing he saw was Ileia being dragged like a ragdoll between two of Lacas' thugs. His mind screamed to help her, but his consciousness fled. A thick, inky blackness surrounded him, suspending him as though he were immersed in honey. A scream pierced the depths of his stupor. His body jerked frantically trying to break free.

I must help Ileia. I must help her... I must ...

CHAPTER 8

Pain radiated through Tere's head and down his body. Attempting to move to ease the searing agony burning across his chest, Tere realised he was secured against a damp, uneven stone wall. Thick, cold, iron chains bit into the flesh of his ankles and wrists. Opening his eyes, he immediately slammed his lids shut against the pain that lanced through his head. When it subsided a little, Tere dared to squint into the dappled darkness again. *Was he in a cave?*

His eyes slowly adjusted to the dimly lit cavern, its rough walls glistening with moisture. Lifting his nose he sniffed. Water. Closing his eyes again, he tried to block out the pain and listened intently. The thunderous sound of water pounding on rocks reached his ears. The waterfall. How long had he been unconscious? He assumed he was back in one of the caves near where he and Ileia had stayed after she'd helped him escape, which was many days from where they'd been captured.

Tere's heart jumped with the memory of their capture. *Ileia!* Yanking viciously at his bonds, Tere's heart thumped wildly. Where was she? When he sent out his senses to find her, another excruciating stab of pain bit through his head. What the hell was suppressing his abilities? Groaning softly, he stilled as the sound of approaching voices reached his sensitive ears. One of them was unmistakable. *Lacas*!

'Ah, my son. You don't look well.' A sinister chuckle slid from Lacas. Moving so close that Tere could feel his hot breath on his face, Lacas sneered. 'Thought I was dead, didn't you?'

Tere refused to show any reaction. Steadily meeting Lacas' cold gaze, Tere mustered a smirk as sinister and cold as his sire's. 'I'd hoped so. At least now I'll be able to watch you die.' He snarled, despite the agony lancing through his head. 'A long, slow, painful death.'

Lacas pulled back his fist and punched Tere viciously on the jaw. Tere's head snapped back, before he spat blood at Lacas. Another smirk curled his bloodied lips.

'Is that all you have? With a punch like that, you're definitely a beta wolf. My grandfather would have—'

Lacas grabbed Tere by the throat. 'Your grandfather died screaming like a subordinate female.'

Tere doubted opportunity to retaliate would present itself again. He would be fortunate to survive the night with Lacas in such a fury. Snapping his head forwards, he slammed it into Lacas' forehead. The crack echoed around the cavern. Lacas staggered back, his eyes glazed. Shaking his head, Lacas roared, launching himself at Tere, his claws extended. His hands inches away from Tere's throat, Lacas stopped, appearing to fight for control. His body shook for a moment, then to Tere's surprise, he pulled away, his hands fisted at his side.

His voice gravelly, Lacas snarled, 'No. You will not taunt me into killing you so quickly. For hiding your alpha status from me and for your mother's complicity, you will suffer.' Turning his head towards the back of the cave, his smirk reappeared. 'Yes, you will suffer more than you can imagine.'

Tere watched Lacas stride away desperately hoping his suffering did not include Ileia. When he heard a pain-fuelled scream, dread and fury penetrated his very soul, his heart thundering. *God, no. Ileia.* The screams continued until Tere thought he might lose his mind. He yanked and struggled against his bonds until blood poured from his wrists and ankles. Hot tears burned the back of his throat. *Not again.*

Images of his mother's murder flashed across his thoughts, then were suddenly replaced by a sickening vision of Lacas raping Ileia. Tere couldn't stop the howl that ripped from his throat. His wolf crouched, ready to kill the moment it was unleashed. The screams peaked with a long, ear-piercing shriek that was eventually replaced by gut-wrenching sobs. Tere's heart broke for the pain inflicted on Ileia.

Tere's inner fury settled into a cold calm as his wolf broke through the restraints, claws protruding through his fingertips. But it couldn't break through the metal bindings. Barely holding himself in check, Tere waited and planned his escape and the revenge he would exact upon Lacas.

When Lacas returned, naked and bloodied, Tere swallowed hard. He wanted to rip him to shreds. Once he was free, there would be no holding back. He didn't know if Ileia was alive or dead. He couldn't feel her because his gift was dampened in the cave. Sorrow threatened to overwhelm him, but he held onto the hope that she lived. Vowing that he would save her, he pulled the ragged edges of his self-control around him like a blanket and steeled himself for Lacas' retribution.

Stunned by who walked in next, Tere forced himself not to react when a small, wizened man shuffled up in front of Lacas, stopping to face Tere. Emanating confidence and oozing the evil stench of necromancy, his sorcery made him seem so much larger than he truly was. An enormous wave of power enveloped Tere as the Sorcerer's pale grey eyes held his. His straggly white beard hung down to the gold, Peridot inlaid buttons at the waist of his dirty, black garb. As he raised his arms and began chanting, the irony of Peridot being a gem reputed to guard against evil momentarily curved Tere's lips in a wry smile.

Tere's eyes flitted to Lacas, standing behind the Sorcerer.

'Have you met Rantec, our resident Sorcerer, my son?' Tere shuddered at Lacas' acknowledgment of their familial connection. 'He's going to help me with your training.'

Lacas smirked, pure malice oozing from him.

Tere's body jerked involuntarily as Rantec resumed his incantation. Lacas moved like lightning, grabbing Tere's jaw and forcing a thick, bitter tasting liquid past his lips. Unable to turn away, he gagged. Lacas held his jaw shut so he could do nothing but swallow. The liquid burned as it rushed down his throat and Tere quickly plummeted into the depths of a fitful sleep plagued by evil nightmares. His last rational thoughts were of Ileia and how he'd failed her.

Tere had no idea how long he drifted in and out of consciousness for. Each time he woke, someone forced the same bitter liquid down his throat as the Sorcerer chanted. His brain was fogged. He was unable to formulate a clear thought and his body ached as though he'd run a marathon. His eyes were dry and scratchy, his lids heavy and unwilling to open more than a slit.

Certain that weeks had passed since his capture, Tere attempted to force his sluggish brain to work. If he'd tried to speak, he was certain his words would be slurred. Tentatively, he poked at his wolf, who growled low and returned to its deep slumber. Managing to open his eyes, he realised he was naked, his body battered and bloody. His gaze slid around the cold, damp cave, and he blinked several times to clear the haze from his eyes.

The reed strewn floor was covered with spatters of blood. Probably his. Wrinkling his nose at the sour odour coming from his body, he spied a jug of water and licked his parched lips. He pulled against his bonds, wincing at the sharp pain of the cold steel biting into his raw skin. The scent of the fresh, cool water and the sharp metallic odour of blood mingled with the stench of sweat and urine.

When footsteps approached, Tere let his head loll to the side, closing his eyes, but used what senses he could muster to stay alert. Hearing a soft clang, he waited. A deep voice quietly spoke his name.

'Tere, wake up. I have water for you.'

Tere's eyes flicked open to see Lupus, one of Lacas' most trusted henchmen, and Anya's father, holding a metal bowl of water close to Tere's lips. Lupus had been one of those who'd held Tere down when Manny had violated him, when he'd been captured, beaten and his mother murdered before his eyes. Lupus had been on the cliff when they'd tossed Ileia over the edge. Tere had no reason to trust him.

'Drink. I wish to help you.'

Tere's head snapped up, which he instantly regretted. Forcing back the bile that rose in his throat at the agony slicing through his head, he grunted and his wolf, finally awake, growled low.

'Why?' he rasped out through parched and torn lips.

Lupus sighed. 'Because I've been wrong. We've *all* been wrong. You should be the one to rule the pack. Lacas has all but destroyed it. You have no reason to believe that I speak the truth, but he...' Lupus paused, his head bowed, then he lifted his angry gaze to Tere's, his voice catching on a barely suppressed sob. 'He took my Anya. He...'

Lupus' voice became low and dangerous, despair etched across his face. 'He raped her, and corrupted her, the bastard. For that, I'll help you kill him and swear loyalty to you, to the pack.'

Tere couldn't believe his ears. 'Is Anya...?' He couldn't finish the sentence.

'She lives as his mate.' Lupus' face contorted with fury. 'Now, drink and regain your strength. I've asked to be the one giving you the potion. I've had a herbal remedy mixed up that resembles the evil smelling concoction that drugs you. In a few days, you should be strong, and we'll escape to plan Lacas' death. Are you with me?'

Tere nodded before Lupus tipped the drink up, letting the cool liquid soothe the parched flesh of his lips and mouth and ease the burn in his throat. He wouldn't let his guard down, but for now, Lupus was his best hope. His only hope. Reluctantly removing his mouth from the metal bowl, Tere asked the question that had plagued him in his brief moments of lucidity.

'Ileia ... Does she live?'

Lupus levelled his gaze at Tere. 'I know not. Lacas alone has access to where she's imprisoned.'

Tere's heart sank as his still ensorcelled brain struggled against despair. A spark of clarity reminded him of his suppressed magic.

'Why can't I access my magic? I could help you.'

Lupus shook his head and pointed to the black leather band secured around his wrist. Strange markings that reminded Tere of glyphs of ancient spells were carved deep into the hard, stained leather.

'When there is more than one band close by, it amplifies the power they possess to suppress magic and render it useless. Rantec had them fashioned for all of Lacas' followers, but for some reason they don't affect the Sorcerer, perhaps because he wears one. The more in the vicinity, the stronger the effect becomes on those with magic. I'll try to get one for you to aid your escape. Now, drink this tea. I hear someone coming. Pretend you're still under the spell or we'll both die in this godforsaken cave.'

Lupus grabbed Tere's jaw, but not as roughly as it appeared, and poured the viscous liquid down his throat. Tere didn't have to feign choking on it as it tasted every bit as foul as the real thing. Lacas approached and Tere spat at Lupus, then let his head loll to the side. He heard Lacas' evil chuckle and the rumble of his voice as he spoke to Lupus. Hope sprang in his chest as Tere began to feel his body starting to heal and recover from the effects of the potion that had been forced on him. Despite the pain of his wounds, he managed to sleep for a few hours, giving his body time to heal.

When Tere woke, the cave was silent. A blessing he supposed. At least Lacas wasn't torturing him or trying to choke him with whatever drug he'd been forcefully administering. He hadn't seen the Sorcerer for a few days, which he was grateful for. His senses swept over the area, the thud of a single pair of boots reaching his sensitive wolf hearing. Cocking his head, he listened, lifting his nose to pick up the scent.

Lupus.

He strode around the corner, heavy metal cutters in his hand. Tere's heart thumped with anticipation of finally being free.

'Hurry. They're all at the main camp, chasing after a group of Fae and human folk. Lacas seems to think they are after the Golden Stone.'

Lupus sliced through the chains at Tere's ankles and wrists. Tere rubbed them to restore the blood flow, grimacing at the pain. Tentatively, he tried to walk, but his legs threatened to buckle beneath him. It had been weeks since he'd been allowed to walk more than a few steps.

'The Golden Stone?' Tere asked, still rubbing his legs and ankles. The blood flow returned slowly, bringing its own burning pain.

'Yes. The stone in which the power of the Fae elders and Rantar, Rantec's father, is stored. 'Tis said to be more power than one man can handle. It is rumoured that the vast power he tried to absorb from it sent Rantar mad. When he was finally captured, after causing great destruction to Therin and the surrounding kingdoms, his powers were extracted and stored in the Golden Stone. It was locked in the Keep at Castle Therin until one of its kings, Eldan, buried it in one of the caves deep in the earth near where we are currently located. Lacas and Rantec had been searching for it for years. Unfortunately, they have recently found it and are calling forth all manner of evil creatures from the bowels of the earth with it.'

'And these people searching for it ... Who are they?' Tere stomped his feet to make them function.

'I'll tell you more when we are out of here ... Can you run?'

'I think so.'

Tere jumped up and down on the spot, testing his legs. He nodded, confirming he could run, and he and Lupus moved cautiously, sliding along the damp cave walls. Lupus walked in front, checking for guards. Without warning, his arm thumped across Tere's chest, forcing him against the rock and back into a narrow crevasse. His wolf's eyes met Tere's in the half light, glowing with warning. The cave echoed with the heavy thud of booted feet approaching. Tere and Lupus pressed themselves against the wall, barely breathing.

Ten massive creatures, marching in unison, rounded the corner. Tere barely suppressed a gasp as he watched the creatures trudge past. They were half-man and half-beast, close to seven feet tall and dressed in oily, black skins and black, studded boots, their bare chests covered in coarse, black hair. Tere shuddered. They would be formidable opponents, albeit not very smart.

When they were out of sight, headed towards the deepest recesses of the cave, Lupus urged Tere on. His heart thudding against his ribs, Tere followed warily, waiting for Lupus to betray him. However, Lupus, true to his word, led Tere out into the sunlight. Blinking rapidly, the brilliance of the sun making Tere's eyes water momentarily, he met Lupus' gaze.

'Now, it's time to run.'

Lupus glanced over his shoulder at Tere, then exploded into a run.

Tere swallowed hard, sucked in a deep breath and followed, determined to keep up, despite the soreness and stiffness in his legs from weeks of abuse and disuse. They ran for almost an hour, staying within the cover of the trees to avoid detection. Stopping briefly to rest and drink some water, Tere caught his breath and eyed Lupus.

'Tell me more about this Golden Stone and those who are trying to find it.'

Lupus didn't answer immediately. Dragging in a breath, he began. 'Lacas believes the new King of Therin has sent some Fae folk to use their powerful magic to retrieve the Stone. He has armed all the wolves at the camp with these magically infused armbands to suppress their abilities so he can capture them.'

He handed Tere an armband. 'Wear this so you can use your magic, if necessary. I've learned that wearing one does indeed negate its power to suppress magic.'

A series of howls sounded in the distance. Lupus swore, grabbed his pack and quickly shouldered it.

'We must go. They've discovered that you've escaped.'

'I'm not going any farther until I find out if Ileia is alive. I won't leave without her.'

Lupus growled. 'I didn't save you just for you to be killed over a woman. Your destiny is to save the pack.'

Tere snarled and moved so close their noses almost touched. Displaying his alpha status he postured, his back ramrod straight, the hair on the back of his neck standing up, a low growl on his lips. Lupus faced him for a moment, breathing hard, then backed down from the alpha he'd now sworn to follow, the alpha who he believed would save the pack.

Lupus pulled in a deep breath. 'What's the plan?'

Tere smiled. 'They won't expect us to go back to the caves. Return to the camp and gather the wolves you believe will swear fealty to me. I'll sneak back in and see if I can locate Ileia.'

Sadness crept into Tere's heart. Would he find her alive? Even with the armband on, he couldn't sense her. Their bond should have led him to her, stretched between them like an invisible cord. Pushing aside the negative thoughts, he nodded at Lupus and sprinted back in the direction of the caves, determined to find his mate.

Cautiously approaching the entrance, Tere scanned the area for guards, listening for the stomp of booted feet that would indicate the presence of the giant beasts he'd encountered earlier. Sniffing the air, he could only detect the foul odour of unwashed humans and the effluvium of the shallow troughs that served as waste pits.

Senses on high alert, Tere crept around to the gaping entrance to the eerie, airless cavern, slipping inside unnoticed. Moving stealthily like the predator he truly was, Tere kept to the shadows as he swept along the wide corridors in the direction that Lupus believed Ileia was being held. Nothing moved. The hairs on the back of Tere's neck stood on end. A sharp tingle of warning skittered down his spine. Not a soul guarded the cavern or the untold treasures within.

Tere froze, the sound behind him so infinitesimal that he almost missed it. Spinning around, his eyes widened as ten enormous beasts, half-man and half-oxen turned the corner behind him, led by the Sorcerer, Rantec. Tere swore silently, fleeing down the corridor all the while praying he'd find another way out. Luck was with him as he noticed dappled light filtering through a small, eye-shaped, bracken-covered exit ahead.

Launching himself through it at full speed, he set his wolf free, transforming in a shower of silver and gold, his clothes shredding and falling away. The sharp spikes of the bracken dragged out tufts of his jet-black fur as his claws ripped through the soft green foliage of the damp, leafy bushes beyond. For the briefest of moments, Tere considered the possibility that the narrow exit might open onto the ravine, but he had no time to explore that notion further as large, filthy, disfigured hands reached through the opening grasping at him. Snarling, he leapt forward, narrowly avoiding being hauled backwards by his tail as the hands groped through the too narrow crack in the rock wall.

Thankfully, the creatures were too large to fit through. Tere heard the Sorcerer shouting orders and the creatures' boots thudding against the solid rock floor as they lumbered towards the main exit.

He ran as swiftly as his wolf legs could carry him, curving up and over the back of the labyrinth of caves to a lightly wooded area that opened onto a short, grassy plain. At the end of the plain, a cliff plummeted hundreds of feet down to the same waterfall that Tere had thrown Lacas into. However, this was much higher than where he and Ileia had originally sheltered after she'd helped Tere escape.

Picking his way down the narrow path covered in sharp, loose, white pebbles, made slick by the mist rising from the waterfall, Tere wound around the side of the cliff, his claws digging in to prevent him from slipping, and found the entrance to their cave.

Remembering that he'd left some clothes jammed in a tight crevice inside, he poked his nose through the leafy barrier concealing the entrance. Smelling nothing of concern, he pushed into the temporary sanctuary. He stretched out on the cool floor, allowing himself a moment to pant and collect his thoughts before he invited the shift to his human form to flow through his body.

Naked, he shivered in the damp chill of the sunless cavern, goosebumps rising on his tanned skin. He allowed his eyes to adjust to the darkness and moved to the place he was certain he'd left his clothes. Shoving his hand into the niche in the wall he pulled out a pair of old, soft, black leather trousers and a light, grey shirt. He sighed with relief as he dragged them on. They weren't overly thick, but they were certainly better than nothing.

Gazing around, Tere was assaulted by a volley of memories of Ileia. He shook his head, silently vowing to go back for her. He would wait for Lupus to bring those loyal to him to fight against Lacas, Rantec and his followers. Realising that he'd need more clothes and supplies, he began formulating a plan to sneak back into his old home. If possible, he'd leave a message with Reine, telling Lupus where he was. Reine was one of the few pack members he knew he could trust with his life.

Feeling marginally better, Tere decided that the best time to attempt his foray into the village was now as night was beginning to fall. He would shift into his wolf if necessary, as the shadows of the evening would easily conceal his dark fur, but for now he would remain in his human form. Carefully sweeping aside the long tendrils of ivy covering the cave entrance he slid them back into place before he jogged down the hill towards home. He wasn't sure what it would feel like going back into the cabin after everything that had happened, but he couldn't deny that it would be the best and easiest place to get the clothes and supplies he needed.

Moving stealthily around the back of the village, Tere arrived at the back of the cabin he'd shared with his mother and Lacas. For a moment, he just stared. His heart thudding as memories, mostly bad ones, flooded his senses. The residual smell of Lacas made his skin crawl, and the faint scent of his mother brought tears to his eyes. He dragged in a breath to settle his raging emotions. Checking that nobody was near enough to see him, Tere darted up the front steps to the wooden door, breathed deeply and pushed inside, his senses on high alert.

The familiar scents that lingered threatened to shatter his fragile emotions. He thrust aside the mantle of sadness that attempted to envelop him and entered his room. Grabbing a bag, he shoved as many clothes in it as he could, then headed for the kitchen.

Pots and pans were strewn across the once neat room, evidence of his final struggle with Lacas. Blood was splattered on the floor. It could have been Lacas' or his own … or maybe his mother's. Tears burned the backs of his eyes as that thought flooded his head with visions of Lacas slaughtering his beautiful, kind mother. His throat tightened and one lone tear escaped, trickling down his cheek.

He whispered into the emptiness. 'I will avenge you, Mama.'

A growl rose in his throat. His wolf agreed. Becoming agitated, it demanded release. Tere ignored that demand with the strength of long years of denial. Grabbing some stale bread, cheese, apples and wrapping a slab of salted meat in a clean cloth, he filled another bag. At the last moment, he grabbed a small frying pan and a pot. Laden with supplies, he checked that no-one was around to witness his exit from the cabin, then quietly made his way down the dusty, wooden front steps. Hiding the two bags behind the cabin, Tere chanted a spell to clear his scent from the area and slipped between the trees towards Reine's home.

Approaching the rear of the well-kept, wooden cabin, Tere heard the voices of Reine's family inside. Listening intently, he was certain one of them was Reine. Tere gathered his determination and let out a short, high-pitched whistle, one he and Reine had used as children to avoid being caught together by Lacas. Tere prayed Reine remembered. A few moments later, Reine appeared around the corner of the cabin calling back to his mother.

'I won't be long, Ma. Love you.'

A pang of something akin to envy spiked through Tere at Reine's comment, but he shoved it down. Reine was lucky to have such a loving family, and despite Lacas' attitude towards their beta status, they had always welcomed Tere into their home.

Reine jogged through the garden and into the trees behind his home. 'Tere?'

Tere stepped out of his hiding place and embraced his friend. Reine hugged him back fiercely.

'We didn't know if you were still alive. Thank God you are. What do you need?'

Tere smiled. Reine had always offered his assistance without question. 'Can you please tell Lupus I'm in the cave to the right of the waterfall?'

Reine's eyebrows lifted in surprise. 'Lupus?'

Tere chuckled. 'Yeah. It's kind of weird for me, too. He saved me from Lacas and his Sorcerer. They kept me drugged for weeks, torturing me for their pleasure. Apparently, Lacas raped Anya and Lupus has sworn revenge.'

Reine nodded thoughtfully. 'It started out that way. We heard Anya screaming when Lacas arrived back in the village. He said you tried to kill him by shoving him into the ravine at the waterfall. Some of us wanted to cheer at that.' Reine chuckled. 'Anyway, Lacas claimed her as his mate, and she's now acting every bit as cruel and vicious as he does. She does despicable things with him in plain sight of everyone, especially her father.'

Tere's mouth fell open. 'Anya? Really? I wonder if he's drugged her or placed a spell on her. This Sorcerer, Rantec, has powerful, evil magic at his disposal.'

'Hmmm, perhaps,' Reine answered thoughtfully, then grabbed Tere's arm and pulled him in for a brotherly hug.

'You'd best be going Tere, before someone sees you. I'll find Lupus and tell him where you are. And Tere, I'm with you. Many of us are. You'll make a great pack leader.'

Releasing Tere and thumping his arm across his heart, a gesture of trust and solidarity, Reine ran off to find Lupus.

Tere smiled. Relief flooded him. He had friends here, those who would follow him. His grandfather had been right. He stood a little taller as he jogged away, picking up his bags of supplies on the way. Next time he returned, he was determined to fight for his rightful place as the pack alpha. For that, he needed Ileia by his side. He must find her and bring her home.

CHAPTER 9

Tere ached to touch her. His heart hammered relentlessly against his ribs, his body shaking with the effort of holding back. His manhood, erect against his belly, throbbed with need, his breath fast and irregular.

Ileia's long, dark lashes rested on her flushed cheeks before they fluttered open. Her green eyes, dark with desire, held his. Slithering out of her clothes, she let them pool at her feet. She moved closer on long, shapely legs, so slowly, so seductively, Tere's heart slammed against his ribs, threatening to break them. He drank in the sight of her lightly tanned skin, the curves that set his body afire, the soft round breasts that he knew fit perfectly in his hands and the vee between her legs lightly dusted with dark red hair that hid a honeyed treasure reserved for him alone. He dragged in another ragged breath.

Stopping a whisper away, Ileia's breath caressed his cheek. Her tongue slid out to moisten her full mouth, and Tere couldn't suppress his groan. A smile twitching at her lips, her small hands came to rest on his chest and their bodies came together intimately.

'Ileia.'

Tere groaned again as his arms snaked around her, pulling her against his overheated body. Lowering his head, he kissed her sweet lips, *his tongue trailing along them, seeking entry. Their tongues duelling seductively as she slid her hands around his neck and ran her fingernails gently up into his hair. Tere shivered, deepening the kiss.*

He laid her gently on the soft fur, crawling over her. Tere sighed as he settled between her hips, covering her body with his and kissing his way down her neck to hard, erect nipples, laving and suckling them. Ileia moaned and writhed beneath him. He was hard and ready, but he would see to her pleasure first. Sliding down her belly, he inhaled the sweet scent of her arousal before he flicked his tongue over her sensitive nub until Ileia screamed his name, her back bowing off the bed.

Unable to wait any longer, Tere positioned himself, nudging at her entrance. He sucked in a sharp breath as her fingers encircled him, guiding him into her throbbing folds. They both groaned loudly as he slid into her slick heat. Ileia howled...

Tere's eyes flicked open. For a moment, he had no idea where he was or why Ileia wasn't with him when only moments before they'd been in the sweet throes of passion. He swore vehemently. It had only been a dream. The pain of losing Ileia shot through him anew, making his chest ache. Ileia wasn't here, Lacas had her imprisoned somewhere deep within the bowels of the cave, and, he'd been woken by a howl. A very close howl. Swearing colourfully again, he yanked on his trousers, jammed his feet into his boots and stuffed what he could into one pack. Exploding out of the cave, Tere barrelled towards the forest, howls and snarls following close behind.

For two days, Tere slept rough, drinking from puddles and creeks, eating sparingly from his provisions, all the while being relentlessly pursued by Lacas' henchmen. On the third day, Tere backtracked, stripped and stuffed his clothes and pack behind a tree near the top of the cliff. Shivering in the biting wind whipping up from the deep ravine, he called forth his wolf.

Shaking the fine droplets of moisture from his thick, black coat he lifted his head, sniffing the chilled air. Surprised that he could no longer detect any wolf scents, he trotted along the edge of the path, staying just out of sight, inhaling the myriad of scents on the breeze. Nothing! He smelled many other things: squirrels, rats, grass, the damp earth and the leaves of the stately elm trees. Finding it difficult to believe that either he'd lost his pursuers, or they'd given up, he loped stealthily along the path that ran around the edge of the precipice leading to the waterfall. On the plain ahead, movement caught his eye.

Riders.

Quickly positioning himself just beyond the tree line, Tere crouched, in his wolf form, behind a dense bush, it's trumpet-like white flowers giving off a strong perfume that tickled his nose. He held back a sneeze as he watched the path, waiting to see who the approaching riders were. The sound of hooves reverberated through the rocky ground as the steeds approached. Keen eyes locked on the four riders. The scent of humans reached Tere's nostrils, a tingle racing up his spine told him that at least one wielded magic. Distracted, he didn't hear the snarling wolves approaching from behind until they were almost on him. Tere's hackles rose. He turned, baring his teeth and burst from the cover of the bushes his trajectory setting him on a collision path with the riders.

Moments before barrelling into the sharp, pounding hooves, Tere's head swung around, his eyes finally focusing on the horses thundering towards him. Sliding to a halt, he prayed that he'd stop in time to avoid the deadly hooves.

A terrified scream rent the air. Swerving around Tere, a chocolate brown mare hurtled towards the cliff, her eyes rolling, foam streaming around the bit in her mouth. The female rider frantically attempted to gain control of her terrified mount. Tere's heart slammed into his throat. The tall, blonde-haired rider in the group of men quickly straightened in his saddle, guiding his black war stallion with his knees alone. Lightning crackled through the air as magic spread, its tendrils streaking through the sky, seeking the woman. Fury radiated from the other men, their stallions – war horses, Tere now realised – stomped and snorted their agitation in response.

'Let us pass, Wolf. We must stop her.'

The warrior stiffened. Tere sensed that the man was gathering his magic again. Calling his human form, Tere shifted. Ignoring his nakedness, he shouted above the roar of the waterfall.

'Hurry. You must catch her. There's a precipice ahead.'

The men spurred their horses forward. Tere shimmered into his wolf form to follow them. Sprinting to the edge of the sheer drop, he noted the mare standing off to the side, her legs wide apart, sides heaving and flecked with foam, head drooped with exhaustion.

The dark-haired man leapt off his steed's back before it halted completely. Dropping to his belly at the edge of the cliff, he frantically searched for the woman, his movements frenetic and panicked. A sob, followed by a war cry, ripped from the man's lips moments before he sprang to his feet and attacked Tere.

Surprised, Tere tumbled onto his side, unbalanced by the impact of the man's body hurtling into his wolf. Remembering the pain that had pierced his heart and removed all rational thought when Lacas shoved Ileia over the same cliff, Tere snarled, protecting himself, but did not bite. Not until he noticed the glint of a knife in the warrior's hand. Managing to clamp his teeth onto the arm that wielded the weapon, Tere softened his bite so as not to penetrate his clothing. They tumbled over and over, the man clearly out of control until a voice of pure authority pierced the air.

'*Daien*! Desist. Ren needs you. She is alive but injured somewhere down the side of the cliff. *Wolf,* stop. Now!'

Daien faltered as the words seemed to penetrate his anger fogged brain. Jumping back, Tere cautiously eyed him, ready to defend himself if attacked again. Daien's blade clattered to the ground. His head dropped into his hands before he lifted his eyes, a glimmer of hope flitting across his expression.

'She's alive? Where?'

The third man, younger but with an obvious air of authority, sheathed his sword, holding out his gloved hand to Daien to help him to his feet. Tere sensed a fierce camaraderie between the men, a strong bond that made him wonder exactly who they were. Grateful he'd stowed his clothes nearby his wolf ran into the bushes, taking the track up to where he'd hidden them behind the tree. When he located the small bundle he called the shift, feeling his body reshape into his human form. Quickly dressing he rushed back to the precipice filled with guilt that the woman had been injured because of him.

Ren? Was that what the blonde warrior had called the woman?

When he reached the group, they'd already lowered Daien over the side of the cliff using a thickly woven rope. The blond warrior's muscles flexed and strained as he gripped the rope. The younger man stood behind him, the end of the rope wrapped around his gloved hands, grimacing with the strain. They both held firm and steadily lowered Daien to reach the woman.

Tere dropped to his stomach on the damp grass at the edge of the precipice helping to guide the rope. He detected a silent conversation going on between Daien and the blond warrior. *Were they using their mind voice?* They obviously weren't human because the tingle of magic surrounded them both like an aura.

Locating the woman about halfway down the side of the wet and craggy rock face, using his own magic, Tere realised her hand was impaled on a huge thorn. *How the hell is that holding her up, and how on earth is she still even semiconscious with the pain she must be experiencing?* For a moment, Tere's thoughts jumped back to Lacas and another woman who he'd rescued from falling to her death in almost the same place. Ileia ... Memories of that terrible day flooded his mind. His heart clenched with sadness as Ileia's face filled his vision, his throat tightening and the back of his eyes burning with unshed tears. Taking a deep breath, Tere dragged his attention to the present.

Looking back over his shoulder, Tere eyed the man who emanated the most authority. He was a little smaller, a little leaner, than the others in the group but definitely a formidable warrior, but there was something about him that made Tere believe this man was a leader, a lord perhaps. He didn't seem to possess magic like the others, but he certainly had an innate air of self-assurance and he'd used mind-speak too. Perhaps the one Tere had thought was the leader wasn't at all. They all wore clothes that told him they weren't serfs. Their steeds were well groomed, and the stallions were war horses.

Who are they and why are they here?

Tere returned his attention to the rope, calling to the others to let them know Daien had her and they should pull them up. The fact that the men had started pulling on the rope before he spoke told Tere that they were using their mind voices again, which meant they had a close bond, maybe even blood ties.

When Daien appeared near the edge, Tere reached over offering his hand to help Daien and the woman onto the slick grass. He witnessed Daien's momentary inner struggle on whether to accept Tere's help, then he reached up, slapping his hand into Tere's. Sweat trickled down Tere's neck as he strained against the weight of two adults dangling over the treacherous rocks and dangerous swirling water below.

The moment Daien and the woman crested the edge and toppled to the ground, the other two men dropped the rope rushing to their side. Swearing at the sight of the woman's hand, torn and bloodied and her battered and bruised body, the tall warrior spoke.

'We're going to need a fire, but we can't light one here. We'll have to head back into the forest to safely tend her wounds.'

Tere responded almost without thinking. 'I know where there's a cave that's safe.'

The blond warrior drew himself up, a challenge in his expression as he eyed Tere.

'What is your name, Changeling? And why should we trust you? You caused this.'

Tere recognised that it was his fault the horse had been startled and he truly wished to help. Not hesitating, he prayed that his willingness would inspire at least some confidence in him. His words tumbled out. 'My name is Tere. I am not part of the local wolf changeling pack ruled by Lacas. They're trying to kill me. I didn't mean to startle your friend's horse. I'm truly sorry. Let me help you. Please.'

Sudden realisation that the wolves chasing him had given up the chase when the riders had appeared made Tere pause. He knew that they'd be back. The question was: when?

'Lacas is dead,' the tall, powerfully built blond man responded in a flat tone. 'I know this because I killed him.'

Tere's attention snapped back to the present. He doubted the words only for the briefest of moments but looking up he met cold, steel-blue eyes, flashing with anger, and knew the truth. However, Tere didn't experience the joy and relief he had expected. He'd been robbed of the revenge he sought. He was certain Lacas deserved his death at the hands of this man, but Tere had waited so long to see the terror in Lacas' eyes as he realised his fate, payment in small part for the years of brutality he'd inflicted on not only Tere and his Mama but the pack, too.

Tere held the warrior's gaze. 'What did he do to you? His life was mine to take.'

Moving up within inches of Tere's face the powerful, blond man snarled. 'His life was forfeit to me when he attempted to rape my sister.'

Tere fought the urge to step back from the intensity of his presence as a warning growl escaped his lips. His alpha wolf lunged demanding its freedom, snarling. The hair on the back of Tere's neck stiffened. Holding his wolf back he clenched his fists, fighting for control but his grandfather's words chose that moment to resurface. *Do not let your anger drive your actions* ... At that moment he knew that how Lacas died no longer mattered. Meeting the man's fierce stare, he replied, his words filled with remorse.

'I'm sorry. He was my sire and I hated him with everything I am, but he deserved to die no matter who took his life.'

Tere dropped his gaze and stepped away. His shoulders sagged and his thoughts turned back to rescuing Ileia before the warrior spoke again.

In a voice laced with authority, he commanded, 'Take us to your cave.'

Daien eyed Tere as he mounted his stallion before they carefully lifted the woman's limp form onto the saddle in front of him. Studying her face momentarily, Tere realised how beautiful she was, despite the dirt, blood and bruises. Her riding attire was expertly sewn, the soft leather of her boots appeared finely crafted and her hair, although tangled and dirty, was obviously well cared for. The dark red strands glowed like a halo around her pale, almost ethereal skin. The damp clothes clinging to her, showed her shapely and firm body. Tere's heart thumped erratically.

She's so like my Ileia.

His body responded as though it were Ileia and he took an involuntary step towards her before he caught himself. Quickly turning away, he stripped stuffing his clothes into his pack and handed it to the smaller man because he seemed the most receptive. The man hung it on the black stallion's pommel, then mounted his steed. Tere moved away so as not to spook the horses and initiated the physical change to his wolf because although he was able to mask his scent so that the horses would tolerate him in his human form, they became skittish if he ventured too close in his wolf coat.

Leading them through a heavily wooded area on the side of the mountain, Tere took the sharp turn down and to the left of the waterfall. The extremely narrow path spiralled around until they came to the partially concealed cave entrance. Once they cleared the long tendrils of ivy and small branches away, the opening was large enough to allow the horses to enter the large area at the front of the cavern.

When they were all inside, the tall warrior gathered the woman, still unconscious, from Daien's arms. Daien slid from his mount and scooped her back into his arms, holding her close to his chest. Planting a gentle kiss on her cheek he waited for the others to create a bed from some soft, dry moss they'd found, covering it with a pile of blankets. When it was ready Daien carefully lowered her limp body onto the makeshift bed.

While the lord, that was how Tere thought of the younger man, lit a small fire in the corner of the cave, tending it carefully so it produced as little smoke as possible, the warrior kneeled beside the bed. Concern etched across his face, he spoke an incantation in what sounded to Tere like the language of the Fae or Elvish, he wasn't sure which, sending what little smoke the fire produced wafting towards the back of the cave.

Daien rummaged in his sack, producing his water bottle, a bowl and a clean cloth to cleanse the woman's wounds. Carefully washing her broken and bloodied hand, emotions played across Daien's face. Tere knew Daien wanted to beat him to a pulp but held onto his control with the strength and honour of a knight. The only real sign of his inner battle was when he raked his free hand through his damp hair. Tere was impressed by the man's restraint, though he knew better than to trust him so soon.

The big man's face drew into a frown and the tingle indicating the use of magic skittered down Tere's spine again. The man was probing, attempting to heal the wound. Tere wondered if he was one of the Elven folk, though elves were usually less muscular and presented a calm, almost arrogant, regal attitude, at least in his limited experience. This man was powerful, and battle hardened, but also showed a great love for the woman, despite the dangerous edge Tere sensed bubbling just beneath the veneer of his control.

Allowing his eyes to wander over the imposing figure bent over the woman as if she were a precious jewel, Tere wondered who this man was. He had shoulder-length, wavy blonde hair, bright blue, intelligent eyes and the demeanour of a proud warrior, yet Tere acknowledged he was a handsome man by human standards and showed great compassion for the woman. The sword hanging at his side had strange markings, perhaps runes. His lips moved in silent incantation. Tere was willing to wager that women fell over themselves for his favour and men faced with his sword would turn and run to escape his wrath. He wondered if these were the Fae folk he'd been told were in the area searching for the Golden Stone.

Eventually, Tere's gaze moved back to the woman, and he noticed something. A resemblance? Could they be related? Maybe brother and sister? His attention was dragged back when the warrior frowned, sitting back on his heels.

'I cannot heal her!'

Turning from the fire, where he stirred the stew, the lord frowned. 'What do you mean?'

The warrior launched to his feet, clearly frustrated. 'Something I can't identify is holding back the healing process.'

Tere moved up from where he had been standing at the mouth of the cave. The three men turned to him.

'The thorn...' he offered quietly, 'I believe it to have been planted there with changeling magic. How else would it have held her up? I felt something while you were pulling her up the side of the precipice but couldn't identify it. Will you allow me to try?'

Daien leapt to his feet and circled around the others, standing face to face with Tere. His anger was evident in his stiff posture, one hand resting on the hilt of his sword, the other fisted by his side.

'You will not touch her, Wolf!'

The lord grasped Daien's arm firmly. 'Peace, Daien. He's trying to help.'

Daien whipped around to argue and pull himself from the other man's grasp, but at that moment, the woman's body shuddered, and she coughed violently. Daien ran to her, quickly lifting her into a sitting position. Settling himself behind her, his legs on either side of her body, he gently wrapped his arms around her.

'It's all right, sweetheart. I have you. Lean on me.'

The coughing subsided as her eyes flicked open, glazed but fully aware. Bending down to touch her forehead, the tall warrior gently prodded a red welt likely caused by a sharp rock during her descent down the cliff face. Checking her eyes for any signs of a head injury, he smiled when her green eyes gazed back at him, clear and alert.

'Welcome back, sweetling.'

Daien's body visibly relaxed when he realised she was conscious.

Lowering himself to the ground, the warrior linked his fingers with the woman's good hand briefly, then handed her an herbal brew made by the lord.

'Aidan has made you some herbal tea. Drink, Tarienne, it will ease your pain.'

So, the lord's name is Aidan and hers is Tarienne ... A distant memory attempted to surface in Tere's thoughts, vanishing just as quickly.

Tarienne accepted the tea, sniffing it and smiling weakly before her gaze trailed to the man at her side. When her eyes met Tere's, she jumped, almost spilling the hot liquid over herself. Her hands began shaking violently. Daien tightened his grip around her waist, pulling her closer, speaking close to her ear and steadying her hand with his.

'It's all right, sweetheart.'

It was meant for her ears only, but Tere's exceptional hearing picked it up. The timbre and emotion he'd heard in Daien's voice told Tere they were intimate. Turning slightly so she could see Daien's face, she again managed a tiny smile and her shaking eased. Daien kissed her cheek lightly and she relaxed back into him, taking a large sip of the warm, soothing tea. The warrior, whose name Tere had not yet learned took the mug from her and grasped her hand, rubbing his thumb gently across her knuckles while he explained.

'His name is, Tere. He helped us rescue you from the cliff face. He also showed us this cave where we could safely tend your wounds.'

Daien growled. 'We wouldn't be here if he hadn't scared Lacey.'

Aidan threw him a sharp look. 'Peace, Daien.'

The warrior motioned him forward and Daien growled like an alpha wolf protecting his territory. Placing her uninjured hand over Daien's, she caressed his knuckles lightly. Daien settled a little, and she tipped her head back to claim a chaste kiss. Tere stepped closer, squatting to meet her gaze.

'Forgive me, my lady. I did not mean to startle your mare. I am Tere, of the Inare wolf pack many miles west of here. I am pleased to make your acquaintance...' He paused. Nobody had formally given him her name yet.

Despite the pain and exhaustion etched across her face, Tarienne responded graciously. 'I am Tarienne.' Her eyes sought the warrior's. When he nodded almost imperceptibly, she continued. 'This is my brother, Raef, over there is Aidan, and behind me is Daien.'

Daien nuzzled her neck possessively, a gesture of ownership not lost on Tere.

'Your brother is having some difficulty healing your wound because the thorn that caused it was forged with changeling magic. I'd like to help.'

She met his eyes, assessing him. When she let her steady gaze drift over his body, it initiated an unexpected response in his loins. He pushed it aside. This was not his beloved Ileia even though she looked remarkably like her. Guilt at his reaction assailed him as her eyes returned to his face but he couldn't stop his mouth from curving into a smile at her examination. He did not flinch from her scrutiny, holding still while she sent her magic to assess him. Mildly amused when Daien scowled at him, he noted Tarienne pressing herself back against Daien's chest, silently reassuring him.

'If you're willing to attempt healing my hand, I would appreciate it.'

'Given that I inadvertently caused your injury, I'm willing, but I'd rather only one other person be present while I do this so I can focus. Perhaps your brother?' Tere looked pointedly at Daien barely suppressing a smirk. He wasn't sure why he felt the need to antagonise Daien except that he felt a strong connection to Tarienne, perhaps because she was so like Ileia. Another pang of guilt spiked through him as he waited for Tarienne's response.

Tarienne caressed the back of Daien's hand, soothing the anger radiating from him. 'All right, but could you all give Daien and I a moment alone, please?'

Rising, they exited the cave, waiting. It wasn't too long before Daien brushed aside the tendrils of ivy hiding the entrance to the cave, aiming a glare at Tere. Raef and Tere moved back inside the cave and lowered themselves to the ground on either side of Tarienne. Tere held his hand out in invitation and Tarienne nervously lifted her injured hand, placing it in his flinching at the first pulse of his magic. When she met his eyes, a gentle, encouraging smile curved her lips.

Tere's pulse beat erratically as he met the gaze of this breathtakingly beautiful woman. Tearing his eyes away, he tamped his reaction down, angry at himself, and focused his attention on Tarienne's hand. His fingers and magic gently probed, feeling for the extent of the damage. Unconsciously, he swirled his scent around her to calm her as he had done once before with Ileia. Hearing Raef grumble a warning, he quickly withdrew it.

He sent Tarienne an apologetic glance, realising his natural fragrance had affected her more than he'd anticipated. When her gaze refused to leave his face his pulse skittered and his body tightened. Forcibly returning his attention to her hand, Tere circled his fingers lightly around the wound. Gently massaging her hand to stimulate the blood flow, he released small amounts of magic into the damaged bone and muscle to stimulate the healing process. Suddenly, he scented her arousal. Tere paused, meeting her scrutiny, a slow burn searing his loins.

Glancing at Raef, Tere realised he hadn't noticed the interaction this time, so he carefully wrapped another wisp of his scent around her. Tarienne sucked in a little breath. Tere's heart thumped erratically again.

What the hell am I doing?

He swore silently when his body hardened in response. This was definitely going to be a problem. He was experiencing some trouble differentiating between Tarienne and Ileia. His thoughts of Ileia blurred and he shook his head slightly to clear them. With difficulty, he once again focused his attention on healing Tarienne's hand.

The intense concentration required eased his arousal. Until Tarienne spoke in what sounded to him like sultry tones.

'Raef, could you get me some water, please? I'm so thirsty.'

Raef nodded and rose immediately, exiting the cave. The moment he was out of sight, Tarienne placed her hand high on Tere's upper thigh. Sliding her thumb up and down, perilously close to his growing erection, she whispered, 'Thank you.'

Dark with arousal, her eyes held his. Tere wanted to lean in and take her lips. His body hardened painfully and he couldn't hold back a growl. When Tarienne licked her lips Tere shook with the effort of resisting the temptation to kiss her. His body recognised her as Ileia and Tarienne was obviously more affected by the pain than anyone had realised. When Raef entered with the water she'd requested, she slipped her uninjured hand back into her lap and accepted the cool liquid. Tere couldn't pull his gaze away as Tarienne closed her eyes, allowing the water to slide down her throat. Swallowing hard, he looked away and pulled in a few steadying breaths.

Raef examined Tarienne's partially healed hand and nodded at Tere. 'It is healing well already. Thank you, Tere.'

Tere finished the healing session, certain Raef could sense the tension emanating from him. When Tarienne relaxed, her eyes fluttering closed, Tere moved away, striding outside. He needed some fresh air.

Returning inside after a brisk walk to clear his thoughts, Tere dropped to the dirt floor, his back pressed against the cold, rock wall, unable to pull his eyes away from Daien and Tarienne. The tenderness they shared was palpable. They touched and whispered. Rarely were they far apart. When Tarienne spied him watching, her brow crinkled briefly before she sent him a small smile and returned her focus to Daien, leaning into him as she ate.

Tere wondered if Tarienne remembered what had happened during the healing session. Judging by her lack of reaction, he doubted it. Perhaps she'd hit her head when she fell, or his magic muddled her thoughts. Her devotion to Daien was clear but she had definitely reacted to his nearness as he'd worked on her hand. What he was struggling with was why he'd reacted to her. Deciding to clean the knives he kept hidden in his boots, he pondered their earlier interaction.

When she had finished eating, Tere could not resist approaching her again. Something inexplicable drove him to explore her reaction to him even though he knew it was wrong. 'If you're up to it, I'd like to try another healing session.'

Tarienne's focus was on Daien, so she took a moment to respond, her thoughts obviously slowed with the pain she must be experiencing. 'If you think another session so soon will help.'

Tarienne turned back to Daien and smiled. 'Would you leave us for a short while, dear heart?' She tenderly ran the fingers of her uninjured hand down the side of Daien's face. Daien captured them, kissing her palm.

'Are you sure you wouldn't like me to stay?'

Tere's thoughts drifted to another time and place when he and Ileia had shared such tenderness.

She looks so much like my Ileia.

His attention flicked back to Tarienne as she answered Daien.

'No, my love. Tere says he works better alone.'

Daien narrowed his eyes at Tere, then reluctantly turned and stepped through the cave entrance. Aidan followed. Raef stood looking down at his sister.

'Would you like me to stay?'

'No, thank you, brother. I'll be fine.'

The full force of her smile knocked the breath out of Tere. *My Ileia.* Tarienne relaxed back, onto the makeshift bed and Tere dropped onto the dirt floor, cross-legged. Holding out his hand, Tarienne placed hers in his without meeting his eyes. Slowly, he massaged around the wound, allowing his magic to trickle into it, healing the bones and muscles. After a few minutes, he lifted his gaze to hers and tentatively released a finger of his scent, coiling it around her.

Tarienne inhaled sharply. Tere immediately scented her arousal. Intense desire slammed into him. Glancing over his shoulder to make sure nobody was near the cave entrance, he slowly and carefully moved closer, lowering his head as he continued to massage and heal her hand.

Her languid eyes met his. A deep growl rumbled through Tere as he captured her lips for a searing kiss. As their lips touched, he recognised that something was wrong, different, but then she softened, opening her mouth invitingly. He groaned as their tongues touched. *Ileia.* He was so focused on the sensation of her lips sliding across his, her tongue stroking his, he forgot to maintain his tendril of scent around her.

Suddenly Tarienne stiffened, pushing Tere away. Fury in her eyes, she hissed, 'What the hell do you think you're doing?'

For a moment, confusion fogged his brain. *Ileia?* The he realised what he had done, immediately despising his actions and himself. Was he just like his sire?

Tarienne gritted her teeth. 'Your magic affects me. I don't know why. Do *not* take advantage of that again.'

Tere huffed out a frustrated and confused breath and wordlessly returned to healing her hand. When he finished, he strode outside and to the amazement of the others, stripped off his clothes, dropping them to the ground, and ran, shifting into his wolf midstride.

* * *

When Tere finally returned slipping noiselessly through the cave entrance, they were all fast asleep. His gaze ran over Daien and Tarienne entwined in each other's arms. A sudden onslaught of emotion slammed into him and he squeezed his eyes closed. Opening them again, anger, embarrassment and regret filled him for taking advantage of Tarienne, for even thinking that way about anyone other than Ileia. He flopped onto his bed. Frustration washed through him making him want to howl. What was happening? His mind was playing tricks on him; sometimes he saw Tarienne and sometimes he saw Ileia. Groaning, he closed his eyes, seeking relief in sleep, but sleep eluded him. The sky had just begun to lighten when he finally succumbed to slumber, dreaming vivid, erotic dreams.

Her curvaceous, naked form stretched out on top of him as she trailed hot kisses down his body. Reaching his arousal, her hands caressed and stroked, followed by the exquisite sensation of her delicious mouth engulfing him. He groaned. Running her tongue along his length, she drew circles around the throbbing head of his rock, hard erection. His back arched involuntarily. Tere groaned at the exquisite pleasure. His hips pumped and he buried his fingers into her hair. With the force of a tidal wave, his climax surged, long and powerful, his hips rocking as she greedily swallowed his seed.

After taking a few moments to catch his breath, Tere deftly flipped her beneath him. Settling between her legs, he returned the favour, laving her sensitive bud until she screamed with release. Kissing his way up her body, he finally slid into her damp heat with one satisfying thrust, dipping his head to claim a long, passionate kiss as he pumped into her tight sheath. Groaning against her lips, he increased the tempo, circling his hips and working her tight bundle of nerves with one hand until another blistering climax ripped through them both rocking his entire body. Her muscles throbbed around him, milking every last drop of his seed before he lowered his head to claim her lips...

A hand shoving at his shoulder ripped him unceremoniously from his dream, Tere jumped to his feet, shaking his head to clear the lingering haze. A menacing growl rumbled through him. His desire-fogged brain finally registered Aidan standing there, eyes wide. Realising he had been trying to wake him, Tere quickly glanced down and was grateful his shirt was long enough to cover the residual evidence of his dream. He bit out, 'Damn it, man. Don't ever wake me like that.'

Aidan held up his hands. 'Sorry. I just wanted to ask if you were hungry.' Dropping his hands, Aidan stomped away, grumbling something about being ungrateful.

Tere flopped back onto his bedroll, scrubbing his face to wipe the dream from his thoughts. He knew the only way to clear his head was to run. Dropping the soft trousers he wore to bed, he quickly wiped away the evidence of his climax with the soft cloth he kept in his pack. Stripping off his shirt, he tossed it aside, shifted, and hurtled through cave entrance.

Vaguely aware of Tarienne's and Daien's absence, he sprinted to the closest waterhole, intending to wash away the evidence of his dream in the icy water. His wolf froze when his eyes latched onto a naked woman and her lover wrapped around each other in the waist-deep water. Watching from the cover of the trees he was incapable of tearing his eyes away as they made love.

A shower of silver and gold heralded the transformation into his human form. Transfixed by the scene playing out in the water, Tere was unable to force himself to leave as Tarienne and Daien rocked in unison, crying out softly, their intimate whispers audible to Tere's enhanced hearing. When Tarienne and Daien both cried out their release, Tere was tempted to seek relief for his aching body by his own hand.

Clamping his mouth shut so he didn't make any sound to alert them to his presence, he crouched, unmoving. Tarienne gracefully moved out of the water, her wet skin glistening in the sunlight. She was a glorious sight to behold, her long, shapely legs reaching up to the dark red thatch of hair at the apex of her thighs. Her pert, round breasts still heaved from making love with Daien. Rising involuntarily, Tere took a step towards her before catching himself. *This is not Ileia.* Swearing silently, he shifted again, bolting through the trees on the silent pads of his wolf.

After several hours Tere finally stopped running and shifted back to his human form. Dropping to the cool grass, he gazed out over a ravine, his knees drawn up, his arms wrapped around them to ward off the chill of the early Spring morning.

What the hell is going on? Why am I attracted to Tarienne when I love Ileia with everything that I am?

Sitting for what seemed like hours, his mind ran over the events of the past few weeks including his captivity at the hands of Lacas and the Sorcerer, searching for answers. Finally, a memory resurfaced of a foul-tasting liquid being forced down his throat. Manacled by his ankles and wrists to prevent him from shifting, it had taken Lacas' and the Sorcerer's magic to compel him to swallow the liquid to ensure his compliance. The liquid had caused confusion, drowsiness and seriously weakened him, he assumed its purpose had been to ensure his compliance, to remove him as a threat to Lacas' leadership of the pack. Thankfully help had come from an unexpected source, Lupus had saved him by giving him a liquid that smelled the same as the potion created by Rantec but did not ensorcell his brain.

Realisation dawned like a rock slamming into his chest. His reaction to Tarienne was due to the remnants of the potion's effects. That explained the difficulty he'd had differentiating Tarienne from Ileia. That Tarienne looked so much like his beautiful Ileia had added to his confusion. Breaking down, his head dropped disconsolately into his hands. He howled a long, mournful, heartbreaking sound. Hot tears ran down his face.

Ileia. Forgive me.

The image of his magnificent, reddish-brown wolf shifted into a stunning woman with long, wavy red hair and the most beautiful, compelling green eyes...eyes so like Tarienne's.

Tere had not been able to prevent Ileia's capture as he had promised, or find her since his escape from the caves. His greatest fear was that Lacas had raped and murdered her as revenge. His heart had been shattered and empty until he'd meet Tarienne, Raef, Aidan and even Daien and for some inexplicable reason they'd accepted him, despite everything.

As he rested, his thoughts racing with the events of the past few weeks, Tere began feeling much more like himself. The long run must have helped his body burn off whatever was in his system. Shifting into his wolf form again, he knew what he needed to do. He ran as fast and hard as he could back to the cave to ensure any remaining effects of the potion were dispelled. When he arrived at the cave entrance everyone was outside. He padded past them, shifted, then dressed quickly. When Tarienne walked into the cave to pack her things, Tere approached her anxiously, standing a respectable distance away.

'Tarienne?'

Tarienne lifted her eyes to meet his. A small frown wrinkled her forehead.

'I wanted to say that I'm truly sorry for what happened. My captors forced me to ingest a potion. I'm not certain what it was, but it made me act out of character. I think I burned most of it off during my run today.' Tere grasped her uninjured hand. 'Can you forgive me, please?'

Tarienne paused. Tere waited, his brows knitted together in a worried frown.

'I believe you, and you are forgiven.'

Relief washed over Tere until Daien moved into the cave. Tensing again, his stance shifted to a defensive posture. Unbeknown to Tere, Daien had been leaning on the wall at the cave entrance, observing the interaction. Daien sauntered to Tarienne's side, a grin curving his lips.

'Just don't let it happen again, my friend.'

After planting a possessive kiss on her lips, Daien leaned over and gave Tere a friendly clap on the back. Astonishment spread across Tere's face.

'You knew?'

Daien nodded. 'We don't keep secrets.'

Tere ran his hands through his hair. 'I thought you'd try to pound me into the ground again.'

Daien smiled. 'Initially, I wanted to, but Ren can be particularly persuasive when she wants something...' He raised his eyebrows and shot a suggestive look at Tarienne. She rolled her eyes, laughing. He looked back at Tere. 'But, despite everything, I happen to believe you.'

Aidan strode through the entrance of the cave. 'We need to gather our things and leave here. Come on, you lot. We'll never complete this quest if you all keep jibber-jabbering.'

Daien raised his eyebrows, laughing. 'Jibber-jabbering?'

Tere laughed along with them even as a distant memory niggled at him. *A quest? Were they the people Lupus mentioned who searched for the Golden Stone?* Deciding to take a chance that they were, Tere smiled, turning to the others now gathered in the cave to pack their belonging.

'I know things didn't start well between us, but my search for Ileia lies in the same direction as your quest. I'd like to help you if possible and I'd appreciate your company on the way if you're all agreeable.'

Daien, Aidan, Raef and Tarienne shared a look that told Tere they were conversing through mind-speak. Possibly wondering how he knew what their quest was. He chose not to listen in but to wait for their verdict. A few moments passed before Aidan stepped forward, clapped Tere on the back, smiled and gave him their joint reply.

'Your company on our journey is most welcome and we'd very much appreciate any assistance you can provide to help locate the Golden Stone, especially with your knowledge of the area.'

Experiencing a sensation of belonging and acceptance that he'd never known Tere's heart swelled with renewed hope as they set off together.

CHAPTER 10

A few hours later, they stopped to discuss their strategy to retrieve the Golden Stone. Tere offered his knowledge of the caves as a gesture of trust.

'It is rumoured that the stone lies in the heart of the largest cave which is guarded by ten huge beasts. They are half-man, half-oxen and over seven feet tall. They're very strong but not overly intelligent. I'd say there are close to one hundred men and beasts, heavily armed and led by a Sorcerer named Rantec.'

'Rantec?' Tarienne asked, her tone disbelieving. 'Rantar's offspring? But how?'

Raef swore vehemently. 'How did we miss this? We would have ridden to our death if not for Tere. Dammit. The prophecy mentions nothing of a son.'

Surprised by Raef's and Tarienne's reaction when he'd mentioned Rantec, Tere waited, nodding, 'The legend says Rantar took a human woman. She bore his son, then died ... or was killed immediately after the birth. Nobody really knows. Rumour has it that the boy was raised by the Inare pack, but I don't recall seeing any evidence of a human in the pack while I was there.' He added, 'Rantec and Lacas were responsible for the capture of myself and Ileia. Given

137

that Lacas is dead I'm hoping that locating Rantec when we find the Golden Stone will also lead me to Ileia.'

Tere watched Tarienne lay her hand on Raef's arm and sensed the tingle of magic as she soothed her brother. 'How could we have known? We just need to rethink our plan of attack. Aidan?'

Noting how Tarienne deferred to Aidan, Tere realised how well each individual in this group complimented each other. Raef, the powerful Fae warrior. Daien, a clever and skilled knight possessed of steadfast loyalty. Aidan, the strategist, and fearless leader, and the cunning and brave, Tarienne, the glue holding them all together. Each wielded their own brand of magic, loving each other in their own way. Together, they were powerful and dangerous, the perfect team to retrieve the Golden Stone.

'We are outnumbered, so we must be clever about this. Daien, what say you and I set a series of traps? We can draw the men out and take down as many as we are able. Tarienne and Raef can use their magic to disable the rest and enter the cave to retrieve the Stone.' Aidan's gaze touched each member of the group, awaiting their thoughts.

'What part will Tere play?' Daien asked.

Tere was momentarily stunned, yet grateful for Daien's unlikely friendship. He smiled. 'They're looking for me. I can be your decoy and lead them through your traps.'

Aidan nodded. 'You can help us set the traps. That way, you'll know where and what they are so you can avoid them.'

Raef smiled, his moment of self-doubt and barely controlled anger fading. 'We need to take care using our magic. We must not exhaust ourselves before we reach the Stone. It's highly likely that Rantec is in there, waiting for us. We do not know how powerful he is.'

Tarienne appeared lost in thought. 'If he is in there, he'll know the moment we use any magic, so we need to make it count. We must destroy as many of the guards as we can at once. We need something that will achieve this, yet not take too long to gather or drain us too much. We'll need to join our magic if we are to have any hope of defeating him—'

Tere interrupted. 'I can return as soon as I've cleared the last of the traps and back you up.' His gaze drifted around the group, seeking approval. Raef was the first to respond.

'Perfect! Aidan and Daien can follow when they've finished. The last thing we need to decide is which incantation to use.'

Eventually, Tarienne spoke quietly, almost reluctantly. 'There is one spell we could use. We could summon the Blade Spirits.'

Fear tinged Tere's voice when he responded. 'You would summon the Blade Spirits to aid in destroying Rantec and his followers? Their legend has been passed down through the pack for generations. They are to be feared. How do you know they won't turn their magic on you? They are ancient warriors so magically powerful they swore to fight evil for eternity, even after their death. They have been fighting from the afterlife for so long, they have become dangerously unpredictable.'

Raef eyed him. 'What Tere says is true, but Ren is right. It's our best chance. While it will take both of us to call them, it won't overly tire us. I believe they will assist us because we are fighting an evil force, this aligns with the vow that holds them between here and the afterlife. Aidan and Daien, I understand that you know little of the Blade Spirits having little previous experience with magic and magical creatures, so I cannot expect you to help make this decision.'

Aidan and Daien glanced at each other. Aidan swallowed before speaking. 'We have heard a little of them, but given my father was opposed to magic they were only spoken of behind closed doors, away from his notice. It is enough to know that they fight evil as do we. We trust you with our lives, so we will agree with what you believe to be right. I know I can speak for Daien when I say this.'

Daien nodded his agreement. He brought Tarienne's knuckles to his lips, kissing them gently. 'We have already agreed that we stay together, no matter what.'

Tarienne smiled at them, then turned her gaze to Tere. 'You do not have the bond of love that we possess, Tere. Do not feel compelled to do this.'

Tere spoke past the lump in his throat, pausing before he spoke. 'Despite our ... difficult beginning, you have accepted me. I will stand by you and do what I can to help. Hopefully I will also discover something of Ileia's whereabouts from the Sorcerer."

Raef's nodded and his voice hardened, the strength of his magic flowing around him like an aura. 'Then let us be on our way. May the spirits be with us all.'

Placing their hands together in the centre of the circle, they united in their battle cry. *'Gurith geoth riam laie.* Death to our enemies!'

Aidan, Daien and Tere left to set their traps, leaving Raef and Tarienne to dispatch the guards posted at the entrance.

Entering the thick forest bordering the path to the caves, it wasn't long before the crackle of magic made the hair on the back of Tere's neck stand on end. Hoping it was Raef and Tarienne summoning the Blade Spirits, Tere tuned into the vibrations emanating from the powerful magical flow. He picked up the words streaming through their minds as they chanted in unison.

'Yahalla onnia Blenidae en'i Lyuhta.'

Smiling to himself, Tere yanked the rope tight across the

spear-filled trench he, Aidan and Daien had dug across the forest path. Tere's magic had been useful in undertaking the major part of the digging as he'd done before when setting a trap for Lacas and his followers. Aidan and Daien had cheerfully voiced their appreciation that they didn't have to do it all by hand. Gathering brush to cover the hole, he glanced at Daien, bending back a branch farther along the track. He'd strung a thin rope across the path a few feet before the trench, at ankle height. When tripped, it would release the branch into the beasts' backs with hopefully enough force to knock them forward into the trench, skewering them on the spears. This would give Aidan and Daien the advantage they needed to defeat any of the foul creatures who managed to survive. Hopefully none would.

They'd just completed the rest of the traps when the earth beneath their feet began vibrating, heralding the approach of a troop of Rantec's warrior beasts. Six creatures clumped into view. They were heavily armed, but it looked like they lacked any armour that would render their trap less effective.

Moving back into the leafy cover of the thickest part of the forest, Tere, Aidan and Daien watched the creatures stomp along the well-worn path. When the *thwack* of the thick branch forced those at the back to stumble forward, unbalancing the rest of the savage beasts, bellows erupted from the enormous brutes, echoing through the silence of the forest. A tangle of tree-like limbs and unwashed, hairy bodies tumbled into the death pit, their combined weight ensuring their execution on the razor-sharp spears.

Daien, Aidan and Tere stealthily made their way back to the pit to ensure none of the monsters had survived. Tere wrinkled his nose lifting a hand to his face to block the stench of creature, blood and death emanating from the trench, Daien and Aidan doing the same. They didn't have time to cover the bodies. They needed to join Raef and Tarienne in the cave.

Tere stripped, stowing his clothes between two rocks where they were well hidden by some soft, green, leafy undergrowth, then shifted. He sprinted ahead to see if Raef and Tarienne needed any help. Daien and Aidan, hampered by the thick underbrush and thorny bushes, dashed through the trees as quickly as they could. Tere was soon so far ahead, his wolf hearing could barely detect them, their scent disguised beneath the vile odour of the dead savages carried on the soft spring breeze. Tere sneezed as he hurtled into the dank, grey tunnels, pleased when he picked up Tarienne's subtle, sweet vanilla fragrance wafting along the chilled corridors.

Bounding to Tarienne's side, Tere whined softly. His gaze swept over the bodies of the dead beasts as Tarienne kneeled, stroking the soft fur on his head. His body warmed with the joy of acceptance and friendship. He leaned into her leg, needing the contact as much as she seemed to at that moment.

'The Blade Spirits helped us as we'd hoped. Were the traps successful?' she whispered close to his ear.

Tere cocked his head sideways in a wolfish nod. Tarienne giggled softly, her hand on his scruff, absently scratching her nails into his coat. Tere wanted to growl contentedly but instead satisfied himself by arching his back into her comforting ministrations.

Raef, his finger on his lips, motioned them farther into the blackness of the cave. Hiding in the chill of the shadows, they watched a small, insignificant looking man with long, silver hair reverently holding a huge, golden orb. The sphere sent out shards of amber light as he chanted in the old language, the language of magic. This was

Rantec, son of Rantar. Tere shivered as the memories of Rantec's torture assailed him.

Tarienne was so focused on her enemy, she did not hear Tere's soft warning yip until it was too late. The moment she stepped from the shadows, Rantec's hawk-like gaze shot to her. He immediately launched a ferocious blast of deadly magic in her direction.

Without thought for his own safety, Tere leapt in front of her, intercepting the fiery trajectory of the evil incantation. The full force of the spell slammed into his flank. Searing pain shot through his body, like a white-hot poker burning through his organs. A pain-filled yelp ripped from him before he landed hard on his side, the breath leaving his lungs with a whoosh. Darkness clouded Tere's vision. Spots of searing, white light burned into his brain like the heat of a blacksmith's furnace, before the blackness mercifully claimed him.

* * *

Dimmed senses told Tere that someone's hand rested on his flank. *Raef?* A tiny sliver of warmth threaded through Tere's awareness, nudging aside the icy pain. The warmth spread with agonising slowness until Tere became aware that Raef was attempting to heal him. A sense of despair so intense that it threatened to consume Tere too, emanated from Raef. His struggle to remain focused further confused Tere's pain-fogged brain.

Why? He'd saved Tarienne, hadn't he?

Tere's jumbled thoughts began clearing. Although his head ached fiercely, he focused on Raef's thoughts: *I must save the wolf who saved my sister's life. I must save Tere. For Tarienne, for the incredible selflessness and loyalty he demonstrated in throwing himself in front of her, taking the full power of Rantec's blast of evil power.*

Raef's thoughts continually flicked to Tarienne. His fear for her was palpable. Despite the searing pain at the back of his eyes, Tere tuned into Raef's thoughts again: Raef wasn't surprised that Daien possessed the gift of earth magic, having thought he'd caught a spark when he'd filtered through Daien's early memories. He was unbelievably grateful Daien had found his power when Tarienne needed it most.

Why did Tarienne need Daien's power?

Tere struggled to consciousness, his vision blurry, the pain behind his eyes almost unbearable as he observed Aidan reaching into a shallow crevice in the rock wall. Pulling out a glowing golden orb, Aidan yanked a cloth from his pocket, quickly wrapping it around what Tere recognised as the Golden Stone. The stone crackled with the powerful magic encased within it. Nestling it into his pack, Aidan cushioned it with his folded cape, then moved to Raef's side.

Raef jumped slightly when Aidan nudged him. The warmth abated as his hands momentarily left Tere's chest. Tere followed Raef's gaze to where Tarienne lay, a hiss slipping from his lips as he witnessed a soft moss creeping across the bloodied floor to cushion Tarienne's crumpled form. The incantation creating this wonder came from Daien, his arms raised, his stance wide as he chanted rhythmically. Raef's eyes widened. Tere felt his hope blooming, replacing the despair that threatened to consume Raef's usually tight control.

Tere watched as moisture gathered in the corners of Raef's eyes and his lids slid closed for the briefest of moments. When Raef grasped for the barely perceptible sibling bond, barely suppressing a sob at its fragility, Tere gently severed the mind connection with him, not wishing to intrude further on the depth of love between them.

Disbelief filled Tere as ivy gently wove itself around Tarienne's body, cradling her in soft, fresh, green leaves. Tiny crisp, white flowers sprouted from the stems, encircling her head like a crown of white gold on a maiden preparing for her passage into adulthood. When Raef placed his hands back on Tere's chest, agony seared through his body again, despite the warmth flowing through him, he was forced to close his eyes once more.

Raef heaved a sigh of relief as Tere struggled to stand, his wolf whining at the pain. Raef and Aidan gently held him down, urging him to take a few moments to catch his breath.

Tere gazed at his friends through wolfish eyes before dropping his head back to the ground. Rising to their feet, Aidan and Raef left Tere to rest. His eyes followed them, witnessing an exhausted Daien stagger to Tarienne's side, calling to her on a sob.

'Sweetheart, come back to me. Please.'

Tarienne did not respond. Daien's pleading gaze met the eyes of his friends. Despair etched across his face, he fell to his knees, his shoulders slumped. His control shattering, tears of grief tumbled down his cheeks. Tere's heart ached with the anguish of the three warriors.

Daien's voice was barely audible. His fists clenched at his side; his body shook with sorrow. 'Rantec has pulled her spirit into the afterlife with him. I was too late.'

With great tenderness Raef placed his large, calloused hands on either side of his sister's head. Tere sensed the immense power Raef possessed as he sent pulses of magic through her. His panic evident when Tarienne still did not respond.

Hanging his head, despair contorting his handsome features, Raef whispered, his cheeks wet with tears. 'My sweet baby sister don't leave us. We need you. We all need you...'

Aidan grasped Tarienne's wrist, his common sense, even in in the face of his anguish displaying his innate leadership. 'Her heart still beats.' His gaze shot to Tere. 'Tere, you helped her before. I'm sorry, I know your injury is causing you great pain, but can you do anything now?'

Tere could watch this drama play out no longer. In a shimmer of gold and silver sparks, he shifted to human form, his injuries causing him excruciating pain. Nevertheless, he dragged himself to Tarienne's side and placed his hands over her heart. Closing his eyes, he sent out his spirit wolf, searching for her lost soul. He spoke, his head still bowed over Tarienne.

'She does not yet walk the afterlife. Her spirit wanders, lost. I think we can pull her back, if we do it together. Place your hands on her. Let her feel you. All of you. Call her with your mind voice.'

Tere rested his hands on Tarienne's flat abdomen. Raef grasped her hand in his, tenderly rubbing her knuckles with his thumb. Aidan gently held her other hand and brought it to his lips to place a gentle kiss across the back of it. And Daien cradled her head in his lap, caressing the side of her face.

Distantly aware of the others desperately calling Tarienne, Tere's heart clenched as he heard Daien pleading. He knew how it felt not to be able to help the one you loved. Tere's eyes moistened as he thought of his beloved Ileia. When this was over, he'd find her, no matter what. His focus returned to finding Tarienne, who wandered somewhere between life and death.

My beautiful Ren, come back to me. Please, don't leave me to an eternity without you. I love you. You are my soul, my life. Walk towards me, sweetheart. Be with me always. We all need you... Daien broke off, his grief a lead weight crushing his soul. *I can't go on without you, my love. Please...*

Blocking out the thoughts and emotions of the other three men, Tere mustered his powers. Pain seared its way through his body as he searched. His gut burned. His head ached. Slowly, carefully, he searched for Tarienne's lost soul, calling on the spirits of his ancestors to help find her.

When Tere finally found her Tarienne wandered alone, obviously confused.

Tere, is that you? Where am I?

Tere yipped, padding towards her on his huge wolf paws. Gently taking her hand in his mouth, he pulled firmly, urging her towards the voices. Tere's mouth was gentle, yet strong around her wrist. When the spirits of Aidan, Daien and Raef appeared, Tere dropped her hand and yipped again. He rubbed his powerful body reassuringly against her leg, then nudged her forward with his snout watching as she made her way towards the voices of those she loved.

Snapping their focus back to the present, the four men yanked Tarienne with them, holding onto her with a strength borne of fear. Tarienne sucked in a sharp breath, filling her lungs as though starved of air. Her lids fluttered open.

'Sweetheart...' Daien gathered her to him, a choked sob escaping as he hugged her hard. Her attention finally turned to a fully clothed Tere.

Holding his gaze, she whispered, 'Your wolf brought me home.'

Daien, Raef and Aidan exchanged confused glances. Tarienne explained.

'I heard Daien's voice, but I only saw him for a moment and wasn't sure where I was or which way to go. I walked towards where I thought I'd last heard him. Then I heard all of you, but I couldn't seem to reach you until Tere's wolf took my hand and showed me the way. Thank you, Tere. You saved me ... again.'

Tere smiled, an odd sense of humility filtering through him. 'Daien put you on the right path. You just needed some encouragement to continue.'

Aidan's expression became serious as he looked at Tere. 'You have earned our trust, Tere. As such, you should know us for who we really are.'

Confusion filled Tere. He already knew who they were ... didn't he? Witnessing small nods from Raef, Tarienne and Daien, Tere frowned as Aidan continued.

'I am Aidan, King of Therin. Raef and Tarienne are the Crown Prince and Princess of the Fae of Darewood. Daien is the most trusted of my guards, a dear friend, of Druid blood and betrothed to Tarienne.'

Tere's eyes widened. Shock spiralled through him. He was unable to speak as he absorbed what he had been told. Aidan's strength in a crisis and the way they all consulted him on matters of strategy now made sense.

Tere bowed low. 'I am humbled and honoured to be in your presence—'

'No!'

Tere's head snapped up. Tarienne held his gaze and continued, her tone softening. 'As Aidan said, you have earned your place. We told you who we are to prove our trust in you, not to change your attitude towards us. We are still Tarienne, Raef, Aidan, and Daien. No more, no less.'

Tere nodded, smiling. 'I thank you all for your trust and friendship.' Tere didn't offer more information about himself. Not yet. Glancing around the cave, he asked, 'Aidan, do I remember seeing you pick up the Golden Stone?'

Aidan nodded, producing a cloth from his pack. He carefully unwrapped it to reveal the amber glow of the Golden Stone pulsing in his hands. Covering it quickly, he rose to his feet.

'We should get as far away from here as we can before reinforcements arrive. Ren, are you well enough to travel?'

'I think so.' Daien and Raef helped Tarienne to her feet. She stood for a moment, testing her legs.

'I feel quite well, considering.' Eyeing Daien speculatively, she asked what everyone else was wondering. 'What did you do?'

Daien shrugged. 'To be honest, I don't really know. Apparently, I called the earth spirits. I had no idea what I was doing. The power just flowed through me when I saw you being pulled into the afterlife.'

Tarienne's smile spoke of her love for Daien. 'My wonderful Druid.'

Slipping his arms around her, Daien pulled her close, stealing a long, tender kiss.

Aidan cleared his throat loudly, glancing at Tere. 'Take no notice. They're always doing that.'

Tere and his new friends laughed as they collected their belongings in readiness to leave. Raef moved up beside Tarienne, capturing her hand in his. Tarienne turned to face her brother, moving into his open arms. Tere overheard as Raef hauled in a deep breath, burying his face in her hair. His voice broke as he whispered, 'I thought I'd lost you, sweetling. Please, never do that to me again.'

Tarienne hugged her brother fiercely, and Tere sensed the flow of courage and love through their sibling bond. Tere drew a deep breath, profoundly affected by the emotion, and withdrew, leaving them to their private moment.

A few moments later, Raef and Aidan rounded up the horses as Tere stripped behind a tree, handing his clothes to Daien. He was still mildly surprised at the unlikely friendship developing between them. Shifting, he broke into a run to put a little distance between himself and the horses. They thundered down the side of the mountain glad to leave behind Rantec's headquarters and his vile, barbaric followers. As he ran Tere's thoughts turned back to Lacas. Residual annoyance sliced through him that his was not the last face Lacas saw. Tere had wanted Lacas to know how powerful he'd become, and he'd wanted to feel the satisfaction as Lacas had realised his fate at the hands of the son he'd abused. And now Rantec was dead too, how would he find Ileia? Despair and the lingering desire for vengeance warred with the words his grandfather had spoken to him. Tere did not want to be like his father and live his life in anger as Lacas had. It was time to turn his thoughts to more positive pursuits and rescue his precious Ileia no matter how difficult it seemed right now.

* * *

Almost an hour later, the landscape started to level out and saplings covered with fresh, green leaves appeared on either side of the track. When a chilling howl pierced the air, they hastily reined in their mounts and waited, listening. Daien walked his stallion up beside Tarienne, his hand tense on the hilt of his sword. She sent him a worried glance.

Tere's wolf burst from between the trees, panting hard. His tongue lolling out of the side of his mouth, he hurtled towards them, shouting into their minds.

Run! Wolves!

Wheeling their horses around, the group raced in the opposite direction, pushing their steeds to run as fast as they possibly could. Instead of following the path, Tere led them down the side of the incline and through a thick line of tall, straight trees. Emerging onto a short, grassy plain leading down to the river, Tere skidded to a halt, scattering dirt and stones. Coming face to face with a huge, slate-grey wolf, the hackles along Tere's back rose. Standing erect in a clear alpha posture, his lips drew back in a snarl. At least thirty other wolves of various colours and sizes fanned out on either side of the leader, ready to attack. Tere growled low, daring one of them to move first.

Across the river, close to one hundred riders sat with deadly crossbows aimed in their direction. Aidan and Daien swore as they yanked their stallions to an abrupt halt. Drawing their swords, they ripped their shields from where they were strapped onto their saddlebags. Daien's shield caught on the heavy metal buckle. Raef murmured the beginnings of an incantation. Tarienne pulled Lacey up hard as several things happened simultaneously.

Growling menacingly, Tere and his opponent launched into a vicious battle as the archers across the river unleashed their arrows. Raef stood in his saddle, shouting the last words of his incantation. At Tarienne's scream, Tere turned for a split second to see Aidan diving to intercept an arrow flying towards Daien, who was momentarily distracted as he struggled to release his shield.

Chaos erupted as Raef unleashed his power with a thunderous boom, creating a shockwave that rocked the ground beneath their feet. The surrounding trees creaked and groaned in protest, shuddering against the immense blast. Wolves and riders were thrown to the ground. The army scattered in confusion.

Raef leapt from his stallion racing towards Tere who was still locked in battle with the grey wolf. Blood ran down the grey's muzzle. Plunging his hand between them, Raef grabbed the huge wolf by the scruff, grunting as the muscles of his arm and chest bunched with the effort. He hauled the wolf off Tere, hurling it towards the closest tree. The beast slammed into the huge trunk, bones cracking. The breath expelled from the animal's lungs on a yelp and a death rattle gurgled past its lips as the grey wolf dropped to the ground, motionless.

Raef's hawk-like gaze landed on Tere, his eyes dark and stormy with the fury raging through him. Tere shifted into his human form and collapsed to the ground, his chest heaving. His neck bled from the puncture wounds inflicted by the grey wolf's jaws. A quick mental assessment of his body told Tere that his injuries were not life-threatening and would heal quickly.

His gaze moved to Aidan lying on the ground, an arrow in his chest, a pool of blood beneath him. He sucked in a sharp breath. Tarienne cradled Aidan's head, frantically uttering healing spells.

Sensing the immense power of the fury engulfing Raef and pushing the Fae warrior's control to breaking point, Tere flung his magic into the maelstrom. Raef swirled the incantation around him, harnessing its power. Daien rose from Aidan's side, his rage coiled tightly, like a snake ready to strike. Moving up beside them, Daien brought the tip of his drawn sword to his forehead before gripping the jewelled hilt, then lifting the blade aloft, his knuckles white as he called on the power of the earth and tree spirits.

The immense combined power blasted into their attackers, forcing them to a dead stop. The small army turned to retreat, realisation of the vast power they faced driving them back. Panic spread as they desperately scrambled over one another to save their own lives. A thick, churning mist swirled menacingly around them. Beasts and men alike coughed violently. Those who ran were driven to their knees. Horses reared, dumping their choking riders to the ground. The viscous, magical fog crept slowly up the bodies of the terrified army. Tere watched the fear cloud their eyes before the dense, white mist enveloped them completely. A wicked satisfaction filled him.

The ground rumbled beneath the embattled army as Raef's chanting escalated. Magnificent and terrifying in his wrath, Raef finally bellowed a triumphant battle cry. Jamming his raised sword into the ground, Daien shouted, '*Bás!*' Tere wasn't sure how, perhaps Daien had translated it in his thoughts and Tere had heard, but he knew it was the Druid word for death. A crack spread from Daien's feet, opening a wide chasm in the earth. The screams of the men and beasts falling into its depths pierced the dense cloud of fog. When the chasm finally closed with a crack, the mist dissipated, leaving no sign of the army, just dust and silence.

Yanking his sword from the hard ground, Daien sheathed it. His features were drawn into a deep frown. Raef spun towards Aidan, racing to his side. Daien also sprinted to Aidan, dropping to his knees beside his King's pale, still form. Tere dragged his battered body to Aidan's feet. Laying his hands on Aidan's legs, he searched for his life force. It was weak and thready. Aidan barely clung to life.

Tarienne lifted her eyes for the briefest of moments, then quickly returned to her attempts to heal the extensive damage the arrow had caused. Daien reached over and gently used his thumb to wipe away the tears streaming down her face. Reluctantly moving away to give her room to work, Daien and Tere began gathering wood for a fire. They worked silently to build a makeshift camp, light the fire and cook a meal. The camaraderie, despite being borne of difficult circumstances, once again filled Tere with the warmth of acceptance. He was determined to help his new friends, all of them, survive to fulfil their destiny.

What seemed like hours later, Tarienne and Raef beckoned Daien over.

'When we tell you, can you pull the arrow out, straight up? You need to remove it as quickly as you can so we can stop the bleeding.'

Tere moved up close as Daien braced himself over Aidan, his hands tightly grasping the arrow shaft. Fear and anguish rolled off Daien in palpable waves, its scent filling Tere's nostrils.

'Now!'

Daien grunted, exerting such force on the arrow that he almost lost his balance when it broke free from Aidan's chest, the bright red blood flowing freely again. Tere steadied him. Daien straightened, regaining his balance and inspecting the bloodied shaft of the arrow. Holding it out to Tere, an unexpected grin curved Daien's lips.

'Thank you, Tere. I'd have landed flat on my backside if you hadn't caught me.'

They chuckled quietly, briefly lightening the moment. Taking the arrow, Tere examined the tip. He sniffed it and whispered, 'I can detect no evidence of any poison.'

Eventually pulling away from Aidan, Tarienne and Raef collapsed near the warmth of the crackling fire.

Daien's brow furrowed with concern. 'How is he?'

Raef responded, his tone flat, 'He's alive. That's all we can say for now. We need help. Even together we do not have the ability to heal him completely.'

Raef crawled onto the bedroll Daien had laid out for him. Tarienne returned to Aidan, barely able to walk through the sheer exhaustion. Her face drawn, her eyes held a deep sadness. Daien crouched beside her, offering her a cup of hot soup they'd made from the root vegetables they had left over, and a rabbit Tere had caught while they were attempting to heal Aidan.

'Sweetheart, drink this. There's no more you can do right now.'

Tere rose, handing Raef a mug of the soup, as Daien took the cup from Tarienne's freezing hands, placing it on the ground. Daien hauled her onto his lap and resting his back against the maple tree, grasped her hands, rubbing them gently to warm them. Tarienne immediately curled up, her head on his chest, and Daien enveloped her in a strong embrace. Leaning back, he closed his eyes.

Tere's gaze drifted over his exhausted companions. His ribs burned and his neck throbbed as his escalated changeling healing repaired his injuries. Trying to find a comfortable position to rest, he winced as he closed his eyes, attempting to seek the peace and healing sleep would bring.

After they'd rested a while, Tarienne rose from Daien's lap to check on Aidan, placing her hand on his head.

'His body is so hot.' Her gaze slid over the others; concern etched across her face. 'Do you think there could have been something on the arrow? Poison maybe?'

Tere's eyes lifted. 'Changelings often poison their arrowheads, I have helped make such a poison when I was in the pack, but the riders were not changelings. Plus, Daien and I checked the arrow after it was pulled from Aidan's chest. I could not detect the scent of any poison on it.'

Raef sat up. 'Whatever the cause of his fever, we need to get

Aidan to someone who can help him more than we are able to. We're about one week from Darewood. I suggest we get Aidan there as soon as possible.'

Tarienne turned to face Raef. 'But how are we going to transport him?'

'We can build a litter and I could ride his horse,' Tere offered.

They all considered Tere's suggestion for a moment, then Daien asked the question they'd all been thinking. 'You can ride a horse with the ... wolf thing?'

Tere chuckled. 'Horses don't seem to mind me in human form. I am able to mask my wolf scent so I don't frighten them.'

'Good. We'll rest for a few hours, then build the litter and be on our way.'

Raef leaned back and closed his eyes. Tere overheard as Raef sent his thoughts out to Darewood. Their sister, Arivaelle was the only one who could help Aidan.

Raef spoke, his eyes still closed, 'You should all get some sleep. I've set wards that will alert us if anything or anyone approaches.'

Tarienne curled up on Daien's lap again. His arms snaked around her, tucking her into the protection of his body. Pain sliced through Tere's chest at the memory of Ileia snuggled against him. Shoving them aside, he vowed he would find Ileia, dead or alive. He prayed she was alive.

* * *

When they'd finished building the litter the next morning, under Tere's expert guidance, they strapped Aidan on securely. Raef and Tarienne spent a few moments on some more healing spells. Tarienne wiped Aidan's face again with a cool cloth, dribbled some water into his mouth and checked the bindings. Talking to him as she worked, Tarienne spoke of her sister, Arivaelle, who would heal his wounds. They all desperately hoped that she'd reach Aidan in time.

Moving around to face Aidan's stallion, Tere quietly spoke a few words of magic to mask his wolf's scent, then hauled himself up into the saddle, grimacing slightly at the lingering pain of his wounds.

Three days into their journey, a lone rider appeared in the distance, heading towards them. Halting, Tarienne focused.

'Arivaelle!' Raef's face split into a huge grin. Tarienne excitedly explained to Tere. 'Rivi's our sister and the best healer there is. She'll heal Aidan!'

Urging Lacey forward Tarienne raced ahead, Raef was close behind. As they came closer the siblings leapt from their mounts, rushing into each other's arms.

The three siblings approached the others arm in arm. Tere noted their similarities, yet they were also very different. Arivaelle's eyes were vibrant green like Tarienne's however, she had white-blonde hair and pale, creamy skin, giving her an ethereal appearance. She radiated a sense of gentle confidence, but Tere also perceived a formidable power simmering through this young Fae woman. Tarienne led her sister forward, proudly introducing Daien.

'Arivaelle, this is Daien, my betrothed.'

Daien bowed slightly. 'It is indeed a pleasure to meet you, Arivaelle.'

Arivaelle smiled, sweetly. 'And you, dear Daien. Welcome to our family. We have been looking forward to meeting you since our brother sent word to us you of your betrothal just before you left Therin on your quest.'

Hugging Daien softly, she then turned her attention to Tere.

Tarienne beamed. 'This is our friend, Tere.'

Arivaelle smiled again, assessing Tere briefly. 'It is a great pleasure to meet you, wolf changeling.'

Tere bowed low, feeling somewhat nervous. 'The pleasure is all mine, milady.'

Her focus quickly snapped to the purpose of her ride, 'Now, where is King Aidan?'

Tarienne lead her to Aidan, strapped to the litter. Arivaelle gasped, placing her hands gently over Aidan's weeping wound as she closed her eyes and softly chanted words that caused the air around Aidan to gently vibrate. The immediate change in Aidan's colour was obvious and the palpable tension in the group eased a little.

After a few minutes, Aidan's eyes fluttered open. Arivaelle asked for some water. Supporting Aidan's head, she drizzled a small amount into his mouth. Aidan licked his lips.

When his gaze finally focused on Arivaelle, his eyes held a question. 'I must be dead. I'm being cared for by an angel,' he said. Grinning weakly, he drifted back to sleep. The friends laughed with relief.

Daien raised an eyebrow and chuckled. 'He seems to make a habit of being rescued by beautiful Fae women. I think he's going to be just fine.'

* * *

Almost one week to the day that Aidan was injured, the group arrived in Darewood to a joyous greeting of friends and family. Entering the inner circle of the Fae city, Tere was struck by its beauty. It was ethereal and magical, just like its inhabitants. He also felt somewhat anxious, wondering if the Fae would accept him. The Fae and the

Changelings had not always had the best of relationships because of Lacas. He'd heard that Lacas had conducted raids in the area. Now that Tere knew about the Golden Stone he assumed that's what Lacas had been looking for but his sire's motive for aggression had rarely been simple nor clear.

When a tall, willowy, elegant blonde with deep blue eyes appeared between the columns of the silver trees lining the entrance to the Royal rooms, Tere and Daien glanced at each other, wondering who she was. She seemed to be waiting. Stunning, her cream robes floated around her slim body, her feet bare and her almost white hair curled around her face like a halo. Their question was answered moments later when Raef's gaze caught hers.

His voice rough with emotion, a joyous smile transformed Raef's face. 'Elyssia...' He all but ran to her, scooping her into a crushing hug. Lifting her feet off the ground, he held her close, then slid her down his body. The kiss they shared leaving no doubt of their love to anyone who saw them. Without looking back, they walked away hands clasped, speaking in soft whispers.

Leaving Raef and Elyssia to their reunion, Tarienne, Daien, Arivaelle and Tere whisked Aidan to a warm room in the infirmary where he could rest and recuperate under Arivaelle's watchful care. When they were certain Aidan was comfortable and well cared for, Tarienne showed Tere to a room not too far from her own, promising to show him around after they rested.

* * *

The next morning, they were all summoned to the meeting hall before Tarienne's mother and father, Queen Aistarenne and King Thalion.

The King was around six feet tall with intelligent, twinkling blue eyes, shoulder-length, dark blond hair. Tarienne had told Tere her father had ruled Darewood for many hundreds of years. Although he nine hundred in human years, he didn't look much older than Raef.

Tarienne began the introductions of Daien and Tere to her family. 'You've met Arivaelle...' She turned as Raef and Elyssia entered behind them. 'And this is Elyssia. You saw her briefly last evening when we arrived.' Tarienne smiled at Raef, not elaborating further.

Elyssia moved gracefully from Raef's side to greet Daien and Tere, reminding Tere of a swan gliding on a lake.

Authion, the youngest son of Aistarenne and Thalion stood by his father, looking every bit the formidable warrior you would expect of the leader of the Fae army of Darewood. As he was introduced, he stepped forward extending his hand to Tere and Daien. Accepting the warrior's clasp Authion offered first Tere noted his green eyes assessing him even as he smiled. Tere smiled in return noticing as Authion turned to greet Daien that his long black hair was secured in many small braids around his head. He wondered if it was just a pragmatic choice or denoted his position.

As Tere pondered that thought Kyre, the third child in the family, was introduced as the one who loved playing jokes on his family. Tere could see that he too moved with the grace and surety of someone who could be depended on in battle despite his deep sea-blue eyes twinkling with mischief.

They all turned to face Queen Aistarenne and King Thalion when they stepped down from their thrones, hand in hand. Approaching Tarienne and Daien first, the Queen took Tarienne's hand in hers, her long red hair not unlike her daughter's, albeit tamed.

'Welcome home, my beautiful daughter. We have missed you.'

Tarienne stepped in hugging her mother tightly. Tears clung to her long lashes. 'I have missed you all so much.'

Kissing Tarienne on the cheek affectionately, Aistarenne then turned her attention to Daien, holding her hands out to him. He grasped her fingers gently and smiled a little nervously.

'Do not fear, dear Daien. You are most welcome here. Know that you are part of our family now, though you may not wish it so at times.'

Aistarenne looked around at the rest of her family and raised an eyebrow, her soft, green eyes twinkling with amusement. The others chuckled as Daien grinned at her.

'I am very happy to be here and to meet you all.'

Aistarenne smiled at him again, then looked around. 'Where is Tere, the wolf changeling?'

Gulping, Tere replied, 'Here, your Majesty.'

Everyone turned to see Tere standing with Authion. Authion nudged him forward and nodded silently reassuring Tere that all would be well. Dropping to one knee, Tere bowed his head respectfully. Keeping his eyes lowered, he spoke.

'Your Majesty, it is an honour to meet you. To be granted entry into your Kingdom is a great gift. I realise that my people have not always been kind to the Fae people, but—'

Aistarenne moved forward, placing her hand on his head. 'Rise, Tere. You are welcome here. We have heard of your deeds and wish you to be at ease with us. We would be pleased if you would treat Darewood as you would your home.'

Tere rose slowly, fleetingly meeting the Queen's eyes. 'I have never had a place I could call a real home. I would be honoured to be accepted by your people. You are most gracious, your Majesty.' His thoughts turned momentarily to the cabin where he had lived. Mama had tried to make a home for him, but it had been impossible with Lacas' cruelty, so this meant a great deal to Tere. What he really wanted however, was a home with Ileia, and a family.

Bowing low, Tere felt the warmth of acceptance seep through him. He desperately wished Ileia were here to share what he'd craved all his life. Swallowing hard, he held back the emotion tightening his throat and blinked rapidly to dispel the moisture gathering at the corner of his eyes before he lifted his head. The Queen's eyes met his. He sensed that she knew everything about him from that one long, assessing gaze.

* * *

Later that afternoon, after a tour around Darewood, they all visited Aidan. He looked so much better despite still appearing a little pale, and his cheerful smile was back. Tere gently slapped Aidan on the back in greeting. Aidan returned the greeting gripping Tere's arm and squeezing it firmly. They all sat and chatted for much of the afternoon, filling in the gaps for Aidan on what had occurred after his injury. After a while Aidan seemed restless.

'I wouldn't mind a walk. I'm getting quite tired of sitting,' Aidan groaned, looking hopefully at Arivaelle.

Arivaelle nodded and smiled, helping Aidan up.

As they strolled through the grove of silver and gold trees forming an archway through the centre of Darewood, Tere noticed Arivaelle's hand tucked into Aidan's and smiled. They walked and chatted and when it was time to walk Aidan back to the infirmary, they turned, coming to a sudden halt as they witnessed Arivaelle wrapped in Aidan's arms. He whispered close to her ear then lowered his head, their lips meeting in a gentle kiss. Daien let out a whoop and everyone chuckled. Aidan raised his head grinning back at them then clasped Arivaelle's hand in his and walked slowly back to the infirmary without a word. The King had been healed in more ways than they had anticipated.

* * *

For the next few days, they rested, secure in the knowledge that the Golden Stone was safe in the deepest vault of Darewood, placed there by Raef and King Thalion. One week after their arrival in Darewood, Queen Aistarenne and King Thalion summoned them all to a meeting to discuss their plans to return the Golden Stone to Therin.

Tere arrived, bowing deeply, then relaxed and sauntered over to sit next to Aidan. Daien, Raef and Tarienne entered together and positioned themselves on the remaining seats. Authion and Kyre sat beside their mother and father, no longer looking like Tarienne's easy-going brothers. They displayed a regal bearing and an almost stern look, betraying their total focus on the problem at hand.

Tere had found Kyre to be an amusing companion. He had laughed more since he arrived than he could ever remember laughing his entire life. Tere grinned at him. Kyre responded with a grin of his own, then schooled his expression into one of focus so quickly, Tere almost snorted out loud.

The room fell silent, and Raef stood, moving up next to his father.

'The Golden Stone was created when, several hundred years ago, the Elders of the immortal races fought a deadly magical war against a powerful Sorcerer named Rantar. Half-Fae/half-Elven, Rantar sought to hold the balance of magic for himself. His greatest desire was to destroy the Elders and gather their power for himself. He managed to kill five of the twelve Elder Council and, drawing on dark magic, extracted their power from them as they died. This was no easy feat, given they have always been the most powerful and experienced among us.

'The sheer intensity of the power Rantar gathered eventually drove him deeper into insanity than he already was. The rest of the Elder Council gathered an army, finally managing to kill him. Unfortunately, many of the creatures he'd created had already escaped. The Council spent many years tracking down these fell beasts, and, using powerful containment spells, secured them in caverns deep in the bowels of the earth.

'Before Rantar died, the Elders were able to extract the power he had stolen, yet they did not absorb it themselves for fear they, too, would be driven mad. The decision was made to contain this immense power in a magically created Golden Stone and leave it where no-one would think to look for it...in the care of a human King. For many years, it was kept safe in the Keep at Therin.'

Raef paused, drawing in a deep breath. 'Aidan, as you know, when your father became King, he buried everything he believed to be magical in a deep cavern several weeks' ride from Therin. Unfortunately, it appears someone or something has found the cavern and the Golden Stone and, using its power, has begun systematically freeing the creatures that were magically trapped beneath the earth.

'The creatures have bred in their dark prison, creating twisted breeds that possess dark magic. The Fae and Elven folk sensed the change in the balance and began moving to Therin, where they believed their people would be safe. Until recently, they hid their presence, for fear you were like your father and would seek to hunt and destroy them, but the tales they had heard of your tolerance and fair judgment encouraged them to seek safety behind the city walls.

'Aidan, when we realised it was to be your destiny to return the balance of magic to Therin, we knew we had to protect you at all costs. We have watched over you to keep you safe until we could assist you to return the balance of magic to the kingdom, but it seems we must now move with haste before the situation worsens any further.'

Aidan nodded as Raef spoke. Raef had explained the situation to him before they left Therin to find the Stone but now, they needed to work out the next steps.

King Thalion stood to speak as Raef returned to his seat..

'We have called this meeting to discuss how best to proceed with the problem of the Golden Stone and the creatures that have been called with it.' He looked around the room at Daien, Aidan, Raef and Tarienne. 'We believe the best option is for you all to return to Therin and place the stone deep within the Keep. It will require powerful magical wards to protect it which we can assist with.'

Raef listened to his father, his elbows resting on his knees, his fingers steepled in front of his face. 'And what of the creatures summoned by the magic of the stone?'

Raef's voice was calm and measured, yet Tere sensed the buzz of his immense power. King Thalion continued.

'Authion and Tere have discussed what they believe to be a viable plan and wish to present it to you here today.'

Raef nodded his approval. The warmth of trust and acceptance once again spread through Tere's chest, making him draw in a deep breath to steady himself.

Raef nudged his arm reassuringly., Tere stood, briefly meeting Authion's steady gaze. Nodding, he moved to the front of the room beside Authion and readied himself to present their plan to the group. Tere's racing pulse echoed in his ears. Sucking in a breath, he began, noting a surprised expression on Tarienne's face as his gaze skittered across his friends in the vast hall. Raef raised one eyebrow at her, which she acknowledged with an almost imperceptible nod. Tere would ask them why later. Looking around the room, he pulled in a deep breath.

'Aidan has spoken with us at length about Therin and the ability to lock it down to create a stronghold. Authion, Aidan and I have devised a plan to draw Rantec's minions to Therin, ambush them, then return them to their prison beneath the earth.'

Tere outlined the plan in detail responding to questions as they came up, then made eye contact with Authion, nodded and sat down to let him speak. Authion rose, his eyes sweeping the room as he spoke.

'As Tere has indicated, we believe we can recapture these creatures by moving the people to safety behind Therin's walls. We will strategically place an army of fae, elves and men away from Therin so they are hidden until required. We need Rantec's followers to believe the stone has not yet reached Therin and allow them to believe they have almost caught up with it. The army will then move in and overtake the creatures. After their capture will then summon the Elder Council and return the beasts to their eternal prison.'

Aidan stood, signalling his intention to speak. 'Then I must return to Therin to bring the people in and ensure there is food and water enough to sustain them while they're within the castle walls. I would ask for one of you to accompany me.'

Without a moment's hesitation, Daien shot to his feet. 'I'll go with you, sire.'

His acknowledgment of Aidan as his King brought a smile to Aidan's face. 'Thank you, Daien.'

Tarienne and Raef stood. Raef glanced at Tarienne, then spoke for them both. 'We, too, will accompany Aidan back to Therin. Authion, who do you suggest as the decoys?'

Authion eyed Raef for a moment, steely determination glinting in his eyes. 'The creatures believe the stone to be with the five of you, another team of five will be needed to actually transport the stone.'

Tere stood immediately. 'I will go and help see this quest through before I resume my search for my mate, Ileia. Returning the balance of magic to the Kingdom will aid my search for her and will hopefully destroy whatever power continues to hold her captive.'

Authion nodded his approval as did several others in the room. 'Thank you, Tere.'

Raef waited, a slight frown on his face. 'And, who else?'

A feminine voice spoke from the back of the room, strong and sure. 'I will accompany Tere and the others transporting the Stone to Therin.'

Every eye turned to Arivaelle standing in the doorway. Gasps and chatter filled the air. Arivaelle was a healer not a warrior. She strode determinedly to Aidan's side. Aidan, Raef and Tarienne all spoke at once protesting her announcement. Holding her hands up, Tere jumped when she shouted into their minds.

Stop!

Stunned, they all stopped midsentence.

'I have discussed this with Mother, Father, Authion and Kyre. I fully intend to accompany the party transporting the Stone.' Arivaelle held their gazes, daring them to protest.

Daien snorted. Tere heard him mumble, 'And who does that remind you of?'

167

Tarienne glared at him, then her expression softened, and she chuckled. 'You should be used to this Aidan.'

Tere struggled to hold back the chuckle threatening to escape, then sobered as he watched Aidan's expression crease with worry. Aidan stared at Tarienne for a moment, then turned to Arivaelle.

'Rivi, are you sure about this?' Lowering his voice so only Arivaelle and Tere's wolf ears could detect his words, he added, 'We have not known each other long, but I couldn't bear to lose you.'

Arivaelle walked into his arms circling her arms around his neck, her lips close to his. 'Oh, Aidan, you're not going to lose me. I want to do this for you, for us. I want to come to Therin, if you'll have me.'

Aidan lowered his lips to hers for a scorching kiss. There was a collective gasp. Memories of Ileia assaulted Tere and his eyes misted until he spied Tarienne gazing around the room mischievously.

'Don't worry. They're always doing that!'

Aidan chuckled against Arivaelle's lips. Raef, Tere and Daien laughed heartily, while everyone else's expression furrowed in confusion.

Authion cleared his throat. 'Are we in agreement then?'

Raef leaned forward. 'That's only two. You need five.' He eyed Authion, waiting, the authority of the future king in his demeanour. Authion held eye contact with Raef, seemingly unfazed by his brother's tone.

'Myself, Kyre, and Father will make up the five.'

Raef's gaze swung to his father, who listened calmly, a smile hovering on his lips.

'My son, I am not a decrepit old man yet. It may have been many years since I fought a battle, but I *was* the leader of the army of Darewood long before you were born.'

Before Thalion could say more, Elyssia swept into the room, stopping by Raef's side.

'I, too, wish to accompany you.' When he opened his mouth to protest, she placed a finger over his lips. Gazing up into Raef's eyes, Elyssia rested a hand on his chest. Her soft eyes pleaded with him. 'You have been gone for so long. I don't want you to leave me again. Please, Raef, don't leave me behind again.'

When a single tear slipped down her cheek, Raef gently captured her chin in his hand. He wiped the tear away with his thumb and leaned down to place a tender kiss on her lips. He searched her watery eyes and all there knew he couldn't leave her again.

Tere watched the touching scene before him, the emotions playing across Raef's face telling Tere that he had come to a decision. He, along with everyone else, waited to see what Raef would do. When Raef dropped to one knee in front of Elyssia, her mouth dropped open and she gasped. Tere heard Tarienne suck in a breath, saw Daien pulling her close.

Raef began. 'My darling, Lissy, this wasn't quite the way I meant this to happen, but ... I love you, have loved you since the first day we met. You are my heart, my reason for being. I want to be with you always. Will you accompany me to Therin and marry me once our quest is complete, my beautiful, sweet Elyssia?'

Elyssia dropped to her knees in front of him, tears of joy streaming down her cheeks. 'Yes, Raef! Oh yes!'

Raef captured her mouth in a passionate kiss. The room erupted in cheers. Everyone was aware of how Elyssia and Raef's love had grown since he rescued her after Kind Eldan, Aidan's father had ordered the village where she lived with her family, destroyed. Tarienne had told Tere, Aidan and Daien the story after they saw Elyssia and Raef together the first day that they arrived in Darewood. Everyone was overjoyed for them and the plans for the battle were set.

*   *   *

A few days later, after ensuring all the plans they'd discussed previously were in place, Tarienne, Daien, Raef, Aidan and Elyssia prepared to leave for the long journey back to Therin. Wishing them farewell was more difficult than Tere expected. They had experienced so much together in a relatively short time and had become friends, something Tere's life had not exactly been filled with.

Twilight raced towards the blackness of night as Tarienne hugged Tere tightly, dropping a kiss on his cheek. 'Stay safe, Tere.' She pulled him into one more fierce hug, then moved back into Daien's protective embrace.

Stepping forward, Tere clasped Daien's arm at the elbow. Daien returned the gesture, then slapped Tere on the back. 'Take care, my friend.'

Tere watched as his friends departed, his enhanced sight tracking them deep into the forest. The trees parted, allowing them to pass, then closed protectively behind them. The tree spirits, their magic strong this close to the Fae stronghold, would guide the party and afford them safe passage to the edge of the forest. A strange emptiness filled Tere, a sense of impending doom washing over him. They had become such an important part of his life in an incredibly short time.

Sighing, he turned away to see Authion waiting. He wrapped his arm around Tere's shoulders in a gesture of support and understanding, walking with him to the great hall to plan their own departure.

These people were how his pack should be—loving, loyal and supportive, yet strong and dependable. Indeed, many of the pack were like that, they were just too oppressed by Lacas to show it. His dearest friend, Reine, had never let him down. Tere caught Authion eyeing him.

'I know, my friend. I know. You'll see them again soon.'

Tere shrugged. 'I've never really experienced that kind of acceptance, except from Ileia. It seems to have seeped into my very being.'

Authion grinned. 'Tarienne's like that. Gets under your skin ... and not always in a good way. She's amazing and a real pain at the same time. And I miss her every minute she's away.' He laughed, and Tere grinned back.

'Daien and Aidan have been amazing. Raef, too. They could have blown me away with their combined magic. We didn't have the best of starts. I tried to ... seduce your sister, you know.'

Authion punched him in the arm playfully. 'I know. She told me. If Daien can forgive you, so can I. I accept that you'd been drugged. Plus, you did heal her wound. How the hell do you think the changeling magic thorn got there?'

Sucking in a deep breath and hanging his head, Tere answered so softly, Authion moved closer to hear his words, 'I believe my sire, Lacas, the pack alpha, put it there to stop himself from falling...' Tere's eyes tracked up to Authion's, 'when I shoved him over the edge with my magic.'

Authion paused. 'Lacas? The same changeling that Raef killed? He was your sire?'

Tere held Authion's gaze. 'Yes. Unfortunately, he survived the fall over the cliff and the water pounding him onto the sharp rocks below. I have no idea how.'

'Forgive me for asking this question, Tere, but why did you push him over the cliff?'

Tere remained silent for a long time. His hands fisted at his side and his throat moved as he swallowed hard, his shoulders hunched, as if in defeat. When he spoke, pain laced his words.

'Lacas was a violent creature. He all but destroyed the pack with his vicious treatment of anyone who dared displease him. Everyone lived in fear of his violence. He hated me, made my life hell and m–murdered my mother in front of me, then whipped me until I was close to death.'

Authion waited without speaking.

'He didn't realise that by almost killing me, he released the magic that had until then remained dormant, the power inherited from my maternal grandfather. I finally released my wolf. I'd been holding it back for years, hiding my alpha status until I was strong enough to destroy him. He pleaded with me, right before I shoved him over the cliff. It was the only time he really acknowledged me as his son, the moment he realised how powerful I was and that I held his life in my hands. I thought I'd feel pleasure, relief, something when the waterfall swallowed him, but I didn't. I only felt numbness.'

'After I escaped with my Ileia, we were free and happy for a short while ... until we were captured again and held in the caves where the power of the Golden Stone was harnessed to raise the evil army of creatures led by Rantec and some of Lacas' henchmen. I don't know what happened to Ileia. I heard her screams for a while. I looked for her, but I couldn't...'

Tears formed in Tere's eyes. He paused, looking away for a moment, gathering his self-control and rubbing his eyes with the back of his hand. Slowly, he raised his gaze to meet Authion's again.

'Then I met Tarienne and the others. You know the rest. I need to return to my search for Ileia very soon.'

Without speaking Authion hauled Tere into a brotherly hug.

Pulling back, he clasped Tere's elbow in a gesture of solidarity. 'When this battle is won, I will help you find Ileia, my friend. This I vow on my honour and on our friendship.'

Tere gripped Authion's arm fiercely. 'Thank you, my friend. Thank you.'

His throat clogging with emotion, Tere listened to Authion's plan as they strode to the great hall where Kyre and King Thalion already stood, ready to commence preparations for their journey.

Once their plans were finalised, the brothers flanked Tere. Kyre grinned. 'Come on, my friend. We'll see them soon. Now, let's eat and you must tell us more about Ileia.'

Authion and Kyre ate more than anyone he'd ever known. They were lucky they trained so hard, or they'd never maintain their powerful, sculpted bodies. Luckily, his own escalated metabolism burned off the extra food he'd been consuming, though he wished he could shift and run through Darewood. His wolf was restless. Now that he'd experienced freedom, he grew edgy when denied it for too long.

Tere laughed and ate with the brothers, telling them how he and Ileia first noticed each other, how she supported him and rescued him from the cage he was imprisoned in after Lacas killed his mother and almost beat him to death, about their time in the cave alone and their flight and eventual capture by Lacas. Even as he spoke and laughed with Authion and Kyre something niggled at him, something that sent his thoughts across the distance in search of Tarienne and Daien, but he could not find them. Perhaps they were already too far away?

Tere returned to his room, sighing as he closed the door behind him. Stripping, he dropped his clothes to the floor, then slipped between the soft, white sheets. Just as he began drifting into that state of total calm between wakefulness and the oblivion of sleep, the sweet scent of vanilla drifted across his senses. His eyes snapped open, scanning the room. Perhaps it was the beginnings of a dream. Satisfied that he was alone, he flipped onto his side and closed his eyes. Again, vanilla teased his senses.

Sitting up he quickly flung the covers aside certain this time that this was no dream. Poised to shift, he blinked to clear his vision. *Ileia?* A hazy shape shimmered in the corner of the room extending an arm in his direction, beckoning. Approaching cautiously, Tere blinked again, hardly daring to believe Ileia was trying to make contact. Did this mean she was dead? His chest tightened painfully.

No!

Tentatively stepping closer, he lifted his arm, reaching out to touch her fingers, even though he knew she wasn't real.

Tere, I'm waiting...

Ileia? Where are you waiting? Tell me, my love. When he tried to grasp her hand, the cloudy figure wavered. Lunging forward, he tried to stop her leaving. *Ileia. No. Don't leave. Tell me where to find you. Please...*

His hand fell to his side as the shape dissipated like a cloud in the wind. Moisture filled his eyes as he clenched his fists at his side, despair ripping through him like a knife. *I will find you, my Ileia. I promise. I need to help my friends, then we'll find you together. I promise you.*

He walked slowly back to the bed, dropping disconsolately onto its edge. Sighing, he climbed under the covers lying awake for what seemed like hours, memories of Ileia consuming his thoughts. He felt such guilt that he'd been diverted from his search for her for so long. When he eventually fell asleep, Tere dreamed of running with her as wolves, of her steadfast love and support, of how she'd saved him from his father and from himself, and of making sweet, passionate love with her.

Waking to the early morning light streaming through the window onto the soft, green foliage covering the walls of the room, Tere's heart and body ached for Ileia. Dragging himself out of bed he answered Authion's early morning summons to go over the plans for the journey to Therin. His dour mood lifted only slightly by the knowledge that Ileia was at least alive. During the meeting it was decided that they would wait one day before they left to provide the others with a head start, then Tere, Authion, Arivaelle and King Thalion would leave with the decoy Golden Stone. Hopefully it would provide both a distraction and enough time for Tarienne, Raef, Daien, Aidan and Elyssia to safely return to Therin and lock the real Golden Stone deep in Therin's Keep. Meanwhile, Kyre and the others would raise an army of Elves and Fae to assist with the destruction of Rantec's fell army.

The following morning, Tere's mood had improved as the four riders left Darewood, bringing him a day closer to searching for Ileia. They travelled along the well-worn main roads to announce their journey to whomever observed their progress. The first day passed without incident, although they were aware their progress was being observed. They were all on edge, prepared for an attack.

Glancing around at his companions, Tere watched as Arivaelle anxiously fingered the bow slung over her shoulder, ready to use it at a moment's notice. Authion and Thalion were both heavily armed

They were fierce warriors, tall and proud in the saddle. Tere was grateful they were on his side. They rode with one hand on the reins and the other resting on their thigh, ready to draw their weapons in an instant. As the evening approached Thalion slowed his destrier. Sliding to the ground, he scanned the area, his hand resting on the hilt of his heavily jewelled sword.

'We'll make camp here tonight. There is both water and shelter available. Remain alert.'

CHAPTER 11

A day and a half into the journey, the Fae received a mind-speak message from Raef. They had arrived safely at Castle Therin but had been pursued by an army of foul creatures, wolves and evil riders. By his account, Aidan, Daien, Elyssia, Tarienne and himself had only just made it inside the castle gates.

Kyre let them know that he had immediately started assembling the army of the Fae and Elven kind who had chosen to join them. Raef confirmed that King Aidan would assemble his army inside the walls of Therin in readiness for their arrival. The four companions would continue their journey, and the Fae army would catch up with them closer to Therin. Tere was fascinated to see how the Fae communicated using mind-speak. They would gesture, but no words were spoken out loud. Of course, he could hear them if he chose to listen, and communicate with them too due to the magic within him. It just felt strange although he had become somewhat used to it during his time with Tarienne, Aidan, Daien and Raef.

Half a day from Therin, the army joined them. Thousands of regal Fae and Elven warriors in full battle dress were a magnificent and welcome sight, especially when Tere knew exactly what they were facing. Hours before the impending battle, raised voices were heard between Thalion, Authion, Kyre and Arivaelle. Tere started in their direction, but his keen wolf hearing could make out every word well before he reached them. They wanted Arivaelle safely away from the fighting. When Tere joined the group, he barely suppressed a grin. Arivaelle stood with her hands on her hips, arguing with the three Fae warriors, one of whom was King Thalion who finally held up his hand to still her tongue.

'Arivaelle, if you were harmed in battle, your mother and King Aidan would kill us all for not protecting you. What would we do without you, my daughter, should you suffer a fatal wound?'

Arivaelle sighed, seeing the sense in her father's words. 'Very well. What do you propose?'

Tere waited, wondering how they were going to keep her safe. Finally, Kyre spoke.

'The spell of concealment is the only way. We will weave it over you and your mare, then you must ride like the wind to the castle. The magic will lessen as you move farther away from us, so you must not dally. We will let Raef know you are coming.'

King Thalion and his sons moved as close to the castle walls as they dared before jointly weaving the spell over Arivaelle. Tere couldn't suppress a gasp as she and her mare simply disappeared.

Kyre, spoke quietly as a small puff of dust rose from the ground; the only sign of Arivaelle's flight to Therin, 'Ride, Rivi. Ride like the wind. We will hold the spell as long as we are able.'

Tere stood on guard as the three focused on Arivaelle's energy, holding the spell as she rode, beads of sweat appearing on their foreheads as time elapsed. Finally, they all pulled in a deep breath and wiped their foreheads. Tere looked at them, the question on his lips answered before he voiced it.

'She made it safely. Now we can concentrate on the battle ahead.'

* * *

A long, sleepless night was spent moving the Fae army into position and discussing the battle strategy to ensure it was solid. Kyre contacted Raef via their sibling mind connection the next morning, letting him know the Fae army was off to the south of Therin, rested and ready. They heard the fighting begin, Raef's war cry reaching them across the distance. It was the signal for the Fae army to charge and surprise Rantec's forces from behind. The battle horn blared their arrival. Tere stripped and shifted, running alongside the army, staying downwind and a safe distance from the hooves of the war horses.

Taking in the sight of wolves and elves locked in battle and the huge half-man, half-oxen beasts they'd encountered in the caves, Tere dashed fearlessly among the fighting. He snapped and snarled, his teeth ripping into the wolves that attacked the army. Some of them he recognised as Lacas' more dedicated henchmen, and others he had seen in the caves where he'd been held and tortured. Where the huge human warriors had come from, he had no idea, but he felt no remorse for any of their deaths.

The fighting continued long into the night. Tere shifted a few times, taking up a fallen sword when his teeth and claws were not enough. He was so dirty in his human form nobody noticed or cared about his nakedness. He spun and sliced at an opponent when he saw Tarienne surrounded by three enormous men. They thought she was an easy mark. Little did they know!

Running towards her he shifted into his wolf form in a shower of gold and silver sparks. Tere launched himself at two of the men tearing out the throat of the first, then whirled and raked his claws down the chest of the other, watching as he collapsed onto the ground. Using his weight to pin him down, Tere finished off the man he'd felled, then pivoted to see Tarienne slashing high with her sword, cutting the third man's throat and opening his chest on the downward stroke.

Tere recognised the exhaustion etched across her face because he felt it too. Seizing a few precious moments to catch his breath, he leaned against her legs, smiling inwardly as her fingers scraped through his thick, black fur.

'Thank you, Tere, my friend.'

Looking up he gave her a wolfish grin and dashed back into the combat, staying as close to her as he was able amidst the fighting. When a scream pierced the night, he dashed back to her side, reaching her just as her head smashed onto a sharp rock. She collapsed like a rag doll, her eyes quickly drifting shut. He turned to face her assailant, quickly dodging the huge, spiked mace flying past his head. He launched himself onto the creature's back, latching his powerful jaw around its neck and jumped backwards. The momentum ripped out the beast's throat and it dropped to the stony ground, dead. Spitting out the foul-tasting blood, Tere returned to Tarienne, shifted and lifted her into his arms, placing her behind a large grassy mound at the edge of the battlefield. He kissed her forehead, covering her with some soft, leafy bracken as best he could. Hoping she'd be safe there, he shifted back into his wolf form to fight some more for the friends he'd come to love.

The fighting lessened as shards of daylight peeked through the inky darkness. Tere took a moment to look around at the carnage, praying none of the dead were his friends. Just as he turned towards the edge of the forest where he'd left Tarienne, he heard a *whoosh* and leapt sideways, an arrow slamming deep into his flank. He yelped, as searing pain ripped through him, the momentum of the arrow dropping him to the ground. Blood poured from the wound as he lay panting, unable to move. He gritted his teeth, unable to shift for fear the arrow would rip through his heart during the process.

* * *

The day dawned into a cold morning, chilling Tere as he desperately clung to life, growing ever weaker. Hearing somebody calling Tarienne's name, he tried lifting his head. Finally, two shadows stood over him. Authion crouched beside him, and he heard Raef calling for Arivaelle, but he sensed deep down that it was too late for him. His life force was weak, ebbing away as each moment passed. He knew that he must let them know where Tarienne was, at least they could save her. Despite the excruciating pain, he shifted into his human form, crying out as agony sliced through him, barely able to breathe. He hardly felt the warmth of Aidan's cloak being draped over him or Aidan's hand resting on his shoulder as he spoke.

'You fought like a true warrior today, my friend.'

Tere's gaze tried to focus on Arivaelle as she carefully lifted his head into her lap. A coughing fit sent white, hot pain spearing through him, feeling like a thousand knives stabbing his chest. Her cool hand came to rest on his forehead.

'Shhhh, stay quiet.'

But Tere would not be dissuaded. His last act in this life must be to let them know where Tarienne was. As Arivaelle began chanting a healing spell, Tere managed to hiss out one word.

'Tarienne...'

Aidan glanced at the others, then squatted beside him, lowering his head close to Tere's. 'Tere, do you know where she is? We haven't been able to find her.'

Mustering the last of his energy, he nodded and weakly lifted his arm, pointing towards the far edge of the battlefield where the large, grassy mound he'd hidden her behind shielded Tarienne from view. Blackness slowly filled his vision, his arm dropped like a lead weight.

The next he knew he had the oddest sensation that he was floating. His pain was gone.

When his eyes flickered open s, his mother and grandfather were gazing at him.

'Mama?'

'Yes, Tere. I'm here, but you should not be. It is not your time yet.'

Tere's eyes tracked to his maternal grandfather.

Canis smiled. 'It is good to meet you, my grandson. You fought bravely today and will be a strong and compassionate pack alpha.'

'But, Grandfather, how can I be pack alpha if I'm dead? Who will save Ileia now?'

Smiling patiently, Canis spoke again. Tere really liked the deep, soothing richness of his voice. 'Your mama is right, Tere. You should not be here. It is not your time. You need to go back, rescue Ileia, and fulfil your destiny to rebuild the pack. When the Fae release your soul from your physical form, we will send you back.'

Seeing the question on Tere's face, Canis smiled. 'You are nothing like your father.'

Tere gave him a small grin, not completely convinced. 'Grandfather, did Lacas murder you?'

'Yes, Tere. The coward caught me by surprise late one night. But we are safe now.'

Pointing through the mist, Canis drew Tere's attention to the funeral pyre. His friends were giving him a warrior's send-off. Touched by the gesture, he watched and listened as the three Fae women sang the Fae lament. Tears pricked the backs of his eyes. Tarienne, a bandage around her head, clutched the little wooden wolf figure he'd carved for her. Tere smiled.

As his mortal body burned, Tere felt a pull and glanced at his mother and grandfather. Canis smiled kindly.

'It's time for you to go back, my dear grandson. Remember. we love you and will watch over you … always.'

Canis and Alika reached out, both touching his hand moments before Tere was swept away on what felt like a gentle wind carrying him back to the physical plain. He maintained eye contact with his mother and grandfather until the mist swirled around him.

'I love you, Mama and Grandfather Canis. I will make you proud.'

On the wind, he heard a rich, deep voice. 'We already are, Tere. We already are…'

Finding himself standing in the forest, naked, Tere shook his head to clear his thoughts. *Did that just happen?*

Laughter filled his mind, along with the voice of his grandfather. *Yes, Tere, it did. Your clothes are where you left them when you shifted for the battle.*

Tere smiled and turned to search for the tree with the small hollow where he'd stashed his clothes only a few days ago. They were slightly damp, but he pulled them on and dug deeper into the hollow, relief filling him when he found his pack and knives. Suddenly engulfed by extreme fatigue, he looked around for a protected grassy thicket and laid out the blanket he'd thankfully stowed in his pack, placed a magical ward as his Fae friends had taught him, then stuffed his pack under his head quickly drifting off into a deep, restful slumber.

When he awoke the next morning, rays of sunshine penetrated the leafy canopy, playing across his body, providing a modicum of warmth. He relaxed on his blanket, thinking about breakfast. He began digging in his pack for some dried meat when his keen wolf ears heard horses. Stripping, he dropped his clothes on his blanket, shifted and crept towards the forest's edge. He lifted his snout, amazed and pleased by the scent that filled his nostrils.

CHAPTER 12

Tere waited, watching, his black fur the perfect camouflage in the darkness of the thick forest where only occasional patches of sunlight penetrated the leafy canopy. Silently, he observed the Fae Princess Tarienne absently rub her mare, Lacey, behind one ear as the party of Fae moved on. She cantered along the grassy edge of the well-worn road, the King's man, Daien, always by her side, protective. A frown creased Tarienne's brow as she stopped and scanned her surroundings. Tere grinned when he felt her magic probing for a mind connection. A broad smile lit her face when she recognised the familiar thought pattern.

Welcome back, dear friend. I didn't expect to meet you here. We've missed you.

It's good to be back, Tarienne. Congratulations on your nuptials.

Thank you. Won't you join us?

I need to find Ileia. I just wanted you to know I'm back, courtesy of my maternal grandfather, and to make sure you were all safe. Thank you for everything.

Oh, Tere, thank you! I pray that our paths will cross again, dear friend.

You can be sure of it. Once I have Ileia back at my side, we'll visit ... together. Be happy, Tarienne.

With that, Tere's wolf howled, then disappeared between the tall, straight elms. He watched and listened for a few moments more, baring his teeth in a wolfish grin. The party pulled their mounts to a halt when the long, low howl reverberated through the forest.

Daien reined beside Tarienne, a momentary frown quickly turning into a grin. 'Tere's back?'

Tarienne smiled. 'How do you know it was Tere?'

Daien chuckled. 'The trees told me.'

The mirth twinkling in Daien's eyes caused a bubble of laughter to escape Tarienne's lips. Daien chuckled and leaned over, placing a kiss on his wife's lips before they moved on again.

* * *

Tere loped back to where his pack was, shifted and stuffed his clothes into his pack so he could carry his belongings between his teeth. He bounded between the trees for some time, keeping watch over his friends, then he turned, padding deep into the thickest, darkest recesses of the forest. Winding his way to the caves, he finally came upon the place where he'd last seen his beloved Ileia. Not finding her wasn't an option Tere was prepared to accept.

Curled up around his pack against the chill of the early autumn evening, Tere rested. His wolf ears flicked, listening for anything out of the ordinary in the usual forest sounds. Despite his eyes being closed, he remained alert. One eye popped open as a squirrel raced past, completely unaware of the nearby predator. Tere chuckled to himself, his eyes drifting shut once more.

The past few weeks had been life changing for Tere. Meeting Tarienne, Daien, Raef, Aidan and the Fae folk of Darewood had given him the gift of acceptance and the strong friendships he'd always craved. His thoughts drifted over the events of the battle against Rantec's army. He'd watched over Tarienne, saved her life, then suffered a mortal arrow wound. He'd known the wound was fatal, but he'd held on to let his friends know where Tarienne was. When he'd helped her one last time, he hadn't suspected he'd be returned to his life to continue searching for Ileia and to lead the pack as their alpha.

His friends had cradled his broken body, their love surrounding him, easing his journey as his life force ebbed and drifted away. They'd mourned when he'd passed, honouring him with a warrior's funeral. In the castle courtyard of Therin, his spirit had been set free during the funeral pyre when Tarienne, her Fae sisters and Elyssia, Raef's betrothed, had joined their voices to sing his funeral lament. Their crystal clear, sweet voices had united, lifting his spirit wolf from his body, setting it free. Hovering high above the courtyard momentarily, Tere had listened briefly, absorbing the love radiating from his friends, prepared for his journey to the next world. He hadn't anticipated his maternal grandfather's spirit sending him back to the mortal realm.

Tere woke with a start to the chirping of birds. He was filled with a deep sense of serenity, having slept soundly for the first time in a very long time. Smiling a wolfish grin, he silently thanked his mama and grandfather for watching over him, allowing him to rest so he had the strength to renew his search for Ileia. Rising, he grabbed his pack between his teeth and set off, determined to find his she-wolf.

Several days of running as his wolf had Tere feeling wild and hungry; however, unless he was forced to eat it raw, he preferred his meat cooked. After chasing down a rabbit, he shifted back to his human form dressing in the clothes he'd stowed in his pack days ago. It was a little annoying carrying his pack between his teeth when he travelled as his wolf but at least he now had his knives, blanket and clothes when he needed them. He was close to the labyrinth of caves near the falls. It seemed like a lifetime ago since he was last there. So much had happened since he and Ileia had shared some happy moments here.

Shaking out his clothes to remove the wrinkles, Tere pulled on the black leather pants, yanked the faded, wheat-coloured linen shirt over his head and slid his feet into his soft, black leather boots. Unused to the confining sensation of boots after travelling so long on the soft paws of his wolf, Tere wiggled his toes and stretched his legs, then bent to pick up the rabbit.

Grabbing a few twigs and some dried moss, he lit a fire with a tiny flick of magic. He grinned to himself, certain that Reine would love his new-found ability if they ever went camping together again. They'd often talked about finding somewhere remote and setting up camp for a few days. Tere smiled as he realised they could go, now that Lacas was gone. Stoking the tiny blaze, he drew his knife from his boot, grateful that he'd thought to store a spare with his clothes.

After he'd finished cleaning and skinning the rabbit, he poked a sharp stick through it, jammed two sticks into the ground on each side of the fire, forming an 'x', and rested the stick holding the rabbit into the vee shape the sticks created. Settling back onto the ground, he rested by the warmth of the fire while his dinner cooked. He closed his eyes, fanning his magic out in every direction, seeking Ileia.

When a faint whisper reached out to him, Tere jerked to a sitting position. Sending out a stronger pulse of magic in that direction, he waited, listening, his entire body rigid, on edge. It seemed like he waited hours, straining to hear a sound, any indication that Ileia was alive. Nothing reached out to him save the hoot of owls and the rustling of small creatures in the underbrush. Had he wanted to hear his beloved so much that he'd imagined the faint call?

The delicious aroma of the rabbit cooking over the fire, its juices sizzling in the flames, made his stomach rumble, returning his focus to his immediate surroundings. Sighing, Tere turned the meat over and sat with his back against a tall, slender elm tree once again. His elbows rested on his knees, his hands hanging loosely, seeking the heat it afforded in the bitter cold of the early morning. He stared into the red and gold flickering flames, momentarily losing himself in happy memories of Ileia.

His belly rumbled again and brought him back to reality. Using the tip of his knife, he carefully pulled pieces off the sizzling coney, blowing on each morsel before popping the succulent meat into his mouth. He hadn't realised how hungry he was and had soon eaten a large portion. Yanking off the remaining meat and wrapping it in some fresh leaves, he carefully covered it with more leaves to protect it from bugs and any small animals bold enough to enter his campsite.

His belly full, Tere stoked the blaze settling down next to the warmth it emitted and closed his eyes. Almost immediately, he drifted into a light sleep encased in a web of magic, both for protection and to aid his search for Ileia.

Drifting into a deeper slumber, images of Ileia filled his dreams. Memories of them entwined together. Acknowledging his frustration at not having taken her fully as his mate, despite Ileia's pleas, Tere forced aside the thoughts arousing his physical body. Why hadn't he listened? If he'd fully mated with Ileia, he'd have been able to locate her through the strength of their mating bond connecting them like a lifeline. A thin thread of consciousness that would glow between them like a beacon in the viscous dark Tere now waded through searching, calling. At least it partially existed, a faint, incomplete thread leading him in what he prayed was the right direction. Even a faint thread meant she still lived ... didn't it?

Growling low, Tere's magic-induced dream wolf moved forward with the power gifted to him by his maternal grandfather to where he'd caught his last glimpse of Ileia bound and struggling against Rantec's thugs. Her screams penetrated his memories, his hackles rising in response, ready to protect his beloved. Forcing his reaction down, his consciousness battled with his recall of the never-ending torture he had endured in this very cave. Before he realised what he was doing, Tere howled in frustration. The air around him stilled.

Danger!

Senses on high alert, the wolf scrambled back to Tere's sleeping form, limp and helpless without his wolf spirit. Too far. He'd travelled too far! The presence he sensed from afar would reach his body before he could re-enter it. His paws flew as he leapt and dove, an evanescent spectre leaving a swirling maelstrom in his wake. Creatures scattered in fear, not knowing what caused the sudden and dangerous windstorm.

The stranger was there, looming over his body. The dream wolf launched, flying on the wings of desperation. Twisting, he slid into his physical body, growling low and menacingly as the warrior standing at his feet widened his stance. The hiss of steel penetrated Tere's returning consciousness. Snapping his eyes open, Tere clamped his legs around the man's ankles and yanked his knees up, pulling the stranger's feet out from underneath him. Black leather booted feet flailed in the air as the warrior thudded unceremoniously onto the muddy ground, landing on his backside with an 'oof'.

Tere froze as the man guffawed loudly. A vague wisp of recollection infiltrated Tere's brain, even as a snarl escaped his lips.

'Nice move, Changeling!'

'Authion?'

Disbelief flooded Tere. How could Authion have known he was alive?

Authion rose to his feet, brushing the dirt from his dark leather trousers and soft, doeskin jacket. Tere's eyes skimmed his friend.

'A promise is a promise, my friend.'

He blew out a breath. 'You almost scared me to death. I was searching for Ileia when my wolf sensed your approach. I thought you were going to skewer me with your sword when I heard the hiss of your steel.'

Authion chuckled. 'What you heard was me sheathing my weapon. When I realised you were not just sleeping, I didn't want to startle you, which I ended up doing anyway. Damn your wolfy senses!'

Authion let out a belly laugh. Tere couldn't help but chuckle at his friend's amusement. Rising, he clamped Authion's elbow in a warrior's greeting.

'Thank you, my friend. But how did you know I was here, alive?'

'Ah, Tere, have you not yet learned of the capacity my sister has to ensure that we all do what she thinks we must?'

Tere's eyes went wide. 'Tarienne?'

He smiled. 'Yes, my friend. I doubt it was moments after you shared mind-speak with her before she badgered Raef into contacting Kyre and myself. His mind-speak is stronger than most and he was able to contact us on our way back to Darewood. We immediately headed this way to help you search for Ileia. Poor Raef. Thank the Gods he has the patience of a saint with her.'

'Kyre is here, too?'

'He's not far behind. I left him scouting the forest for signs of your woman. He's the best tracker in the Kingdom. If there's any evidence of Ileia, he'll find it.'

A whistle pierced the night, stilling the mournful hooting of the tawny owls.

'Here he is now!' Authion whistled in response.

Kyre approached almost soundlessly, but Tere's keen wolf hearing heard the soft crunching his boots made as they crushed the dried autumn leaves. Smiling broadly, Kyre grabbed Tere's elbow. His deep, sea-blue eyes shone brightly beneath the wisps of blond hair straggling across his tanned cheeks.

'Well met, Tere. It's good to see you.'

Tere returned the warrior's clasp. 'And you, Kyre. I can't thank you both enough for coming.'

Looking between the brothers, Tere grinned. Authion's long, black hair secured in hundreds of tiny braids framed his face and his startling green eyes held a mischievous glint. Tere knew that behind the grin was a most formidable warrior who was, despite his youth in immortal terms, the leader of the Fae army of Darewood. An exceptional tactician, Authion had an uncanny way of knowing what the enemy would do before they did it. Tere wondered if that was his magical strength.

Kyre, on the other hand, had his shoulder-length, unruly, blond hair secured at the nape of his neck. His blue eyes shone with intelligence, and Tere had seen how females reacted when he turned their depths into a weapon of seduction. He was not unlike Raef in his lean, yet muscular build, or in the effect his ready smile and handsome features had on women. He was a joker, always playing tricks and teasing, but he was fearless, loyal, and could wield powerful magic, making him a valuable ally and a foe to be feared. Tere was so very grateful they were his friends and that they had offered to assist him find Ileia.

Kyre's eyes met his friend's. 'Have you found any sign of Ileia?'

Tere shook his head. 'I thought I heard her voice, but maybe I just really wanted to hear something.'

'Where did you say that you last saw her?'

'In the cave system to the north where I was imprisoned and where Rantec held the Golden Stone before it was retrieved. I was searching for her when Authion arrived.'

Tere's gaze tracked from Authion to Kyre. He was tall, but the brothers towered over him.

'If we are to find Ileia, we need to rest. I have leftover rabbit if you're hungry.'

The brothers nodded, settling themselves around the fire. Unwrapping the rabbit, which was still warm, unleashed the delicious aroma of the cooked meat. Authion and Kyre leaned forward, their stomach's rumbling audibly. Tere chuckled.

'How long since you ate? I can hear your bellies protesting from here.'

Authion spoke between bites of the juicy meat. 'We've travelled five days, eating only dried meat and cheese, to get here to appease our sister, Changeling. What else do you expect when you bring out a delicious, cooked coney?'

The three men chuckled, then began discussing their plans to find Ileia. Kyre licked the juice from the rabbit off his fingers, settling on his elbow, his long legs stretched towards the crackling fire.

'So, first we head for the caves. If there are any clues, we'll find them. What did you find when you sent your spirit wolf searching for her?'

Tere's eyes flicked to Authion. 'I was about to enter the caves when Authion arrived, and I was forced to pull my dream wolf back. I tried to find her spirit essence earlier and thought I heard something, a faint call, but before I could lock onto it, it was gone.'

Holding back the despair that made him want to howl again, Tere leaned forward, waiting to hear what Kyre had to say.

'Would you mind if I connected with your memories to see if I can find a clue in what you heard?'

'Of course. Anything that could help.'

Kyre scooted closer, placing his hands on either side of Tere's head, then closed his eyes. Tere tensed his arm and neck muscles as Kyre's presence slipped into the part of his consciousness that held his memories. Distantly, he heard Authion's voice coaxing him to relax so Kyre could access his memories of Ileia.

Willing himself to let go, warmth suffused him, and his memories flowed freely. Visions of Ileia as a young cub playing with her brothers as Tere watched from the steps of his home brought a smile to Tere's lips. Images of his beautiful red wolf gazing at him on the cliffs, and the times when he couldn't protect his mother from Lacas' cruelty squeezed his heart. Quickly, the scene changed to Tere pleasuring Ileia at the river. It seemed so long ago now.

Every moment of his life replayed as though on fast forward through his mind. When his mother lost the baby. When Ileia saved him from Lacas' prison. His anguish at listening to her screams when he'd been tied up and tortured in the caves. Finally, they reached the moment when Tere thought he'd heard Ileia.

There! He heard her. Ileia was alive, her whisper barely audible.

'Tere ... Is that you? I love you, my alpha ....'

Carefully, Kyre withdrew and whistled. His gaze slid to Tere's. When he spoke, Kyre's voice was filled with a quiet fury.

'She's still in the caves, hidden. Damn, Tere, you should have told us the hell you've been through.'

Tere knew his friend's anger was directed at Lacas. Tears pricked the back of his eyes. Nobody except his mother, Reine and Ileia had ever cared enough to be angry for what Lacas had done. The warmth of true friendship bloomed in his chest.

'Lacas is dead now, so it's over. I need to find Ileia and, with her at my side, claim my rightful place as the Inare pack alpha.'

Authion whistled. 'Yes, Raef killed him. Right?'

Authion had obviously observed Tere's memories through his sibling bond while Kyre had been connected to his consciousness. Tere couldn't help the chuckle that escaped.

'Yes.' Sobering, he added, 'When Lacas attempted to rape your sister.'

Kyre and Authion both exploded to their feet, swearing vehemently in what Tere knew was the language of the Fae. Tere caught the scent of their fury as it swirled around them.

His hand gripping the hilt of his sword, Authion bellowed, 'What? The vile bastard. If he weren't dead already, I'd run him through myself.'

Tere growled, the sound low and menacing. His anger towards

his sire a deadly promise of retribution on those who had followed Lacas and unquestioningly carried out his heinous orders.

'You'd have to get in line, Authion. For what Lacas forced myself, my mother, my grandfather, Ileia and the pack to endure, I would have had him die by my hand and mine alone. But Raef took that from me, and initially I was angry that I didn't see the fear in his eyes as I killed him, but then I realised that it no longer mattered. The only thing that matters is that he's dead and can no longer hurt anyone.'

Squeezing his hands into tight fists to stop his claws from sliding out, Tere jumped up, pacing agitatedly around the campfire. Authion's and Kyre's eyes followed him. He finally dropped back to the ground, his jaw clamped so hard, his teeth hurt.

Authion's eyes flicked to Kyre again, a knowing look passing between them. Tere was too agitated as his mind replayed Ileia's screams when they'd been imprisoned in the cave, to comment. Rolling his shoulders and neck to ease some of the tension, he stretched his legs out and forced his hands open, flexing them and holding them towards the warmth of the fire. The gesture was more out of habit than need because his changeling body temperature was several degrees warmer than a human's.

'We should all get some rest. We can leave for the caves at first light.'

Without commenting Kyre lowered himself to a patch of soft grass, dragging his pack under his head to use as a pillow. After punching it several times to make it comfortable, he placed his hands behind his head. His eyes drifted closed, but it was obvious that he maintained a level of alertness.

Authion snorted. 'I suggest you try to sleep now, Tere, otherwise, Kyre's snoring will prevent you from getting any rest at all.'

Kyre, eyes closed, threw a small rock with amazing accuracy at

Authion's head. Authion grinned, snatching it in midair. Observing the brotherly exchange evoked a chuckle from Tere. He settled back onto the hard ground, his anger temporarily assuaged, and closed his eyes, willing himself to sleep. He was anxious to allow his dream wolf to roam in search of Ileia while he had the benefit of his friends' protection.

A pale apparition in the inky darkness, Tere's wolf moved stealthily through the thick bank of trees leading to the caves where he believed Ileia to be imprisoned. Recalling his flight from the labyrinth, he crept towards the tiny slit at the rear of the cave. It overlooked a craggy precipice leading down to the dangerous rocky waterway below, the churning water agitated by the thundering power of the nearby waterfall. His focus drifted, remembering the day he'd shoved Lacas over a similar cliff not so very far from here. Nothing less than he'd deserved. A growl rumbled up through Tere's chest.

How the hell did he survive that?

Returning his attention to the narrow cleft through which he'd escaped just over a week ago, Tere's ghostly figure slid through. There were definitely some advantages to travelling in this form. On the silent pads of the spirit wolf, Tere carefully made his way through the labyrinth. He hadn't seen or heard anyone or anything in the viscous darkness of the cold, damp caves, even with his wolf's enhanced vision. Continuing down the winding path worn into the slimy rock floor, an unnatural shiver coursed through Tere.

Something isn't right.

Inching around the corner that led into a gigantic vault, an icy wind whipped furiously around him.

Wind in a cave?

Tere's senses spiking, his dream wolf shifted unbidden into attack mode. Hackles rising, he choked back a growl and crouched close to the ground. Crawling on his belly to the edge of the precipice, he saw a small community of the foulest creatures he'd ever laid eyes on. In the centre of the roughly hewn platform in the mud and rocks was Ileia, strung naked, hanging between two huge wooden stakes. Her head hung limply against her chest. Tere's heart stopped.

Holding back a howl of despair, he focused on her. She wasn't dead. He wouldn't accept that. There didn't appear to be any movement ... until he noticed an almost imperceptible rise and fall of her chest. Unable to rescue her in his current form, he watched her for a few moments before he allowed a whisper of thought to reach out to her.

Ileia, my love. I've found you. I must leave soon, but I promise I'll be back to free you, to take you home to our pack. Can you hear me, my love?

For what seemed like an age, there was no response. Tere's heart ached with the pain of seeing her like this. His pulse raced, his ethereal form quivering with the need to rescue her, to hold her in his arms, protect her ... ask her to be his true mate. Without Ileia, his life would mean nothing. Holding his breath, he waited.

Slowly, Ileia lifted her head, her eyes scanning the darkness. Her weak voice trickled through Tere's consciousness.

I hear you, my alpha, my Tere, my love. I knew you'd come for me. I just had to wait ...

Moisture filled Tere's eyes. His breath released in a whoosh of relief. Ileia was alive. Joy skittered through him, but he tamped it down, knowing they still had to come back to free her.

The stench of the creatures, like rotten meat and excrement, reached Tere's sensitive wolf nose. He wrinkled it in disgust. Their skin was a mottled red and brown, eyes of varying sizes bloodshot, and their ears and lips appeared barely attached. Tere's skin crawled and he wondered at Ileia's suffering. How had she endured being near them, let alone whatever they had done to her during her imprisonment. Echoes of her screams drifted across his memories. Forcing himself to turn away, Tere allowed himself one last glance at his she-wolf.

I'll be back, my love. Hold on. We'll be together soon.

His heart twisted as Ileia's silent despairing sobs reached him.

Hurry back, please...

Physical pain assaulted Tere at being forced to leave her, but he knew he must because he could not rescue her in his current form. Silently, he padded away, cautiously exiting the cave. Loping through the thickest parts of the forest towards his resting human body, a howl of desolation ripped from his jaws. Tiny creatures scattered at the sound of the nearby predator, the larger nocturnal animals silent, listening, hiding.

There was no urgency this time. Tere knew his sleeping form was protected by his friends. It seemed odd to think of anyone that way, except for Reine and Ileia. This was different. It was a friendship of warriors, forged in battle. Each relied on the other's strengths. The ultimate expression of trust—to put your life in the hands of another.

Slipping back into his body, Tere stirred. His eyes flicked open. Kyre snored quietly, his hands still resting behind his head, his lean, muscled legs stretched out towards the crackling fire. Authion was focused on something in his hand, however, Tere knew he was alert and paying attention to their surroundings. The moment Tere moved and opened his eyes, Authion caught his gaze.

'Any luck?'

Tere nodded. He couldn't contain a triumphant grin, despite the danger Ileia was still in.

'Yes! She's in a cavern deep in the labyrinth. The creatures that hold her ... I've never seen or smelled anything quite so foul. It nearly killed me to leave her there, Authion.'

Eyeing him for a moment, Authion leaned forward, his expression serious. 'We'll get her out, my friend. She'll be with you soon. I'll wake Kyre. You can tell him what you've discovered.'

Kyre stirred at the mention of his name.

Authion snorted. 'He's the only person I know who can be asleep and snoring, yet still be aware of his surroundings.'

Opening one sleepy eye, Kyre peered at his companions. 'Tere, you're back. Did you find her?'

Before Tere could answer, Authion spoke. 'We were just about to wake you to tell you what Tere discovered.'

Kyre stretched slowly, like a cat waking from a long and restful sleep, even though he'd obviously only been napping. Sitting up he leaned back against one of the smooth rocks surrounding their makeshift camp and yawned, scrubbing his face.

'From the smug grin on your face, I'm going to assume you found her and she's all right but being held captive.' Raising his eyebrows, Kyre scanned Tere's face.

Tere couldn't suppress a chuckle, shaking his head at Kyre's uncanny knack of knowing what was going on without being told.

'How the hell do you do that?' Tere asked. Kyre shrugged. 'She's alive, but I couldn't get close enough to determine what injuries she has suffered. She was able to converse a little with me through mind-speak, but she's tied up at the bottom of a huge cavern deep within the cave system, surrounded by the foulest creatures I've ever laid eyes on. I don't know how she's staying sane in that environment. Maybe when we are close enough, she can help us with the movements of the creatures. But she's weak. Very weak.'

Kyre frowned, deep in thought. 'They sound like the remnants of Rantec's army, creatures he didn't have time to finish raising from the bowels of the earth before he was destroyed by Tarienne. Poor Ileia. Tomorrow, we make our way into the caves to rescue your woman.'

Tere smiled gratefully, lowering himself to the ground. 'Given that I've slept, I'll take the watch.'

Authion grinned. 'No need. Now that your dream wolf has returned safely to you, I've set some powerful wards to protect us. Nothing is going to get near us tonight. Sleep, Tere. Your body may be rested, but you need to recover from sending your consciousness so far from your physical form.'

Tere nodded. He had to admit, he was exhausted. The concentration and magic it took to send his wolf searching for Ileia was immense. If he didn't rest, he'd be of little assistance to his friends or Ileia tomorrow.

Dragging a blanket from his pack, Tere stretched out on the hard ground, his feet towards the glowing embers of the campfire, and pulled the soft wool over him. It reminded him of Ileia's silky hair, and he barely managed to suppress a groan as images of her glorious red hair trailing across his chest assaulted him.

Squeezing his eyes shut, he rolled onto his side, bunched up part of the blanket beneath his head as a makeshift pillow and forced himself to relax. Soon, he and Ileia would be together, and he would fulfil his vow to be the Inare wolf pack alpha. He would be a strong and compassionate leader who would make his mother and grandfather proud. Any sign of cruelty or oppression would be dealt with swiftly and surely. Each member of the pack, whether alpha or beta, would be treated with respect, loyalty and love.

Tere dreamed of a happy and healthy pack filled with cubs, some of whom he hoped would be his own. Finally, he drifted into a deep sleep fuelled by both exhaustion and a measure of relief.

* * *

The crisp and clear morning air penetrated both Tere's thin wool travel blanket and his clothes. He wished he'd thought to also hide a jacket in the tree as goose bumps prickled his skin, despite the extra warmth that his changeling blood afforded. Flicking the blanket aside he stretched his sore muscles. He'd have been far more comfortable sleeping on the ground in his wolf form, but he'd been too exhausted to maintain the change all night.

Kyre was already awake, munching on a bright red apple, two more nestled in a small hessian bag at his side. Their skin glistened as the sun's first vibrant rays melted the frost that had settled on them during the night. Tossing one to Tere, he carefully rolled the last one along the ground towards his brother's still sleeping form, managing to stop it under Authion's nose. Tere chuckled as Authion's nose twitched, then sniffed at the aromatic fruit only inches away. Eyes flicking open, his hand snaked out, capturing the apple like a spider snaring its prey in its strong web. Swivelling into a sitting position, Authion took an enormous bite, the sticky juice dribbling down his chin.

'Nice one, Kyre,' he mumbled, chewing the crisp flesh.

Eating in silence, each man lost in their own thoughts, Tere couldn't help but wonder what it was that occupied the thoughts of the warrior brothers. He hadn't known them long enough to guess. After finishing their fruit, both Kyre and Authion dug small holes beneath the protective branches of a huge oak tree at the edge of the clearing. They reverently buried the cores and spoke a few words in the Fae tongue that Tere did not understand.

Authion caught Tere staring and grinned. 'Just returning the seeds to the earth so that what we have used of its bounty will be replenished.'

Fascinated with the concept, Tere could see the good sense of their actions and did the same with his apple core, digging a hole with his knife. Though he did not know the Fae words that Authion and Kyre had spoken, he asked Mother Earth to nurture the seeds and let them grow to feed any future passersby. Re-sheathing his blade into the black leather pouch hanging at his side, Tere drew in a deep breath.

'Ready?'

Kyre and Authion nodded as they grabbed their gear and strode off in the direction of the caves where Ileia was being held prisoner. Leading the way, Tere suddenly slowed his pace when a prickle of something unpleasant travelled up the back of his neck, making the hair at his nape stand on end. A chill spread through his body causing him to shiver. He'd only felt a chill like that once before when he'd seen a wizened old man at the pack's burial site on the outskirts of the village. An unwelcome thought skittered across his consciousness: *had the old man been the necromancer? And had finding Ileia been a little too easy?*

CHAPTER 13

Kyre and Authion exchanged concerned glances at Tere's sudden halt.

Kyre asked, 'What is wrong, Tere?'

Facing his companions, Tere's hand slid to the hilt of his knife. 'Was finding Ileia too easy? I mean, there were no guards except for down in the cavern where they are holding her ... and did you feel the sudden, unnatural chill a moment ago? Something feels ... wrong.'

Closing his eyes, Kyre sent his powerful Fae magic out in a sensory sweep of the area. Authion's stance widened, battle ready, protecting his brother's back. Tere moved to stand in front of Kyre, his wolf senses on high alert. Pulling in a deep breath, Kyre opened his eyes and swiped his hand across his now sweaty forehead, frowning.

'There's something out there. It doesn't seem to have a physical presence, although I sense it, catch a whiff of magic, then it's gone. And, yes, it feels ... sinister.'

Authion eyed his brother. 'Then what say you? Do we continue our mission to rescue Ileia, or do we need to rethink our plan?'

Puzzled, Tere waited. Authion was the leader of the Fae army, yet he was deferring to Kyre on this. Tere prayed that the brothers' decision would be to continue because he was going to rescue Ileia today, no matter what it cost him.

Kyre's gaze ran over Tere assessing, then he grinned.

'We continue, of course. We made Tere a promise I intend to keep.' Clapping Tere on the back, he hefted his pack onto his shoulder. 'Ready?'

Tere grinned back at him, relieved. He pulled three large strips of dried meat from his pack and tossed one to each of the brothers. Chewing on the surprisingly tasty meaty strap, hoisted it onto his shoulders.

Moving quickly through the thick forest, they talked little, focusing on their surroundings and maintaining a silent vigil against the magical presence they'd sensed earlier.

The trees thinned as they approached the plain where the cave system began, forcing the three men to skirt around the perimeter to avoid being seen by whatever was out there. Quietly, they watched, their senses alert, waiting to see if there was any activity at the cave entrance. Tere scanned the darkness, his enhanced lupine vision reaching far into the depths of the labyrinth.

There was no movement, no trail of sorcery that he could identify, just a few lingering scents of familiar wolves and the stench of the foul creatures now guarding Ileia. Cautiously, they approached the mouth of the cavern. Making their way inside, they pressed against the biting cold of the sodden, lichen-covered walls. The pungent, musty odour of damp earth, mixed with the sickening metallic scent of old blood, reached their nostrils.

A shiver skittered down Tere's spine. How long had he been imprisoned here? Time held no meaning during the pain and drug-induced fogginess that had clouded his brain and he'd had no indication of day or night while he was chained against the wall in the inky blackness. The only time he'd woken was to Lacas or the sorceror beating or drugging him for their own twisted pleasure.

Hauling in a deep, silent breath Tere lead Kyre and Authion forward, calling on the memories of his spirit wolf to locate where Ileia was suspended between the two roughly hewn wooden stakes. Even from here, he sensed the fear emanating from her, the panic threatening to engulf her. She held onto her courage by the barest of threads.

Gathering his power, Tere spoke softly into Ileia's mind, a soothing, reassuring voice he prayed would not startle her. Not even a flicker of response returned to him via the mind connection he'd carefully forged with his beloved red wolf. Tere closed his eyes pushing a warm trickle of healing magic through the meagre lifeline strung between them, hoping that nobody in the encampment had the power to sense it. Authion and Kyre shot him a glance, aware of what he'd done and concerned they'd be detected before they were ready.

Ileia's head lifted slightly, the barest of movements. When Tere detected it, his heart leapt. Awareness of his presence filtered through the nexus, brightening the strength of its light, visible only to himself and Ileia. Her mind voice, weak and shaking, tiptoed into Tere's mind so quietly, he doubted he heard it. Focusing his power solely on Ileia, her words became clear.

Tere, you have come for me... She trailed off, as though she didn't have the strength to say more.

Yes, my love. It won't be long now. Hold on, dear heart, we're coming.

The three warriors eased around the back of the encampment behind the largest of the primitive, filthy, cloth tents. The worn canvas was supported by what appeared to be stalagmites or stalactites, snapped off from the depths of the caves where they'd grown for thousands of years. A moment of sadness swept over Tere for the sheer disrespect these creatures showed for something so precious and ancient.

Shuddering at the disgusting stench emanating from the beasts and their belongings, Tere's gaze flicked to his companions. Kyre and Authion wrinkled their noses as they slipped between the roughly erected shelters, winding their way closer to Ileia. Tere's heart thumped against his ribs. They were so close to Ileia now that he could see the cuts and bruises marring her usually smooth, unblemished, creamy skin. She was so pale.

Muting the growl that rumbled through him at the sight of the dried blood caked around her wrists and ankles, he and his companions slid inside the closest tent. Authion silently dispatched the only occupant, a heavily clad creature resembling an ox on two legs. Momentarily surprised by how easily Authion lowered the dead beast to the ground, the slice across its neck bubbling bright blood, its eyes wide with shock, Tere moved to the centre of the tent.

Authion crouched, wiping his blade on the creature's rough clothing. The soft hiss of steel alerted Tere that Kyre had drawn his sword. Their eyes met for a brief instant, an almost imperceptible nod the only indication this was the moment they would confront Ileia's captors. Flinging the ragged tent flap back, the three warriors stepped, abreast, into the midst of the encampment, like avenging angels. Tere dimly registered a gathering cloud of magic, its power growing quickly, swirling around the brothers.

The creatures apparently felt it, too, because even the most fearsome of them turned and fled, trampling anything in their way, including each other, terror etched across their gruesome features. When the warriors reached the structure across which Ileia was strung by her ankles and wrists, Authion and Kyre paused, chanting louder. Their arms spread towards the fleeing beasts, their voices magnified with authority, the brothers spoke the final words of the spell. The air thrummed with the magnitude of the power they wielded.

'Bestiam morden!!'

Blood spattered the damp walls of the cave as many of the creatures simply blew apart midstride. Tere watched, momentarily distracted from his quest to release Ileia.

Ileia's scream wrenched his focus back, his eyes snapping to hers. Confusion filled him as he whipped his knife from the leather pouch hanging at his waist. What was she screaming at? Almost too late, he realised that her terrified gaze was fixed on something behind him.

Cursing his lack of focus, Tere spun around just as a sword arced towards his head. Dropping and rolling, the blade missed Tere by a hair's breadth. He could smell the bitter stench of old blood lingering from the many injuries he knew it had caused, and the tang of uncleansed steel clinging to the sharp blade. Launching to his feet, he scanned the area for a larger blade. His small knife was no match for a sword.

'Tere, use mine!'

Tere snatched Authion's blade in midair, his hand closing around the finely carved hilt of the Fae weapon. His fingers flexing around the grip, he stepped forward. The blade hummed with residual power adding to Tere's natural ability. Ready to face his attacker, his eyes lifted. The sight of the creature he faced halted his forward trajectory. His grip almost faltered around the hilt of the blade he'd raised in preparation to attack his assailant.

'Lacas?'

This could not be Lacas. This creature was enormous, more beast than man. Despite the disfigurement, the face was unmistakable. Without a doubt, Tere knew Lacas had been magically raised from the dead using the dark powers of necromancy and was the cause of the sinister, cold sensation he'd felt as they approached the cave. He shuddered as Lacas laughed maniacally.

From the corner of his eye he noticed Authion and Kyre releasing Ileia from her bonds, wrapping her limp body in a cloak. They recognised this was Tere's fight but were ready should they be needed.

Straightening, Tere's resolve renewed, he tightened his grip on the weapon, his body becoming one with it. He raised the blade high, circling around Lacas, a predator preparing to attack. Gathering his focus, Tere advanced and struck the first blow. His arm shuddered as Lacas easily blocked it, a sinister and unearthly cackle breaking from Lacas' discoloured lips.

'You can't beat me, you fool. I'm already dead. Now it's your turn, you deceitful whelp.'

Lacas lunged. Tere managed to block the powerful blow, but the force of it drove him to his knees giving Lacas the opportunity to drive his blade towards Tere's chest. In his peripheral vision, Tere glimpsed Authion and Kere moving up, swords ready.

No! I need to do this alone!

Wrenching himself sideways, Tere dove and tumbled, but not quickly enough. The wicked blade sliced his side.

White-hot, searing pain ripped through Tere, unleashing a feral howl from his lips. Before he could snatch at his prized control, Tere's wolf exploded free, his body changing form so quickly, he heard the snap of his bones reshaping. Unable to tell if the excruciating pain was from the rapid shift or his injury, he knew this change was different than ever before. He and his wolf had finally become one, the quintessential alpha wolf and the man who would lead the pack. Together, they would defeat the creature that had brought pain and suffering to so many.

Tere stretched his powerful muscles, rejoicing at the unity of spirit that flowed though him, filling his body with warmth and a strength he'd never quite been able to grasp until now. Tipping his head back, he howled.

Lacas seemed to sense the change in Tere, too, his feral grin slipping as he took a step backward. Tere scented his terror. Taking one menacing step towards the now cowering creature, Tere realised his own wolf was bigger, stronger, more alpha than Lacas had ever been. He couldn't hold back the wolfish grin and bared his teeth at his sire. Prowling forward, he snarled viciously, a predator hunting his prey. Dimly aware of the two brothers behind him, ready to join the fight, if necessary, Tere swung his head around, giving them a canine version of a nod, acknowledging their support. Both nodded back.

Lacas scrambled back towards the cover of the now mostly destroyed tents. Tere returned his attention to his sire, briefly wondering why Lacas hadn't shifted to fight him. Had being raised from the dead in this way destroyed his ability? Was Lacas' wolf still alive within, or did it die when Raef pierced Lacas' heart? Remorse spiked in Tere as he considered the death of the noble beast trapped within the soul of the consummately evil creature, Lacas.

Stalking forward, Tere let loose a growl that rumbled through his chest like thunder as he came to a halt in front of the once powerful pack alpha who now appeared pitiful and defeated. Tere wrinkled his nose at the stench of rotting flesh emanating from the creature he once called Father. He felt nothing but disgust. Not even the desire for revenge remained. This pathetic creature was dead already.

Shifting back into his human form, Tere grabbed one of the sharpened wooden tent poles spinning it expertly in his hand.

'This is a far more humane end than you deserve, but I find I no longer care for revenge, just an end to everything you've done. Enjoy life in purgatory, Lacas.'

Lacas raised his hand, a last half-hearted attempt to prevent the stake from piercing his blackened heart. Tere slammed it straight through Lacas' deformed body, jamming it into a crevice beneath the now broken creature who had sired him. Pinned to the cold, rocky ground, what remained of Lacas' life force slowly drained away. Tere didn't wait to see the pathetic creature die. Every evil thing Lacas had done to him, his mother, the pack ... no longer mattered.

Tere needed to see Ileia. Now. Holding her was the only thing that mattered. Dressing quickly, not caring that his clothes were torn from his rapid shift, he strode towards her, barely able to believe she was still alive.

* * *

Lacas struggled to breathe, his eyes glazed, hatred drawing one last snarl from his lips. Glancing sideways, his fading vision caught a wisp of something. He blinked slowly. A small thread of pure evil crept along the rocky ground like a deadly snake, wrapping itself around his leg. A sharp gasp became Lacas' dying breath as the black tendril of malevolence reared up. The viper silently plunged between Lacas' spittle covered, almost black lips, unseen by Tere or his companions.

Tere turned to see Kyre and Authion standing on either side of Ileia.

They had covered her nakedness with Authion's cloak. Kyre squatted beside her emaciated, filthy frame, offering her water. Shaking as she grasped the leather firkin with both hands, she slowly raised it to her parched lips. After a few mouthfuls, she sighed quietly, thanking Kyre with a voice so quiet and scratchy, even Tere's sensitive hearing could barely make out the words.

'Thank you, Kyre. Forgive me. I'm so dirty. I...'

Ileia's voice trailed off when she became aware of Tere's presence. Green eyes lifting to meet his, his world ground to a halt. The pain and suffering he saw tore into his very soul. Suppressing the mournful howl that threatened to escape, expressing the utter desolation he was experiencing at that moment, his shoulders slumped. He'd let her down. Yet even now, Ileia held his gaze, smiling weakly, reaching out to him. He couldn't comprehend her capacity to forgive, to love him after everything she'd been through. Tears tracked down his face, making trails in the dirt and grime as the last vestiges of his tightly wound control slipped away.

Dropping to his knees in front of her he drank in her presence as Ileia's eyes filled with tears. Tere gently gathered her close as she sobbed, her body shaking. He did not care that the brothers saw his tears. Deep down, he knew they understood the depth of his feelings for Ileia and did not judge him as weak. He was dimly aware of them moving away to give them a few moments alone. Before Tere was willing to release Ileia from his embrace, Authion moved up placing his hand on Tere's shoulder.

'Tere, we need to go. There is powerful magic nearby. We've placed a few wards to disguise our presence, but if we don't leave soon, we could be trapped by whatever evil continues to haunt these caves.'

Slowly, Tere raised his head, dropping a kiss on Ileia's forehead before he spoke. 'I can feel it, too. I sensed something similar when Tarienne and Raef battled Rantec, but this is more powerful, even more evil. Can you tell which direction it's coming from?'

Authion's gaze skimmed over Ileia, then flicked back to Tere. 'Being underground, it's difficult to determine the direction from where the power is flowing. Kyre and I believe it to be coming from deeper in the cave network. We need to leave as quickly as we can, especially given that Ileia is not strong enough to walk.'

Ileia's chin tipped up defiantly. 'I will not be a burden to you. I can walk.'

Struggling to her feet, she swayed as she stood for the first time. As she pulled the cloak around her Tere slipped his arm around her waist, tugging her close.

'I will carry her for a while until her strength returns. We need to get far enough away for her to shift to hasten the healing process.'

Ileia opened her mouth to protest, determination shining in her eyes.

Tere smiled at her, pleased to see a spark of the woman he knew and loved. 'No arguments, my love. When you've shifted and healed some more, you can walk. Until then, I'm carrying you.'

Tears filled her eyes again. 'I don't want to be a burden.'

'My love, you will never be a burden. Just accept this, for me ... please.'

Dropping a tender kiss onto her lips, he scooped her into his arms. Authion shouldered Tere's pack and they jogged away, anxious to leave behind the confines of the musty, dank caves, for the fresh, clean scent of the forest.

Ileia soon drifted into an exhaustion fuelled sleep, her head on Tere's shoulder. His heart skittered, her warm body against his invoking a protective instinct so powerful that when Kyre offered to carry her for a while, Tere was forced to suppress a possessive growl.

Authion suddenly barked an order. 'Faster!'

Tere did not need to turn his head to know they were being pursued and what pursued them. Breaking into a run, they turned the corner into the long, straight tunnel that led to the cave entrance. Tere's arms and chest burned, but he tightened his hold on Ileia, sprinting towards the tiny patch of light that heralded their freedom. Flanked by Authion and Kyre, Tere ran, the sinister cloud pursuing them, swallowing everything in its wake. Darkness consumed the labyrinth behind them, a fetid nebula of evil magic devouring what little light reached into its depths.

Spreading its heinous tendrils towards them, the cloud began sucking the oxygen from the cavern. Stray wisps wrapped around Tere, slowing him, choking the breath from his lungs. Ileia spasmed in his embrace, coughing violently. Looking over Tere's shoulder, her eyes opened wide with fear. Struggling against the viscous fog threatening to envelop them, Tere could not pull his knives without releasing Ileia. He gathered what was left of his strength and leapt forward. Suddenly, a clear patch of air appeared in front of him. Propelling himself forward, he saw Kyre and Authion shrouded in a white light, wielding their swords in wide arcs. The mist cleared a little, seeming to retreat. Tere broke through the wall of darkness just inside the cave entrance. Clean air whooshed into his lungs, making him gasp. Ileia's chest heaved against him. Whether from fear or lack of breath, he wasn't certain. He was just grateful she was still breathing.

Unable to hold her any longer, Tere walked a safe distance from the cave mouth and lowered her gently to the ground where she would be partially hidden by some bushes covered with fresh, glossy green leaves.

'Wait here, Ileia. You'll be safe.'

Pulling on the last reserves of his fortitude, Tere drew his twin knives, dragged in a long breath and stomped back to the mouth of the cave to aid his friends. The clear patch of air around them pulsed and shifted like a living entity, slowly growing as the power they manipulated between them drove the evil mist back into the tunnels.

Sweat poured off the brothers as they swung their swords, wielding their power, depriving the malicious fog of its quarry and reinforcing the strength of the pure magic, driving the heinous cloud back. Tere stepped into the bubble of light, echoing the incantation the brothers repeated over and over. He didn't know what they were saying but it didn't matter because the moment he joined his power with theirs, the light burst outward. A deafening roar bounced off the cavern walls, the blackness sucked away with a scream making their ears ring.

Exhausted and panting, they momentarily leaned against each other, drawing support. The tips of the brothers' swords lowered slowly to the ground, the enchanted steel still glowing with the power they had wielded.

Finally able to speak, his voice roughened from thirst, Kyre rasped, 'What the hell was that?'

Authion straightened, pulling in a deep breath. 'I believe Rantec and the creatures he's managed to gather have raised his sire, Rantar. Well, perhaps not completely. His magical essence was not powerful enough for him to take on a physical form. We've only subdued him, and it took the three of us to achieve that. To defeat him, we'll need to return with Father, Raef and the other remaining Eldar. Fortunately, he didn't seem to be able to move past the cave entrance. We should block it to ensure he remains contained until we are able to return.'

A metallic ring echoed through the cavern as Kyre sheathed his weapon. 'I'd wager Rantec was trying to return the power of the Eldar held within the Golden Stone to Rantar.'

Tere slid his twin knives back into their leather sheaths and turned to the cave entrance. 'Thank the Gods that the Stone is now safely locked in the Keep at Castle Therin.'

The brothers nodded in agreement. All three drew a deep, cleansing breath of fresh air. Striding to where Ileia huddled beside the bush, Tere squatted down to face her, grasping her hand and kissing her fingers, then leaned close to steal a chaste kiss.

'It's time for you to shift, my love. You'll heal more quickly in your wolf form.'

Extending his hand to help her rise, unsteadily, he watched her nod, then glance anxiously at Kyre and Authion. She was nervous about dropping the cloak to shift in front of the brothers, even though she'd been naked when they found her. Tere grinned, even as a wave of possessiveness swept through him.

Mine! 'Ileia is going to shift, my friends. Could you provide us with some privacy, please?'

The two Fae nodded, moving away, dropping to the ground a short distance away, their backs facing Ileia and Tere. Tere helped Ileia remove the cloak, wishing he had some clean garments for her. She was so weak and unsteady, she leaned on him heavily.

'Shift now, sweetheart.'

Ileia closed her eyes, willing her inner wolf to surface. The change usually initiated immediately, but nothing happened. Tere wondered if Ileia's wolf was sick or injured from her ordeal.

Suddenly, Ileia cried out. The shift was unusually long and arduous, and although not usually painful for her, she panted and groaned this time, sweat trickling across her pale skin until the shift was complete. The dark red wolf's head hung low, her feet wide apart, her sides heaving.

Concern spiralled through Tere as she swayed, then dropped to her haunches, unable to stand. Sitting cross-legged beside her, Tere ran his hand reassuringly through the soft fur of her head as she lay down. A soft whine escaped before her head drooped to rest on her front paws and she sighed deeply. Tere opened his mind, searching his beloved's body to ensure that there were no serious injuries he'd missed.

Kyre appeared beside him. 'She's exhausted, Tere. Let her sleep. I'll wash your spare clothes in the nearby stream. By the time Ileia wakes, the sunshine should have dried them. Authion has returned to the cave and is collapsing the rocks at the entrance to prevent the evil cloud from spreading for now at least.'

Tere looked up at the tall warrior, who had a heart of gold buried beneath the tough exterior. He wondered briefly if Kyre ever listened in on his thoughts, but he was certain he would have felt the intrusion into his mind. This was Kyre's gift. Tere realised the fierce and powerful warrior was an empath. His strength and power balanced by his ability to perceive the needs of those he cared about. Tere couldn't help but wonder how the two worked together.

'Thank you, Kyre. Ileia would very much appreciate that. You are a good friend.'

Kyre blushed and mumbled, 'Just trying to help.' It was followed by a few expletives as he picked up the clothes and walked away. Tere couldn't hold back a chuckle.

Shifting to sleep beside Ileia, he noticed that her posture was more relaxed and her breathing more even. Her wolf was working on healing her.

* * *

When Tere awoke, the sun had only just breached the horizon. The thin rays penetrating the leafy canopy offered no warmth. Rising, he ran his gaze over Ileia. She had shifted back sometime in the night but seemed more at ease, her breathing deep, her heart beating stronger and more rhythmically. For the first time in months, Tere relaxed. Ileia was here with him, safe. Now to return to the pack and take his rightful place as alpha. Anticipation tingled through him, his wolf restless at the thought. He'd waited so long to assert his alpha status, Tere wondered what the reaction of the pack would be when he laid claim to the leadership of the Inare wolves.

Shifting then laying back down, he wrapped the blanket and his arms possessively around Ileia, her back resting against his chest, his knees caging her protectively. Her long imprisonment had stolen her lush, womanly curves. She was thin and frail, when she'd once been so strong. A growl rumbled through him at the thought of what she'd suffered.

Ileia woke, turning in his arms, the movement bringing a slight wince to her beautiful, but drawn face. Frowning at the growl vibrating through his body, Ileia sent Tere a questioning glance. The pain he knew she was still experiencing brought a grimace to her face, but she lifted her head so that she could meet eager lips. He could hardly believe she was here with him. During those long months while she'd been captive, he'd almost given up hope of ever seeing her again.

Pulling back he shook his head. Guilt and anger for everything that had happened to her consumed him.

'Tere?' His eyes held hers. Swallowing hard, she continued in a low voice. 'I love you, Tere.'

His eyes filled with moisture and a lone tear trickled down his cheek. He tightened his hold on her. His entire body shook. He was close to losing his usually tightly gripped control.

'None of this was your fault, Tere. We are both alive and back together. That's all that matters now.'

A strangled sound slipped past his lips as he buried his face in her hair and pulled her tightly against him. Shoving at him gently, she loosened his arms and swivelled so that she straddled his lap, wrapping her arms around his neck. Their company forgotten, they held each other, releasing the months of fear, guilt and pain in silent, gut-wrenching sobs.

When they finally pulled apart, Tere cupped her chin, kissing her so tenderly her tears began afresh.

'No more tears, my beautiful Ileia. I love you and we're together. While we were apart, I promised myself that if we had the opportunity, I would, with your consent, make you my mate in the true sense of the word. Will you be with me always, my Ileia?'

Tears trickled down Ileia's cheeks again. Unable to speak for a moment, she nodded, wiping her eyes. 'Oh Tere, yes. It has only ever been you. Make me your mate, my love.'

Shaking his head, Tere couldn't believe they were finally going to take the step to formalise their joining, to make them mates for life, joined by a bond so strong that they could converse and feel each other's emotions telepathically.

'As soon as you are well enough, sweetheart.'

'Now, Tere. Please?'

Tere's gaze slid to Authion and Kyre, who appeared to be sleeping, their backs towards them. Tere smiled, silently thanking the two warriors for their discretion. His focus warred with his escalating desire. When desire won, Tere slid from beneath Ileia, rising and scooping her into his arms. Striding purposefully towards the stream, he rounded the bend, out of view of the campsite.

'Sweetheart, we're both dirty. Do you feel strong enough to bathe with me?'

Ileia nodded. Lowering her feet to the ground, Tere helped her undress, then quickly stripped, dumping their clothes beside a large boulder. Her hand firmly in his, he led Ileia into the icy, swirling water. She gasped quietly. Goose bumps ran up her arms, and her nipples beaded enticingly.

Finally, waist-deep in the clear stream, Tere turned to Ileia, drawing her close for a long kiss that quickly deepened. Ileia moaned softly, parting her lips, allowing his tongue entrance to her sweet mouth. Sighing as the tension of the last few months slipped away, Tere's hands roamed over her soft skin, eventually settling on her deliciously firm buttocks. She rocked her hips rubbing against him. Smiling against her lips before he plundered her mouth, their tongues duelling as Ileia's arms slipped around his neck, her nails grazing his scalp, sending a shiver down his spine.

Lifting his head, Tere gazed into her beguiling green eyes, then began trailing kisses down her neck and across the top of her firm, round breasts. Bending his head, he drew a tightly puckered nipple into his mouth. One hand slid around to cup the other breast, the other caressed her bottom. Panting, Iliea hooked one leg over his hip. The invitation too much to ignore, Tere's hand trailed from her breast down her flat stomach until it reached the thatch of dark red hair between her thighs. Stroking, her soft nub swelled beneath his touch. He slid one finger inside her heat, Ileia's needy moans firing his desire.

Ileia gasped and moaned. Capturing her mouth again, Tere swirled his tongue around hers, then licked her lips. She writhed against him. He wanted her so badly that it took every last shred of his resolve to bring her to climax first. Despite the cool water, the hot moisture between her legs indicated her readiness as his swollen member rested against her belly.

Swirling his fingers inside her, he worked her sensitive bundle of nerves with his thumb. Her muscles tightened and began rhythmically squeezing his fingers moments before she cried out, bucking against him. Before her climax subsided, Tere lifted her, wrapping her legs around his hips, and slid into her welcoming heat.

Unable to suppress a loud moan, Tere's hips thrust back and forth, creating a rhythmic friction that quickly built into a powerful tide of sensation. His lips crushed against hers. Her fingernails clawed his back. Their hips ground together. Tere's fingers dug into her buttocks as he exploded. Ileia cried out again, her muscles squeezing him and dragging out his orgasm, stealing his breath with its intensity.

Panting heavily, they clung to each other, their foreheads touching. Finally, Ileia managed to speak. 'Tere, I always knew that truly being with you would be the most amazing experience of my life, but...' The worry that creased Tere's expression tore at her heart, so she pressed on to reassure him. 'Tere. I love you. You know that don't you?'

His frown deepened. Tere didn't understand what she wanted. *Just say it.* Ileia gulped, dragging in a deep breath. Ileia looked into Tere's eyes, her love shining like a beacon of hope for him.

'I'm not doing a very good job of explaining myself, am I? Tere, we just made love, and it was beautiful, but why didn't you bite my neck and take me as your lifelong mate?'

Relief washed across Tere's face. Tightening his grip around her, he pushed their hips together, his burgeoning arousal sliding deeper within her sheath. She gasped, and Tere grinned.

'Ileia, I want to, but if I do that, we are bound so closely that if either one of us dies, the other will likely not survive.'

Ileia wriggled, tightening her legs around his waist. 'I understand, my love. We've been through a great deal together and I love you so much. I wouldn't want to live if anything happened to you.'

He'd begun circling his hips as she spoke, and her words ended on a soft moan. No more words were necessary as their lips met in a soul-searing kiss. Ileia ground her hips into his as Tere thrust faster and harder than before. A groan rumbled through him as he tipped his head back, increasing the tempo. Ileia cried out, their pleasure building to a crescendo. Just as he sensed Ileia was about to crest the wave of passion, Tere bit her neck gently, piercing the skin next to the spot where her pulse fluttered, and a pleasure filled scream ripped from her lips.

Tere thrust several more times releasing his hot seed into her. The howl his climax drew pierced the quiet of their surroundings.

Licking the place where his teeth had penetrated, to aid its healing, Tere supported Ileia, his arms around her, her legs obviously wobbly after the scorching passion they'd just shared. He understood because his body also pulsed with aftershocks. There was a tangible difference between them now as they embraced, their hearts galloping, their breath coming in quick gasps. He could feel her heartbeat, sense her emotions. They were bonded in a way that nobody who had not performed the bonding ceremony could comprehend. He could now sense Ileia deep within his consciousness, and his love for her burned like a lantern in the dark. There was no way they could ever doubt their feelings for each other their souls were now connected.

When she released her shaking legs Tere lowered her until her feet touched the fine silt of the stream bed. His lips met hers. The emotion contained within that kiss told him their newly forged bond affected her as deeply as it did him.

Drawing her against him, Tere wrapped his arms tightly around Ileia's tiny frame. Tears moistened his eyes at the trust she'd placed in him. She was finally his, forever. His mate. He threw his head back and howled with joy. Scooping her into his arms, he strode to the bank, an uncontainable grin forming on his lips. Lowering Ileia onto the large, smooth rock where he'd dropped their clothes earlier, Tere began drying her with his clean shirt. She shivered and, he reached for the cloak, realising it had been replaced by his now clean, spare clothes. Tere grinned to himself. Obviously, Kyre had substituted the clean clothes for the dirty cloak while they had been ... otherwise occupied.

Sliding the shirt over her head, Tere laced it together at the front, then dragged his own down one of her legs, dropping to one knee to dry her properly. Their eyes met and Tere stretched up to kiss her again.

'I love you, Ileia.'

'And I you, Tere.

Tere helped her into her clean clothes and quickly dressed himself before scooping her into his embrace and carrying her back to camp. He lowered her near the heat of the campfire and sat on the ground, before hauling her into his lap.

Neither Kyre nor Authion spoke. However, Authion grinned,

raising one eyebrow at them. Ileia wriggled closer against Tere's firm body, the spike of desire flaming through him again. Completion of the mating had heightened their desire, their need for each other. Her cheeks reddened and Tere chuckled certain that Kyre and Authion knew exactly what she was thinking. Tere definitely knew what she was thinking.

CHAPTER 14

Hindered by Ileia's lingering injuries, their progress was slower than usual. When darkness fell the first evening, Tere urged her to shift again to hasten the healing process, despite her exhaustion. Stripping alongside her in the privacy of a stand of young elm trees he called the shift, feeling his bones lengthen, his skin stretch. Tere nudged Ileia into a gentle run parallel with the river, ensuring they didn't stray too far from the camp and the protection of their friends. That night they both slept more soundly than they had in a very long time.

Each day, Ileia's wounds healed a little more. Gradually, with Tere's gentle encouragement and Kyre and Authion's patience, her strength and confidence returned.

One week after her rescue, the four companions made camp several leagues upwind of the Inare wolf pack settlement. Ileia's wounds had almost healed completely. She now sat cross-legged on their blanket, watching Tere pace the perimeter of their campsite. Kyre and Authion rested on the cool, damp grass chewing on dried beef strips, seemingly unperturbed by Tere's agitation. Understanding the reason for his unrest, Ileia rose to her feet. She approached, resting one hand on his arm.

'Oh Tere, have faith in the pack. They know you're nothing like your sire...'

Frowning as Tere continued his pacing, the gentle breeze wafted the scents from the Inare village in their direction. Ileia turned her head and inhaled, smiling. He knew why she smiled. The familiar, comforting aroma of cooking fires, meat searing over them, made her mouth water. The scents of young and old wolves, male and female, the wooden cottages hewn from the local trees, the dusty roads meandering between the homely cabins, the more distant scent of water from the small lake where she and Tere had first explored their attraction. Momentarily distracted from his anxiety, Tere's focus suddenly snapped back and he stopped pacing, posturing as a low growl rumbled through him.

Kyre and Authion responded immediately, jumping to their feet, their hands poised over the hilts of their jewelled Fae swords. Tere's gaze searched the surrounding trees, his nostrils flaring and drawing in the scent his keen wolf senses had picked up. Ileia focused her attention on that direction too. There was something familiar about the scent. Suddenly, Tere sprinted into the thickest part of the forest noting as he left that the brothers closed protectively in protectively around Ileia, their hawk-like gazes watching for signs they were needed.

The air was still. Not even a bird song pierced the silence. Finally, after what seemed like an eternity, Tere reached the source of the whiff that had alerted him to a presence nearby and a low, rumbling laughter bubbled up as he realised why the scent had been familiar. He embraced Reine before they strode through the forest back to the camp where Tere had left his friends and Ileia wondering what had caused him to sprint away. Kyre and Authion were both grinning as

Tere and Reine entered the campsite. Ileia rushed to Reine, hugging him, then melted into Tere's awaiting arms.

'Tere, you scared me when you ran off like that,' she scolded.

Burying her face into his shoulder, she slipped her arms around his waist, then looked up, smiling at his joyful laughter after his earlier dour mood.

Reine offered his hand in greeting to Kyre and Authion, stiffening momentarily as Kyre pulled him into a quick hug, grinning. Laughing, Reine relaxed and clapped Kyre on the back.

'We have heard much about you. Any true friend of Tere's is a friend of ours. Come. Sit. Tell us about the feeling in the pack. Has anyone attempted to take over its leadership?'

Reine grinned, dropping onto the cool grass, cross-legged. Tere, sat with Ileia anchored against his side. Kyre and Authion slid effortlessly to the ground, Kyre with his back against a straight, young elm tree. Authion leaned forward, his elbows on his knees, eager to hear information about the pack.

'It's good to see you both safe. In answer to your question, Kyre, the pack is in disarray. Nobody is certain if Lacas is dead or not. His henchmen never returned after they set out to find Tere. Except for Lupus. He has changed. He has been trying to keep the pack together, telling them you'll be back to lead us. I thought it was another of Lacas' tricks, but he has done his best to maintain order until your return. Of course, many believe you were murdered by Lacas. We've been trying to reassure them, but you've been gone for so long, Tere. We need you to assume your rightful place as the pack Alpha. Will you come back with me?'

Four pairs of eyes watched Tere expectantly, awaiting his reply. He hesitated briefly then smiled. 'I will! It is why we are here.'

Everyone leapt to their feet. Reine slapped Tere on the back, congratulating him. 'It's where you belong, my friend. It's where you've always belonged. It's your destiny to rule the pack and bring it back to prosperity. I should tell you, though, that Anya has become vicious like Lacas, especially since they became bonded mates. As of late, she has not been seen outside their cabin, leading many of us to believe Lacas is dead. Her father's the only one who dares visit her. I believe she'll do her utmost to ensure that and sabotage your leadership.'

Surprise lifted Tere's brows. His gaze briefly tracked to Ileia. 'Bonded mates? Well, we'll have to deal with Anya and her offspring. I think it best that we return at first light. That will be a good time to gather everyone and let them know I'm back and intend to assume the role of pack Alpha. If anyone puts forward a challenge, leadership will be determined before sunset.'

Reine nodded. 'I doubt there'll be a challenge, Tere, but if there is, I have no doubt you will defeat it and be our rightful leader by sundown.'

CHAPTER 15

The next morning, Reine returned to the campsite just after sunrise. He seemed excited to be leading their new Alpha back to the village. He told Tere that when he'd returned to the village last night, he'd rushed to find Lupus to tell him he'd found Tere and that he was coming to claim his place as Alpha of the pack. Relieved, Lupus had decided to wait until this morning to gather everyone in the village square. Reine had left the gathering crowd, full of anticipation. He told them he hoped there wasn't a challenge for leadership, but that Tere was strong, and he was certain that he'd be their leader before the end of the day.

Tere's heart thumped as they approached the gathered crowd. Flanked by Kyre and Authion, with Reine leading them and Ileia at his side, Tere straightened, gripping his resolve as a few of the pack turned at his approach. Murmurs rippled through the gathering. A few cheers broke out. The crowd surged forward. Before he knew it, Tere was surrounded by friends clapping him on the back, greeting him. He'd never imagined the warmth of his welcome home. He hadn't known the way others in the pack felt about him. How could he? Lacas had them all too scared to even look at him. Reine and Ileia had been the only one's brave enough. Tere glanced at them both, renewed pride at their bravery, their loyalty.

Lupus stepped into the crowd and approached Tere. For a moment, the crowd hushed, nobody daring to breathe. Then Tere grabbed Lupus' hand and shook it. Tere grinned and spoke so that everyone could hear.

'Thank you for keeping the pack together. I'm sorry I've been gone so long, but we had some ... business we needed to attend to.'

Grinning at the cheer that went up, Tere continued shaking hands and speaking with the pack members. As he glanced around, he noticed Manny standing off to the side with another wolf. They watched him anxiously before Tere made his way over to them, pulled in a deep breath and held out his hand. Manny smiled tentatively then spoke.

'Tere, I'm so very sorry for what I did. Lacas was holding Mac,' he turned to look at Mac, nodding at him, 'and had threatened to kill him if I didn't ... didn't...'

'I understand, Manny. You and Mac are both welcome here if you can promise your fealty to me.'

'We will, gladly.' They replied in unison, both now smiling. 'And thank you.'

Reaching out, Tere grabbed first Manny's, then Mac's hand and shook them before moving on to greet others eager to welcome him home until Lupus motioned him onto the central speaking platform. A hush fell over the pack.

'You all know why I'm here. To take over leadership of the pack. Lacas is dead, finally killed by my own hand.' He paused when cheers erupted. 'Never again will this pack be ruled by fear, cruelty and viciousness. I wish to honour my maternal grandfather and my beautiful mother, who protected me from the cruelty of Lacas and died at his hand. I promise to rebuild the Inare wolf pack to be as happy and prosperous as it once was. I wish to honour you, the pack members, and pledge my loyalty to you.' Beckoning Ileia up to stand beside him, he took her hand in his. 'And I pledge my loyalty and love to Ileia, my one true, and bonded, mate.'

Kissing her hand, he dropped to one knee before her. 'Ileia, my love. Will you honour me by ruling by my side as the mate of my heart?'

Ileia blushed deeply, then dropped to her knees, too. 'Always, my love, my mate, my Alpha.'

Another cheer rose from the assembled crowd.

Tere beamed as he stood and faced the crowd again. 'We must vote. Everyone must vote, not just the remaining leaders. I will not be your true leader unless that is what everyone wants.'

Another roar from everyone brought a grin to Tere's face. Lupus made eye contact with him, nodded, then began organising the collection of votes from everyone, even children, to decide if they wished Tere to be their pack alpha.

Suddenly, the milling crowd parted, and a heavily pregnant, haggard looking woman pushed through the gap. Tere couldn't withhold a gasp.

'Anya?'

She approached, snarling. 'How dare you return. You killed my Lacas but now his pup will be the alpha, not you. You murdered your father, the leader of your pack, and expect to be voted in as alpha?!' She screamed at him now. 'You've plotted to kill him for years. You hated that he was so strong. A strong, proud alpha who sired you ... supposedly. I dispute your claim to the leadership. You are no alpha. You're probably not even his son. That slut of a mother of yours probably slept with every horny male in the pack.'

Tere stepped forward, barely maintaining control of his temper at the way Anya spoke of his mother. 'Anya, if you promise to behave with respect, you will be looked after.'

'Me?! Behave with respect? You killed my bond mate. I challenge you for leadership.'

Tere drew in a sharp breath. No wonder she looked so haggard. Lacas and Anya had truly been bonded mates. Glancing at Ileia, Tere stepped towards Anya again, one cautious step at a time.

'Anya, I understand how you feel, but I will not fight you.'

'Coward!'

She spat at him, ripped her clothes off and shifted. Snarling, she lunged. Tere had no other option than to shift himself. He was no match as a human against a vicious she-wolf. He circled her, unwilling to fight. Anya lunged again, and Tere moved quickly to avoid her bite. She was slow because of her advanced pregnancy. Tere took advantage of that. Swiping at her back paws, he tripped her and jumped, landing on top of her, pinning her down, his jaws inches from her throat. The onlookers gasped.

Tere knew this was a significant moment. He could easily kill her. That was what Lacas would have done. But he needed to show the pack he was going to be a more compassionate and fairer leader. Growling, he shook his huge, black wolf head, holding her on her back in a submissive position with his enormous paws, hoping desperately that she'd capitulate.

Finally, she calmed. Slowly moving back, he maintained eye contact with her shifting into his human form. Authority in his voice he spoke.

'Anya, shift so we can talk about your future position within the pack.'

She did as she was asked. Both stood there, naked, maintaining eye contact. A battle of wills. Finally turning to dress, he took a few steps towards his clothes and heard a snarl and several gasps. Before he could defend himself, Anya attacked in her wolf form. Tere did not have time to shift. All he could do was use his strength to hold her snapping jaws away from his throat. He was dimly aware of shouting, then something flew into Anya, knocking her sideways, pulling a yelp from her.

Tere jumped to his feet to see Lupus in his wolf form fighting with his daughter. There was silence, except for the snapping of jaws. Tere couldn't believe his eyes. Anya yelped but fought back like a demon. Finally, Lupus pinned her with his huge grey wolf body, his jaws around her throat.

'Lupus, no!'

Lupus growled, his massive grey canine head swinging towards Tere. Tere stood, his legs wide, his back ramrod straight, posturing, maintaining eye contact and showing his alpha status. In Lupus' moment of indecision, Anya slithered out of his grip and jerked her jaws towards his throat.

'Anya! Stop this! Now!' Tere bellowed, his voice slashing through the air.

Anya paused for the briefest of moments before her eyes rolled, showing the whites. She snarled and her jaws snapped around Lupus' throat. An arrow hissed past Tere, embedding itself in Anya's chest. She yelped, loosening her jaws. Blood poured around the arrow shaft, matting her thick, chocolate brown fur.

Lupus sat back on his haunches, blood dripping from the puncture marks around his neck, and let out a long, mournful howl. Shifting, he collapsed, sobbing over his daughter. As Anya's life force ebbed away, she shifted back into her human form, Kyre's arrow protruding through her rib cage. A collective gasp arose from the crowd.

'My daughter, I'm sorry. I love you. Bond mating Lacas sent you mad. You would have never stopped. You would have never...' His gaze lifted and he nodded at Kyre. 'Thank you for doing what needed to be done. I'm not certain that I could have...' Lupus' shoulders sagged, and his eyes lowered again to his daughter's lifeless form.

Nodding at Kyre in silent gratitude, Tere motioned the pack away to give Lupus time with his daughter. Ileia handed Tere his clothes and wrapped her arms around him, crying quietly. He looped his arm around her and walked back to Kyre and Authion, who stood at a respectful distance. Tere's thoughts drifted back to the Anya he'd once known, the Anya he'd made love to at the Coming-of-Age ceremony.

A tug on his sleeve brought Tere back to the present. It was Merico, the healer.

'Tere, I need to help Lupus and I may be able to save the pups. Anya has carried them almost to term, but I must act quickly. They are Lacas' pups...' Her words trailed off, waiting.

Tere did not hesitate. Striding to where Lupus sat holding his daughter's lifeless hand, Tere crouched and spoke softly so only Lupus could hear.

'Lupus, I'm sorry that it ended this way. Merico must tend to your wounds, and she may be able to save the pups, but it's your choice. Do you wish her to try? Would you accept them and raise them as your own? The pack will help you...'

Slowly, Lupus turned red-rimmed eyes to Tere. 'Yes, I wish it. Perhaps something good can come out of this. New life, a new beginning.'

Tere nodded to Merico, placing his hand on Lupus' shoulder. 'We must act quickly. You may not want to watch.'

'She may be gone, but she is still my daughter. I will stay and be the first to see and hold the pups if they survive.'

Resting his hand on Lupus' shoulder again, Tere nodded. He had no need for grand gestures, no desire to grandstand in front of the pack. This moment was about supporting Lupus through something that should have been joyous, the birth of the pups, but was shrouded in grief at the loss of his daughter.

'Then I will stay with you.'

Tere motioned the crowd to create a circle around Anya at a respectful distance, facing outward. Kyre and Authion ensured Merico had enough room to work unhindered. Merico cleaned and bandaged Lupus' neck, then, armed with the several wads of cloth, clean water and blade she'd brought with her, she carefully sliced open Anya's belly. Lupus held Anya's hand as the pups were born. Two healthy girls and a boy, all chocolate brown. The male pup had a black patch on his ear, the only hint of Lacas' midnight black fur. Holding the wriggling pups, tears dripped down Lupus' face. Tere momentarily wondered why they were born as wolf pups when their mother was in her human form. Before he could ask, Merico smiled softly and spoke.

'They will shift after they are fed. They are wolves because Anya shifted only moments before her passing. I have a mother from the pack who has volunteered to help with feeding them. They need to feed as quickly as possible.'

Lupus nodded and stood, placing the pups in the wicker basket Merico held. 'Wait.' Lupus strode to where the shreds of Anya's clothes were, then tucked some unbloodied pieces around the pups. He sighed. 'They should know the scent of their mother.'

Tere placed his hand on Lupus' shoulder again and squeezed gently.

'She shall have a proper burial, my friend. These last few months should not taint her memory.'

'Thank you, Tere. You are our alpha now. I know you'll be a wise and compassionate leader.' He turned to Kyre. 'Thank you, again.'

Climbing up onto the speaking platform, Lupus called the crowd to order. Tere wondered at his composure in the face of his grief. Lupus had much to teach him about leadership

'Let this day not be about sadness and loss. Let it be about new beginnings. You have witnessed the strength and compassion Tere shows us all. He is the rightful pack alpha, and anyone who does not agree can leave now.'

Slowly, the crowd began to chant, softly at first, then louder. 'Tere! Tere! Tere!'

Not one pack member walked away. Lupus thumped his arm across his chest in a gesture of loyalty. The rest of the Inare pack did the same, cheering their new alpha. Kyre and Authion stood off to the side, grinning. When the pack tipped their heads back and howled as one, Kyre and Authion whooped their approval, too.

CHAPTER 16

The next day, Anya was burned on the traditional funeral pyre of the pack. It was believed the burning of the body set the wolf spirit free to roam the forests of the after world. Tere's thoughts wandered momentarily to his own funeral pyre in Therin after the battle for the Golden Stone. Thankful that the great spirits had believed in him enough to bring him back from death to take his rightful place as pack alpha, Tere slipped his hand into Ileia's, squeezing it gently as they watched Lupus light the fire. The flames quickly licked around the raised wooden structure holding Anya's body. The fire roared, soon hiding Anya's body from view beneath the flickering orange-red flames and the shimmering heat. Reine and his family sang the farewell lament, their melodious voices rising with the flame in perfect harmony. It wasn't the poignant song of the Fae that Tarienne and her sisters had sung at his funeral, but a haunting wolf song of life, death, and rebirth.

A collective gasp rose as Anya's spirit drifted slowly up from her physical body, hovering over the crowd fleetingly before it disappeared like a wisp on the wind. Sadness washed over Tere as Lupus said farewell to his only daughter, his lips moving in a silent tribute that only he could hear. Finally, Lupus blew a kiss in her direction.

Tere remained to support Lupus, watching the flames burn down to embers, consuming the body that Anya held in life. Ileia stood beside Tere in her rightful place, her fingers threaded through his. When the embers had burned down to a soft glow, she gently tugged on Tere's hand, pulling him away to allow Lupus some final moments alone. Nodding at Kyre and Authion, who stood respectfully in the shadows, Tere's gaze drifted to the cabin where he'd spent much of his young life. He wasn't certain he could confront the memories tonight. As always, Ileia knew what he needed, gently guiding him to her home and up the four wooden steps to the entrance.

Pausing, she smiled. 'I didn't think you'd want to face the ghosts tonight. My room is small but clean, and my parents have prepared it for us.'

Pulling Ileia into his arms, Tere kissed her. A tender kiss, a grateful kiss. 'Thank you for always knowing what I need without me having to say it. I love you, Ileia.'

'I love you, too, Tere. Now, let's get some sleep.'

Thanking Ileia's parents, Ranger and Keana, they closed the bedroom door, stripped and climbed into bed. It was the first real, comfortable bed they'd slept in together, but they were too exhausted to do more than kiss and drift off to sleep wrapped in each other's arms. There would be plenty of time to explore their love, but tomorrow would be another big day.

The sun rose bright in a clear, blue sky, its rays filtering through the window of Ileia's room heralding the new day. Tere looked over at Ileia and smiled, her long, titian hair spread across his chest, one leg looped across his, a small smile touching her deliciously soft lips. Tempted to spend some time waking her in the best way he knew, Tere gently tipped her face up to steal a taste of her sweet lips. Ileia woke, responding to him in a way that set his body on fire. Holding one finger to her lips to tell him he should stay quiet so her parents did not hear them, she moved to straddle him. Tere suppressed a groan when she leaned over to kiss him, her firm, round breasts so close. Ending the kiss, he pulled Ileia farther up his body, his hands circling her tiny waist, laving each nipple with his tongue, drawing each tiny bud into his mouth. Ileia groaned softly, her damp sex sliding along his erection.

Sitting up, Ileia shook her head, her long, rich auburn hair floating around her like a ruby halo. Tere lifted her onto his straining erection, biting his lip to keep from crying out at the sweet pleasure as he slid into her. He almost chuckled at Ileia's strained expression, her mouth pressed tightly together to prevent her moans from escaping. Tere flexed his hips as Ileia rose and fell, their rhythm escalating to a frantic pace just before the exquisite crescendo. Moments later, Ileia's inner muscles began pulsating around him, and his climax exploded, a low moan escaping his lips. Collapsing together, Ileia giggled, settling on his chest. Tere chuckled and shushed her.

When they'd fully recovered from their lovemaking, they dressed, gathering fresh clothes so they could bathe in the lake.

When they returned, breakfast was ready, the tantalising aroma drawing Tere to the kitchen table. He thoroughly enjoyed chatting with Keana and Ranger over the delicious breakfast they'd prepared of eggs and field mushrooms with freshly baked bread. They were interested in what had happened in the months Tere and Ileia had been missing and were keen to fill them in on what had happened in the pack during their absence.

Tere left out the worst parts. There was no need to traumatise Ileia's parents now that their daughter was home safe and sound.

Keana and Ranger expressed how proud they were of Ileia for being brave and of Tere for never giving up on her. They thanked him for taking care of Ileia, even though Tere didn't believe he had. He was overwhelmed by the unfamiliar feeling of acceptance and belonging, something he'd never had from his own father.

A knock on the door had Tere jumping to his feet before he detected the scent that told him it was Kyre and Authion. Tere and Ileia walked out onto the long, polished, redwood verandah that crossed the front of the cabin.

Kyre spoke first. 'It's time for us to return home, Tere. You have the backing of the pack. The rest is up to you. Never fear, we'll be back to visit. Mayhap we'll bring Tarienne and Daien with us.' Kyre's eyes twinkled mischievously. 'I'm sure you'd love to meet the new addition to their family.'

Tere grinned. 'New addition? Is Tarienne with child?'

Authion and Kyre both nodded breaking into wide grins. Kyre spoke. 'We're going back to Darewood to pick up Mother and Father, then on to Therin, where we'll stay until after the birth. Be happy, dear friend.'

Authion and Kyre each pulled Tere into a quick hug, then did the same to Ileia.

'I can't thank you enough. Without you both, I very much doubt Ileia and I would be home safe and sound, looking forward to life with the pack. Please, feel free to visit whenever you can. You will always be welcome.'

Kyre and Authion grinned, both promising to return soon and leaving with a wave. Tere and Ileia watched them stride down the street, speaking to everyone they passed. Tere chuckled, then turned to Ileia, pulling her into his arms.

'I'll miss them, but we have much to do, my Ileia. Today, we're going to purge my cabin of bad memories and make it ours. I wish to hear laughter and little paws in the future. Lots of them!'

Grinning as Ileia looked up at him, Tere kissed her and grasped her hand, leading her across the sandy road to the cabin where they would raise their family. Pulling Ileia inside, he dropped the wooden latch to lock the door behind them. He chuckled at her surprised look.

'The good memories start here.'

Backing her up against the door, he caged her with his body and kissed her so passionately, Ileia's head swam. Wrapping her arms around his neck and her legs around his waist, she smiled lovingly up at him.

'And hopefully the little paws,' she whispered before Tere swept them to a new beginning filled with passion and beautiful memories.

CHARACTERS:

Aidan (fiery)-pronounced *ay-den* – King of Therin. Six feet tall with bright blue eyes and short blond hair, Aidan is handsome and takes as much pleasure in honing his body as his skill with a sword. He is dedicated to making the lives of the people of Therin safe and better than when his father was alive.

Aistarenne (blessed and gracious in High Elvish)-pronounced *ay-eest-ar-enn* – Queen of Darewood and mother to Raef, Tarienne, Kyre, Arivaelle and Authion. Tall with dark red, waist-length, wavy hair, and pale skin, Aistarenne is a serene, calming influence, yet a strong warrior in times of need. Her skill with the bow is renowned.

Alika – pronounced *All-ee-ka* – She is Lacas' mate and Tere's mother. Her father was Canis who was pack alpha before Lacas.

Anya – pronounced *ann-ya* – She is the daughter of Lupus and is a chocolate brown wolf when she shifts. She is attractive but ambitious and is paired with Tere for the Coming-of-Age ceremony.

Authion (war in High Elvish)-pronounced *awth-i-on* – Youngest son of Aistarenne and Thalion. He is six feet tall with long, black hair tied in many small braids around his head and vivid green eyes. He is the leader of the Fae Army of Darewood and a formidable warrior.

Arivaelle (sunlight in High Elvish)-pronounced *ar-ee-vay-ell* – Second youngest child of Aistarenne and Thalion. Nicknamed Rivi by her family. Gentle and always happy, Arivaelle is tall and beautiful with pale skin, white-blonde hair, and vivid green eyes. She has a very ethereal appearance, like her mother, and a formidable latent power in times of need. She is also the most skilled healer seen in recent times. Her chosen weapon is the bow and arrow.

Baras – pronounced *bar-ass* -One of Lacas' staunchest followers and part of the wolf council for the Inare wolf pack.

Canis – pronounced *Carn-is* – Canis was the Inare wolf pack leader before he was murdered by Lacas and is Alika's father and Tere's grandfather.

Daien- (gift in Druid)-pronounced *day-en* – King's Guardsman. Around six-foot-two with shoulder-length, chocolate brown hair and deep brown eyes. He has Druid blood from his mother's side, though he knows little about his heritage as his parents were killed when he was quite young.

Elyssia-pronounced *el-is-ee-ya* – Nickname, Lys. Half-Fae, half-Elven, she is Raef's lover and soul mate. Tall and blonde with blue eyes, she is passionate, elegant, extremely gentle. Exquisitely beautiful, even by

Fae standards, and lives in the Fae Kingdom of Darewood with her brother, Fienn.

Ileia – pronounced *eye-lee-yah* – Lived opposite Tere in the Inare village and caught his eye at a young age but did not become his mate until after Lacas' death. She is a red wolf with bright green eyes,

Kyre (flawless in High Elvish)-pronounced *keer* – Third child of Aistarenne and Thalion. Like his siblings, Kyre is tall, his long, blond hair falling to his waist, his eyes a deep, sea-blue. He moves with grace and certainty, and his muscular build and fearless demeanour make him a dangerous enemy but an extraordinary ally.

Lacas-pronounced *lay-cas* – Wolf changeling. Tall with short, black hair and ice-blue eyes in his human form. Lacas is the cruel alpha of the Inare wolf pack and Tere's sire. His wolf is jet-black and huge.

Lupus – pronounced *Loo-puss* – He is Anya's father and was initially a staunch follower of Lacas and a member of the wolf council of the Inare wolf pack.

Reine – pronounced – *rain* – A member of the Inare wolf pack and a true friend to Tere despite being a beta wolf and therefore reviled by Lacas.

Raef (strong in High Elvish)-pronounced *ray-f* – Tarienne's eldest brother. Crown Prince of the Fae of Darewood. Over six-foot-three, muscular, with light blond, shoulder-length hair, and bright blue eyes. He is incredibly handsome a valiant and intimidating warrior, yet patient and compassionate. He also has strong magical and mind-speak abilities.

Rantar-pronounced *ran-tar* – A powerful Sorcerer, half-Fae and half-Elven, who tried to hoard the balance of power by killing five of the twelve members of the Elder Council several hundred years ago. Killed by the remaining Elder Council, the power he had gathered was contained in a Golden Stone and left for safekeeping with a human King.

Rantec-pronounced *ran-tek* – The son of Rantar. His mother was a human who died when Rantec was born. He was raised by Lacas' wolf pack for the sole purpose of using the Golden Stone to gain power.

Tarienne (adventurous in High Elvish)-pronounced *tar-y-en* – Nicknamed Ren by her family and close friends. Crown Princess of the Fae of Darewood. At five-foot-ten, she has waist-length, deep red hair, and vivid green eyes. Her skin is pale, but she is less ethereal than her sisters. She has a quick temper and is, like her mother, a strong and formidable warrior, as well as an accomplished swordswoman.

Tere-pronounced *t-air* – Wolf changeling of the Inare wolf pack with ice-blue eyes and black fur in his wolf form. In human form, he is six feet tall, his hair black and spiky. He is extremely handsome and extraordinarily strong as an adult and inherits strong magical abilities from his grandfather, Canis. His sire Lacas was a cruel alpha of the pack. Alika is his mother and Lacas' mate.

Thalion (strong in High Elvish) – pronounced *Tha-lion* – King of Darewood and father to Raef, Tarienne, Kyre, Arivaelle and Authion. A strong and fair King to almost one thousand Fae, Thalion is around nine hundred years old, but because immortals age extremely slowly, does not look much older than Raef. He is six feet tall with twinkling blue eyes and shoulder-length, dark blond hair.

GLOSSARY OF TERMS

Bestiam morden – A Fae spell to kill/destroy whatever is named. In this case *Bestiam i.e. beasts.*

Gurith geoth riam laie-Fae battle cry meaning "Death to our enemies."

Yahalla onnia Blenidae en'i Lyuhta-a spell to summon the Blade Spirits, fearsome ancient warriors who swore to fight evil for eternity, yet have been fighting so long, they have become dangerously unpredictable.

Darewood (pronounced *de-ara-wood*)-the birthplace of Tarienne and Raef. It is home to the Fae ruled by King Thalion and Queen Aistarenne. There are approximately one thousand Fae in Darewood.